PENGUIN BOOKS

# CLEAR LIGHT OF DAY

Anita Desai was born in 1937. Her father was Bengali, her mother German, and she was educated in Delhi. Her published work includes *Fire on the Mountain* (Penguin, 1981), for which she won the Royal Society of Literature's Winifred Holtby Memorial Prize and the 1978 National Academy of Letters Award, a volume of short stories, *Games at Twilight* (Penguin, 1982) and several books for children. *Clear Light of Day* was nominated for the 1980 Booker McConnell Prize. Anita Desai is married, with four children, and lives in Bombay.

# Clear Light of Day

ANITA DESAI

Penguin Books
*in association with* William Heinemann Ltd

Penguin Books Ltd, Harmondsworth, Middlesex, England
Viking Penguin Inc., 40 West 23rd Street, New York, New York 10010, U.S.A.
Penguin Books Australia Ltd, Ringwood, Victoria, Australia
Penguin Books Canada Ltd, 2801 John Street, Markham, Ontario, Canada L3R 1B4
Penguin Books (N.Z.) Ltd, 182–190 Wairau Road, Auckland 10, New Zealand

First published in Great Britain by William Heinemann Ltd 1980
First published in the United States of America by Harper & Row, Publishers, Inc., 1980
Published in Penguin Books in Great Britain 1980
Reprinted 1981, 1984
Published in Penguin Books in the United States of America by
arrangement with Harper & Row, Publishers, Inc., 1982



LIBRARY OF CONGRESS CATALOGING IN PUBLICATION DATA
Desai, Anita, 1937–
Clear light of day.
Originally published: New York: Harper, 1980.
I. Title.
[PR9499.3.D465C56 1982] 823 81-23422
ISBN 0 14 00.5860 5 AACR2

Made and printed in Great Britain by
Richard Clay (The Chaucer Press) Ltd,
Bungay, Suffolk
Set in Times Roman

Grateful acknowledgment is made for permission to reprint the following: Lines from "The Waste Land" and "Little Gidding" from *Collected Poems 1909–1962* by T. S. Eliot; reprinted by permission of the publishers, Faber & Faber Ltd and Harcourt Brace Jovanovich, Inc. Lines from *Collected Poems* by Emily Dickinson; reprinted by permission of the publishers, Little, Brown & Company and Faber & Faber Ltd. Lines from "The Ship of Death" from *The Complete Poems of D. H. Lawrence*; copyright © Angelo Ravagli and C. M. Weekley, Executors of the Estate of Frieda Lawrence Ravagli, 1964, 1971; reprinted by permission of Laurence Pollinger Ltd, the Estate of Frieda Lawrence Ravagli, and Viking Penguin Inc.

*For Didi and Pip*

Memory is a strange bell –
Jubilee and knell –

*Emily Dickinson*

See, now they vanish,
The faces and places, with the self which, as
it could, loved them,
To become renewed, transfigured, in another pattern.

*T.S. Eliot*

# 

The koels began to call before daylight. Their voices rang out from the dark trees like an arrangement of bells, calling and echoing each others' calls, mocking and enticing each other into ever higher and shriller calls. More and more joined in as the sun rose and when Tara could no longer bear the querulous demand in their voices, she got up and went out onto the veranda to find the blank white glare of the summer sun thrusting in between the round pillars and the purple bougainvillea. Wincing, she shielded her eyes as she searched for the birds that had clamoured for her appearance, but saw nothing. The cane chairs on the veranda stood empty. A silent line of ants filed past her feet and down the steps into the garden. Then she saw her sister's figure in white, slowly meandering along what as children they had called 'the rose walk'.

Dropping her hands to pick up the hem of her long nightdress, Tara ran down the steps, bowing her head to the morning sun that came slicing down like a blade of steel onto the back of her neck, and crossed the dry crackling grass of the lawn to join her sister who stood watching, smiling.

The rose walk was a strip of grass, still streaked green and grey, between two long beds of roses at the far end of the lawn where a line of trees fringed the garden – fig and silver oak, mulberry and eucalyptus. Here there was still shade and, it seemed to Tara, the only bit of cultivation left; everything else, even the papaya and lemon trees, the bushes of hibiscus and oleander, the beds of canna lilies, seemed abandoned to dust and neglect, to struggle as they could against the heat and sun of summer.

But the rose walk had been maintained almost as it was. Or was it? It seemed to Tara that there had been far more roses in it when she was a child – luscious shaggy pink ones, small crisp white ones tinged with green, silky yellow ones that smelt of tea – and not just these small negligible crimson heads that lolled weakly on their thin stems. Tara had grown to know them on those mornings when she had trailed up and down after her mother who was expecting her youngest child and had been advised by her doctor to take some exercise. Her mother had not liked exercise, perhaps not the new baby either, and had paced up and down with her arms folded and her head sunk in thought while the koels mocked and screamed and dive-bombed the trees. Tara had danced and skipped after her, chattering, till she spied something flashing from under a pile of fallen rose petals – a pearl, or a silver ring? – and swooped upon it with a cry that broke into her mother's reverie and made her stop and frown. Tara had excitedly swept aside the petals and uncovered – a small, blanched snail. Her face wrinkling with disgust, her mother turned and paced on without a word, leaving Tara on her knees to contemplate the quality of disillusion.

But here was Bim. Bim, grey and heavy now and not so unlike their mother in appearance, only awake, watchful, gazing at her with her fullest attention and appraisal. Bim laughed when she saw Tara panting slightly in her eagerness.

Tara laughed back. 'Bim, the old rose walk is still here.'

'Of course,' said Bim, 'only the roses grow smaller and sicker every year,' and she bent to shake a long spindly branch from which a fully bloomed rose dangled. It came apart instantly, revealing a small naked centre and a few pathetic stamens clinging to the bald head while the petals fell in a bunch to the chocolate earth below.

Tara's mouth opened in dismay at the destruction of a rose in full bloom – she would never have done what Bim did – and then she saw the petals that had clung together in a bunch in their fall part and scatter themselves. As she stared, a petal rose and tumbled onto its back and she saw uncovered the gleam of a – a pearl? a silver ring? Something that gleamed, something that flashed, then flowed – and she saw it was her childhood snail slowly, resignedly making its way from under the flower up a clod of earth only to tumble off the top onto its side – an eternal, minature Sisyphus. She brought her hands together in a clap and cried, 'Look, a snail!'

Bim watched her sister in surprise and amusement. Was Tara, grown woman, mother of grown daughters, still child enough to play with a snail? Would she go down on her knees to scoop it up on a leaf and watch it draw its albuminous trail, lift its tiny antennae, gaze about it with protruding eyes and then, the instant before the leaf dipped and it slid downwards, draw itself into its pale pod?

As Tara performed the rites of childhood over the handy creature, Bim stood with lowered head, tugging at the hair that hung loosely about her face as she had done when she had sat beside her brother's bed that summer that he was ill, with her forehead lowered to the wooden edge of the bed, a book of poetry open on her lap, reading aloud the lines:

> *Now sleeps the crimson petal, now the white;*
> *Nor waves the cypress in the palace walk;*
> *Nor winks the gold fin in the porphyry font:*
> *The firefly wakens . . .*

Her lips moved to the lines she had forgotten she remembered till she saw the crimson petals fall in a heap on the snail in the mud, but she would not say them aloud to Tara. She had no wish to use the lines as an incantation to revive that year, that summer when he had been ill and she had nursed him and so much had happened in a rush. To bury it all again, she put out her toe and scattered the petals evenly over the damp soil.

Now Tara's hand trembled, the leaf she held dipped and the doomed creature slid soundlessly back to earth.

They both stood staring as it lay there, shocked and still.

Tara murmured 'You looked so like Mama from a distance, Bim – I mean, it's so – the sun –' for she realised at once that Bim would not like the comparison.

But Bim did not seem to hear, or care. 'Did you sleep at all?' she asked instead, for last night on arriving from the airport Tara had laughed and chattered and claimed to be too excited to sleep.

'How could I?' cried Tara, laughing, and talked of the koels in the morning, and the dog barking in the night, and the mosquitoes singing and stinging in the dark, as they walked together up the grassy path, Tara in her elegant pale blue nylon nightgown and elegant silver slippers and Bim in a curious shapeless hand-made garment that Tara could see she had fashioned out of an old cotton sari by sewing it up at both sides, leaving enough room for her arms to come through and cutting out a wide scoop for her neck. At the feet a border of blue and green peacocks redeemed the dress from total shabbiness and was – Tara laughed lightly – original. 'How he barks,' she repeated. 'Don't the neighbours complain?'

'I think they've grown used to him at last, or else they've realised it does no good to complain – I never will chain him up and, as I tell them when they do protest, he has such a beautiful voice, it's a pleasure to hear him. Not like the yipping and yapping of other people's little lap dogs,' she said with a toss of her grey head.

Although they spoke softly, no louder than a pair of birds to each other, the dog must have heard his name or realised he was being discussed. When Tara had come out onto the veranda he had been asleep under the wooden divan, hidden from her by the striped cotton rug with which it was covered, and he had only twitched his whiskers when he heard her pass by. Now he was suddenly out there on the grass walk with them, standing with his four legs very wide apart, his nose diving down into the clods of earth where the snail still lay futilely struggling to upright itself. As it finally flipped onto its edge, he gave a thunderous sneeze.

'Badshah!' cried Bim, delighted with his theatrical performance, and his one eye gleamed at the approval in her voice while the other followed the snail. But it disappeared under the rose petals once more and he came lolloping towards them, stubbed his moist nose into their legs, scuffed his dirty claws into their heels, salivated over their feet and then rushed past them in a show of leadership.

'He does like to be first always,' Bim explained.

'Is he nine now, Bim, or ten?'

'Twelve,' exclaimed Bim. 'See his old whiskers all white,' she said, diving forwards at his head and catching him by the ears, making him stand still with his head against her thigh. He closed his eyes and smiled a foolish smile of pleasure at her attention, then drew away with a long line of saliva dribbling from his jaws onto the grass, more copious and irregular than the fluent snail's. 'He is Begum's son, you know, and she lived to be – fourteen?'

Tara lifted her hair from the back of her neck and let it fall again, luxuriantly, with a sigh. 'How everything goes on and on here, and never changes,' she said. 'I used to think about it all,' and she waved her arm in a circular swoop to encompass the dripping tap at the end of the grass walk, the trees that quivered and shook with birds, the loping dog, the roses – 'and it is all exactly the same, whenever we come home.'

'Does that disappoint you?' Bim asked drily, giving her a quick sideways look. 'Would you like to come back and find it changed?'

Tara's face was suddenly wound up tightly in a frown as if such a thought had never struck her before and she found it confusing. 'Changed? How? You mean the house newly painted, the garden newly planted, new people coming and going? Oh no, how could I, Bim?' and she seemed truly shocked by the possibility.

'But you wouldn't want to return to life as it used to be, would you?' Bim continued to tease her in that dry voice. 'All that dullness, boredom, waiting. Would you care to live that over again? Of course not. Do you know anyone who would – secretly, sincerely, in his innermost self – *really* prefer to return to childhood?'

Still frowning, Tara murmured meaninglessly 'Prefer to what?'

'Oh, to going on – to growing up – leaving – going away – into the world – something wider, freer – brighter,' Bim laughed. 'Brighter! Brighter!' she called, shading her eyes against the brightness.

Tara's head sank low, her frown deepened. She could not trust Bim to be quite serious: in her experience, the elder sister did not take the younger seriously – and so all she said was a murmured 'But you didn't, Bim.'

'I?' said Bim flatly, with her eyes still shaded against the light that streamed across the parched lawn and pressed against the trees at the fringe. 'Oh, I never go anywhere. It must seem strange to you and Bakul who have travelled so much – to come back and find people like Baba and me who have never travelled at all. And if we still had Mira-*masi* with us, wouldn't that complete the picture? This faded old picture in its petrified frame?' She stopped to pluck the dead heads off a rose bush dusted grey with disease. 'Mira-*masi* swigging secretly from her brandy bottle. Baba winding up his gramophone. And Raja, if Raja were here, playing Lord Byron on his death-bed. I, reading to him. That is what you might have come back to, Tara. How would you have liked that?'

Tara stood staring at her silver toes, at the clods of upturned earth in the beds and the scattered dead heads, and felt a prickle of distrust in Bim. Was Bim being cruel again? There could be no other motive. There could be no reply. She made none and Bim swung away and marched on, striding beside Badshah.

'That is the risk of coming home to Old Delhi,' she announced in the hard voice that had started up the prickle of distrust that ran over the tips of the hairs on Tara's arms, rippling them. 'Old Delhi does not change. It only decays. My students tell me it is a great cemetery, every house a tomb. Nothing but sleeping graves. Now *New* Delhi, they say is different. That is where things happen. The way they describe it, it sounds like a nest of fleas. So much happens there, it must be a jumping place. I never go. Baba never goes. And here, here nothing happens at all. Whatever happened, happened long ago – in the time of the Tughlaqs, the Khiljis, the Sultanate, the Moghuls – that lot.' She snapped her fingers in time to her words, smartly. 'And then the British built New Delhi and moved everything out. Here we are left rocking on the backwaters, getting duller and greyer, I suppose. Anyone who isn't dull and grey goes away – to New Delhi, to England, to Canada, the Middle East. They don't come back.'

'I must be peculiar then,' Tara's voice rose bravely. 'I keep coming back. And Bakul.'

'They pay your fare, don't they?' her sister said.

'But we *like* to come, Bim. We *must* come – if we are not to lose touch, I with all of you, with home, and he with the country. He's been planning this trip for months. When the girls arrive, and we go to Hyderabad for the wedding, Bakul wants to go on from there and do a tour of the whole country. He did it ten years ago and he says it is time to do it again, to make sure –'

'Of what?'

The question was sarcastic but Tara gave her head a toss of assurance and pride. Her voice too had taken on the strength and sureness that Bim noticed it usually did when she spoke of her husband. She told Bim evenly 'That he hasn't forgotten, or lost touch with the way things are here. If you lose touch, then you can't represent your country, can you?' she ended, on an artificial note.

Bim of course detected that. She grunted 'Hmph. I don't know. If that is what they tell you in the diplomatic service then that is what you must say.'

'But it's true,' Tara exclaimed, immediately dropping artificiality and sounding earnest. 'One has to come back, every few years, to find out and make sure again. I'd like to travel with him really. But there's the wedding in Raja's house, I suppose that will be enough to keep us busy. Are you coming, Bim? You and Baba? Couldn't we all go together? Then it will be a proper family reunion. Say you'll come! You have your summer vacation now. What will you do alone in Delhi, in the heat? Say you'll come!'

Bim said nothing. In the small silence a flock of mynahs suddenly burst out of the green domes of the trees and, in a loud commotion of yellow beaks and brown wings, disappeared into the sun. While their shrieks and cackles still rang in the air, they heard another sound, one that made Bim stop and stare and the dog lift his head, prick up his ears and then charge madly across to the eucalyptus trees that grew in a cluster by the wall. Rearing up on his hind legs, he tore long strips of blue and mauve bark off the silken pink tree-trunks and, throwing back his head, bellowed in that magnificent voice that Bim admired so much and that soured – or spiced – her relations with the neighbours.

'What is it?' called Tara as Bim ran forwards, lifting the peacock-edged nightie in order to hurry.

It was her cat, crouched in the fork of the blue and pink tree, black and bitter at being stranded where she could not make her way down. Discovered first by the mynahs and then by Badshah, she felt disgraced.

Bim stood below her, stretching out her arms and calling, imploring her to jump. Badshah warned her not to do anything of the sort in a series of excited barks and whines. Tara waited, laughing, while the cat turned her angry face from one to the other, wondering whom to trust. At last Bim coaxed her down and she came slithering along the satiny bark, growling and grumbling with petulance and complaint at her undignified descent. Then she was in Bim's arms, safely cradled and shielded from Badshah's boisterous bumps and jumps, cuddled and cushioned and petted with such an extravagance of affection that Tara could not help raising her eyebrows in embarrassment and wonder.

Although Bim was rubbing her chin on the cat's flat-topped head and kissing the cold tips of her ears, she seemed to notice Tara's expression. 'I know what you're thinking,' she said. 'You're thinking how old spinsters go ga-ga over their pets because they haven't children. Children are the *real* thing, you think.'

Tara's look of surprise changed to guilt. 'What makes you say that? Actually, I was thinking about the girls. I was wondering –'

'Exactly. That's what I said. You think animals take the place of babies for us love-starved spinsters,' Bim said with a certain satisfaction and lowered the rumpled cat to the gravel walk as they came up to the house. 'But you're wrong,' she said, striding across the sun-slashed drive. 'You can't possibly feel for them what I do about these wretched animals of mine.'

'Oh Bim,' protested Tara, recognising the moment when Bim went too far with which all their encounters had ended throughout their childhood, but she was prevented from explaining herself by the approach of a monstrous body of noise that seemed to be pushing its way out through a tight tunnel, rustily grinding through, and then emerged into full brassy volume, making the pigeons that lived on the ledge under the veranda ceiling throw up their wings and depart as if at a shot. It was not Bakul who was responsible for the cacophony. He was sitting – flabbily, flaccidly – in one of the cane chairs on the veranda with the tea tray in front of him, waiting for someone to come and pour. The noise beat and thrummed in one of the curtained rooms behind him. 'Sm-o-oke gets in your eyes,' moaned an agonised voice, and Tara sighed, and her shoulders drooped by a visible inch or two.

'Baba still plays the same old records?' she asked as they went slowly up the wide stairs between the massed pots of spider lilies and asparagus fern to the veranda.

'He never stops,' said Bim, smiling. 'Not for a day.'

'Don't you mind the noise?'

'Not any more,' said Bim, the lightness of her tone carefully contrived. 'I don't hear it any more.'

'It's loud,' complained Tara in a distressed voice. 'I used to look for records to send Baba – I thought he'd like some new ones – but they don't make 78s any more.'

'Oh he doesn't want any new records,' said Bim. 'He wouldn't play them. He loves his old ones.'

'Isn't it strange,' said Tara, wincing at the unmodulated roar that swept across the still, shady veranda in an almost visible onslaught of destruction.

'We *are* strange, I *told* you,' laughed Bim, striding across the tiled floor to the cane chairs and the tea tray. 'Oh, Bakul – *bhai*, you're up. Did you sleep?' she asked carelessly, sitting down in front of the tray. But instead of pouring out the tea she only lifted the milk jug and, bending down, filled a saucer for the cat who crouched before it and began to lap even before Bim had finished pouring so that some drops fell on her ears and on her whiskers, a sight that made

Bim laugh as she held the jug, waiting for the cat to finish the milk. Then she bent and refilled the saucer. Tara, who had poured out a cup of tea for Bakul, waited for her to surrender the milk jug. When she did, there was very little left in it for Bakul's tea. Tara shook it to bring out a few reluctant drops.

'Is that enough?' she asked uneasily, even guiltily, handing the cup to Bakul.

He shrugged, making no reply, his lower lip thrust out in the beginning of a sulk. It may not have been the lack of milk, though, it might have been the din that stood about them like sheets of corrugated iron, making conversation impossible. As he stirred his tea thoughtfully with a little spoon, the song rose to its raucous crescendo as though the singer had a dagger plunged into his breast and were letting fly the heartfelt notes of his last plaint on earth. Then at last the rusty needle ground to a halt in the felt-embedded groove of the antique record and they all sighed, simultaneously, and sank back in their chairs, exhausted.

The pigeons that had retreated to the roof came fluttering back to their nests and settled down with small complaining sounds, guttural and comfortable. The bamboo screen in the doorway lifted and Baba came out for his tea.

He did not look as if he could be held responsible for any degree of noise whatsoever. Coming out into the veranda, he blinked as if the sun surprised him. He was in his pyjamas – an old pair with frayed ends, over which he wore a grey bush-shirt worn and washed almost to translucency. His face, too, was blanched, like a plant grown underground or in deepest shade, and his hair was quite white, giving his young, fine face a ghostly look that made people start whenever he appeared.

But no one on the veranda started. Instead, they turned on him their most careful smiles, trying to make their smiles express feelings that were comforting, reassuring, not startling.

Then Bim began to bustle. Now she called out for more milk and a freshly refilled jug appeared from the pantry, full to the brim, before Bakul's widened eyes. Baba's cup was filled not with tea at all but with milk that had seemed so short a moment ago. Then, to top it, a spoonful of sugar was poured in as well and all stirred up with a tremendous clatter and handed, generously slopping, to Baba who took it without any expression of distaste or embarrassment and sat down on his little cane stool to sip it. Even the cat was transfixed by the spectacle and sat back on her haunches, staring at him with eyes that were circles of sharp green glass.

Only Bim seemed to notice nothing odd. Nor did she seem to

think it necessary to speak to or be spoken to by Baba. She said, 'Look at her. You'd think I had given her enough but no, if we take any ourselves, she feels it's come out of her share.'

After a minute Tara realised she was speaking of the cat. Tara had lost the childhood habit of including animals in the family once she had married and begun the perpetual travels and moves that precluded the keeping of pets. It was with a small effort that she tore her eyes away from her brother and regarded the reproachful cat.

'She's too fat,' she said, thinking pet-owners generally liked such remarks. It was not a truthful one: the cat was thin as a string.

Bim put out her toe and scratched the creature under her ear but the cat turned angrily away, refusing such advances, and kept her eyes riveted on Baba till he had sipped the last drop of milk and put the cup back on the saucer with an unmistakably empty ring. Then she dropped sulkily onto the tiles and lay there noisily tearing at her fur with a sandpapered tongue of an angry red.

While the two women sat upright and tense and seethed with unspoken speech, the two men seemed dehydrated, emptied out, with not a word to say about anything. Only the pigeons cooed on and on, too lazy even to open their beaks, content to mutter in their throats rather than sing or call. The dog, stretched out at Bim's feet, writhed and coiled, now catching his tail between his teeth, now scrabbling with his paws, then bit at fleas and chewed his hair, weaving a thick mat of sound together with the cat who was busy with herself.

Bakul could bear it no longer. When his expression had grown so thin and so sour that it was about to split, he said, in a voice meant to be sonorous, 'Our first morning in Delhi.' To Bim's wonder and astonishment, Tara smiled at this radiantly as though he had made a profound remark on which he was to be congratulated. He gave her a small, confidential smile in return. 'What shall we do with it?'

Bim suddenly scratched her head as if the dog had started up something there. 'I don't know about you,' she said, 'but I have some of my students coming over this morning.'

'Students? But Bim, I thought your summer vacation had begun.'

'Yes, yes, but I wanted to give them some reading lists so they don't waste all their time walking up and down the Mall in Simla or going to the pictures. Then they reminded me I had missed a tutorial and had to see some of their papers. You see, it isn't just I who make them work – they make me work, too. So I asked them to come down here – they love to come, I don't know why. I'll go and get ready – I'm late. And you? You two? What will you do?'

Tara gazed at her husband for answer till he finally lowered his eyes by careful inches from the plaster moulding under the ceiling where the pigeons strutted and squatted and puffed themselves, and said 'Perhaps I could ask my uncle to send us a car. Then we could go and call on some of my relations in New Delhi. They will be expecting us.'

'I'll get ready,' said Tara, instantly getting to her feet as if in relief.

Bim, who remembered her as a languid little girl, listless, a dawdler, noted her quick movements, her efficient briskness, with some surprise, but said nothing. Instead, she turned to Baba and drawled, slowly, 'And Baba,' as she bent forward and started stacking the cups onto the wooden tray. The others got up and stretched and walked about the veranda except for Baba who sat calmly with his long white hands dangling loosely on either side of him. When Bim said 'Baba' again, he smiled gently at the floor. 'Baba,' she said again in a very low voice so that Bakul, standing on the steps and scrutinizing the bougainvilleas at the pillars, would not hear her, 'do you think you might go to the office today?'

Tara, who was at the door at the end of the veranda, about to lift the bamboo curtain and go in, paused. Somehow she had heard. Even in her rush to get dressed and be ready for anything her husband might suggest, she paused in shock to find that Bim still made attempts to send Baba to the office. Considering their futility, she thought they must have been given up long ago. She could not help stopping and turning round to see Bim piling up the tea tray and Baba seated on his small child's stool, smiling, his hands helplessly dangling, the busy dog licking, scratching, while the morning took another stride forward and stood with its feet planted on the tiled floor.

'Won't you go today, Baba?' Bim asked softly, not looking at him, looking at the tea cups. 'Do go. You could catch a bus. It'll make a change. We'll all be busy. Then come home to lunch. Or stay if you find it interesting.'

Baba smiled at the bare tiles. His hands swung as if loose in their sockets, as if in a light breeze. But there was no breeze: the heat dropped out of the sky and stood before them like a sheet of foil.

Then Bim got up and lifted the tray and went barefoot down the other end of the veranda to the pantry. Tara could hear her talking to the cook in her normal speaking voice. She turned and went into the room herself, unable to face the sight of Baba alone and hopeless on the veranda. But Baba did not stay either. He must have gone back to his room, too, for in another minute or two she heard that ominous roar pushing its way through the tunnel and emerging as the maudlin clamour of 'Lilli Marlene'.

'Now this is precisely what I told you,' Bakul said, bustling into the bedroom after making his phone call. 'I pointed out to you how much more convenient it would be to stay with my uncle and aunt, right in the centre of town, on Aurangzeb Road, how it would save us all the trouble of finding a car to travel up and down in . . .'

Tara, who was bending over the bed, laying out his clothes, straightened and said in a strained voice 'But I had not meant to go anywhere. I only wanted to stay at home.'

He flicked his silk dressing gown open and said impatiently 'You know you can't do that when there's so much to do – relations to visit, colleagues to look up, all that shopping you had planned to do –'

'I'll wait till the girls come. I'll go shopping with them,' said Tara with an unaccustomed stubbornness. She held up a cluster of ties and waited, a bit sullenly, for him to choose one.

He put out his hand and picked one of broadly striped raw silk and said 'You surely don't mean that. You can't just sit about with your brother and sister all day, doing nothing.'

'But it's what I want – just to be at home again, with them. And of course there are the neighbours – I'll see them. But I don't want to go anywhere today, and I don't want to go to New Delhi at all.'

'Of course you will come,' Bakul said quite sharply, going towards the bathroom with an immense towel he had picked up. 'There's no question about that.'

When the bathroom door had shut, Tara went out onto the veranda again. The veranda ran all around the house and every room opened out onto it. This room had been hers and Bim's when they were girls. It opened onto the dense grove of guava trees that separated the back of the house from the row of servants' quarters. Bright morning sounds of activity came from them – a water tap running, a child crying, a cock crowing, a bicycle bell ringing – but the house was separated from them by the thick screen of low, dusty guava trees in which invisible parrots screamed and quarrelled over the fruit. Now and then one fell to the ground with a soft thud. Tara could see some lying in the dust with chunks bitten out by the parrots. If she had been younger – no, if she had been sure Bakul would not look out and see – she would have run down the veranda steps and searched for one that was whole. Her mouth tingled with longing to bite into that hard astringent flesh under the green rind. She wondered if her girls would do it when they arrived to spend their holidays here. No, they would not. Much travelled, brought up in embassies, fluent in several languages, they were far too sophisticated for such rustic pleasures, she knew, and felt guilty over her own lack of that desirable quality. She had fooled Bakul into believing that she had acquired it, that he had shown her how to acquire it. But it was all just dust thrown into his eyes, dust.

Further up the veranda was Baba's room and from behind the light bamboo curtain that hung in the doorway came the guttural rattling of 'Don't Fence Me In'. For a while Tara leant her head against a pillar, listening. It was not unfamiliar, yet it disturbed.

A part of her was sinking languidly down into the passive pleasure of having returned to the familiar – like a pebble, she had been picked up and hurled back into the pond, and sunk down through the layer of green scum, through the secret cool depths to the soft rich mud at the bottom, sending up a line of bubbles of relief and joy. A part of her twitched, stirred like a fin in resentment: why was the pond so muddy and stagnant? Why had nothing changed? She had changed – why did it not keep up with her?

Why did Bim allow nothing to change? Surely Baba ought to begin to grow and develop at last, to unfold and reach out and stretch. But whenever she saw them, at intervals of three or five years, all was exactly as before.

Drawing away from the pillar, she moved towards his room, propelled by her disturbance, by her resentment at this petrified state in which her family lived. Bakul was right to criticise it, disapprove of it. Yes, he was right, she told herself and, lifting the dusty bamboo curtain, slipped into Baba's room.

He was sitting on his bed, a string cot spread with a cotton rug and an old sheet, that stood in the centre of the room under the slowly revolving electric fan. He was crouched low, listening raptly to the last of 'Don't Fence Me In' unwinding itself on the old HMV gramophone on a small bamboo table beside his bed. The records, not so very many of them – there must have been breakages after all – were stacked on a shelf beneath the table in their tattered yellow sleeves. The string cot, the table, the HMV gramophone, a canvas chair and a wardrobe – nothing else. It was a large room and looked bare. Once it had been Aunt Mira's room, and crowded. Baba looked up at her.

Tara stood staring, made speechless by his fine, serene face, the shapeliness of his long fingers, his hands that either moved lightly as if in a breeze or rested calmly at his sides. He was an angel, she told herself, catching her lip between her teeth – an angel descended to earth, unsoiled by any of it.

But then why did he spend his days and years listening to this appalling noise? Her daughters could not live through a day without their record-player either; they, too, kept it heaped with records that slipped down onto the turntable in a regular sequence, keeping them supplied with an almost uninterrupted flow of music to which they worked and danced with equal ease. But, she wanted to explain to him, theirs was an ever-growing, ever-changing collection, their interest in it was lively, fresh, developing all the time. Also, she knew they would outgrow their need of it. Already Maya had friends who took her to concerts from which she returned with a sheen of uplifting pleasure spread across her face and talked of learning to play the flute. Soon it would be behind her – this need for an elemental, primitive rhythm automatically supplied. But Baba would never leave his behind, he would never move on.

Her anguish and impatience made her say, very quickly and loudly, as the record ground to a halt and before Baba could turn it over, 'Are you going out this morning, Baba? We've sent for a car – can we give you a lift?'

Baba lifted the smoothly curving metal arm off the record and sat with his hand resting on it, protectively. It was clear he would have liked to turn over the record but he hesitated, politely, his eyes cast down, flickering slightly as if with fear or guilt.

Tara too began to squirm with guilt at having caused him this panic. 'Are you, Baba?'

He glanced at her very quickly, with a kind of pleading, and then looked away and shook his head very slightly.

This made her cry out 'But don't you go to the office in the mornings?'

He kept his head lowered, smiling slightly, sadly.

'Never?'

The room rang with her voice, then with silence. In the shaded darkness, silence had the quality of a looming dragon. It seemed to roar and the roar to reverberate, to dominate. To escape from it would require a burst of recklessness, even cruelty. Was it to keep it at bay that Baba played those records so endlessly, so obsessively? But it was not right. She herself had been taught, by her husband and by her daughters, to answer questions, to make statements, to be frank and to be precise. They would have none of these silences and shadows. Here things were left unsaid and undone. It was what they called 'Old Delhi decadence.' She knotted her fingers together in an effort to break it.

'Do you think you will go to the office today?' she persisted, beads of perspiration welling out of her upper lip.

Now Baba took his hand off the gramophone arm, relinquishing it sadly, and his hands hung loosely at his sides, as helplessly as a dead man's. His head, too, sank lower and lower.

Tara was furious with herself for causing him this shame, this distress. She hated her probing, her questioning with which she was punishing him. Punishing him for what? For his birth – and for that he was not responsible. Yet it was wrong to leave things as they were – she knew Bakul would say so, and her girls, too. It was all quite lunatic. Yet there was no alternative, no solution. Surely they would see there was none. Sighing, she said in a tone of defeat 'I'll ask Bim.'

She had said the right thing at last. Quite inadvertently, even out of cowardice. It made Baba raise his head and smile, sweetly and gently as he used to do. He even nodded, faintly, in agreement. Yes, Bim, he seemed to say, Bim will decide. Bim can, Bim will. Go to Bim. Tara could not help smiling back at his look of relief, his happy dependence. She turned to leave the room and heard him lift the record and turn it over. As she escaped down the veranda she heard Bing Crosby's voice bloating luxuriantly out into 'Ah-h'm dream-in' of a wha-ite Christmas . . .'

But now something had gone wrong. The needle stuck in a groove. 'Dream-in', dream-in', dream-in'' hacked the singer, his voice growing more and more officious. Shocked, Baba's long hands moved with speed to release it from the imprisoning groove. Then he found the needle grown so blunt and rusty that, as he peered at it from every angle and turned it over and over with a melancholy finger, he accepted it would do no longer. He sighed and dropped it into the little compartment that slid out of the green leather side of the gramophone and the sight of all the other obsolete needles that lay in that concealed grave seemed to place a weight on his heart. He felt defeated and infinitely depressed. Too depressed to open the little one-inch square tin with the picture of the dog on it, and pick out a clean needle to insert in the metal head. It remained empty, toothless. The music had come to a halt. Out in the garden a koel called its wild, brazen call. It was not answered so it repeated the call, more demandingly.

For a while Baba paced about the room, his head hanging so low that one would have thought it unnatural, physically impossible. Now and then he lifted his hands to his head and ran his long bony fingers nervously through his white hair so that it was grooved and furrowed like the lines of an aged face. The silence of the room, usually so loud with the rollicking music of the '40s, seemed to admit those other sounds that did not soothe or protect him but, on the contrary, startled him and drove him into a panic – the koel calling, calling out in the tall trees, a child crying in the servants' quarters, a bicycle dashing past, its bell jangling. Baba began to pace up and down faster and faster as if he were running away from it. Then, when he could bear it no longer, he went to the cupboard and pulled open its door, searched frantically for clothes to wear, pulled out whatever seemed to him appropriate, and began to dress hurriedly, dropping his pyjamas onto the floor, flinging others onto the sagging canvas chair by the bed, hurriedly buttoning and lacing and pulling on and off till he felt sufficiently clothed.

Without a glance into the mirror on the cupboard door or an attempt to tidy the room, he fled from it.

Tara, still sitting on the steps with an arm around the veranda pillar, waiting for Bakul to emerge so that she could go in and dress, saw a pale elongated shape lurching and blundering down the veranda and onto the drive, bent almost double as if in pain or in fear – or perhaps because of the sun beating down with white-hot blows. She stood up in fright and it took her a minute to realize it was Baba.

By then he was already at the gate and had turned out of it into the road. Tara hurried down the steps onto the drive, shading her eyes, her mouth open to call him, but she stopped herself. How old was Baba now? If he wanted to go out, ought he at his age to be called back and asked to explain?

If she had, Baba would have been grateful. If anything, anyone had stopped him now, he would have collapsed with relief and come crawling home like a thirsty dog to its water bowl. Once, when he had ventured out, a bicycle had dashed against him as he stood hesitating at the edge of the road, wondering whether to cross. The bicyclist had fallen and cursed him, his voice rising to a shrill peak and then breaking on Baba's head like eggs, or slivers of glass. Another time, he had walked as far as the bus stop but when the bus had arrived there was such a scuffle between those trying to get off and those trying to get on that people were pushed and bumped and shoved and when one man was somehow expelled from the knotted mob, Baba saw his sleeve torn off his shirt, hanging limply as if he had no arm, were an amputee. Baba thought of the man's face, of the ruined shirt. He heard all those shouts again, the shouts that had been flung at his head, knocking into him till he was giddy with blows.

He was small. He was standing on the dunes. There was nothing here but the silver sand and the grey river and the white sky. But out of that lunar stillness a man loomed up, military in a khaki uniform and towering scarlet turban, and roughly pushed past him shouting '*Hato! Hato!*' to make way for a white horse that plunged up out of the dunes and galloped past Baba, crouching on his knees in the sand, the terror of the horse hooves beating through his head, the sand flying back into his face and the voice still commanding '*Hato! Hato!*'

His knees trembled in anticipation, knowing he would be forced down, or flung down if he continued down the road. But it was as if Tara had given him a push down a steep incline. She had said he was to go. Bim had said he was to go. Bim and Tara, both of them, wanted him to go. He was going.

His feet in their unfastened sandals scuffed through the dust of Bela Road. Sharp gravel kept slipping into them, prodding him. His arms swung widly, propelling him along. His head bobbed, his white hair flopped. His eyes strained and saw black instead of white. Was he going to faint? Would he fall? Should he stop? Could he? Or would they drive him on? '*Hato! Hato!*'

Then he heard the crash he knew would come. Instantly he flinched and flung up his arm to protect his face. But it was not he who had crashed. It was a cart carrying a load of planks that had tipped forwards as the horse that drew it fell first onto its knees, then onto its nose and lay squirming in the middle of the road. Baba shrank back, against the wall, and held his arm before his eyes but still he saw what happened: the driver, a dark man with a red rag tied about his head, leapt down from the mound of planks and raised his arm, and a switch or a whip, and brought it down with all his force on the horse's back. The horse gave a neighing scream, reared up its head with the wet, wringing mane streaming from it, and then stretched out on the stones, a shiver running up and down its legs so that it twitched and shook. Again the man raised the whip, again it came down on the horse's back, neck, head, legs – again and again. Baba heard screams but it was the man who screamed as he whipped and slashed and beat, screamed abuse at the animal who did not move but seemed to sink lower and lower into the dust. 'Swine! Son of a swine!' the man panted, red eyes straining out of the dark face. *Suar! Sala! Suar ka bachcha!*' All the time his arm rose up in the air and came down, cutting and slashing the horse's flesh till black stuff oozed onto the white dust and ran and spread, black and thick, out of the horse.

Baba raised both his arms, wrapped them about his head, his ears and eyes, tightly, and, blind, turned and stumbled, almost fell but ran on back up the road to the house, to the gate. His shoulder hit the white gate-post so that he lurched and fell to his knees, then he rose and stumbled, his arms still doubled over his eyes so that he should not see and about his ears so that he should not hear.

Tara saw him as he came climbing up the steps on his knees and ran forwards to help him to his feet. Tugging at his arms to drag them away from his face, she cried 'Are you hurt? Baba, Baba, say – are you hurt? Has someone hurt you?' Pulling his arms away, she uncovered his face and saw his eyes rolling in their sockets like a wild horse's, his lips drawn back from his teeth as if he were racing, and the blue-black shadows that always lay under his eyes spreading over his face like a bruise, wet with his tears. Then she stopped demanding that he should speak, and helped him to his room, onto his bed, rushed out and down the veranda in search of Bim, in search of water. There was no one on the veranda or in the kitchen. The cook had gone out to market. She tilted the earthen water jar to fill a tumbler and hurried back with it, her legs cutting into her nightgown and the water spilling in splashes onto the tiles as she hurried, thinking of Baba's face. She lifted his head to help him drink but most of it ran down his chin into his shirt. When she lowered his head, he shrank into a heap, shivering, and she stayed a while, smoothing his hair and patting his cheek till she thought he was quieter, nearly asleep, then went to find Bim.

But Bakul stepped out of their room, his tie in one hand and his shoes in another, to ask 'Aren't you getting ready, Tara? We'll be late. The car will be here any minute and you know Uncle is very punctual. We mustn't keep him waiting.' He went back to finish dressing without having seen Tara's face or anything there to stop him.

He noticed nothing – a missing shoe-horn and frayed laces having presented him with a problem meanwhile – till she came in, her shoulders sloping, her hair hanging, and sat down on the foot of the bed instead of going in to dress. Then he spoke more sharply. 'Why aren't you getting ready?'

'I don't think I'll come after all,' she mumbled. She always mumbled when she was afraid, as if she hoped not to be heard.

She expected him to explode of course. But even for Bakul it was too hot, the atmosphere of the old house too turgid and heavy to push or manipulate. Bending down to tie two perfect bows, he merely sighed 'So, I only have to bring you home for a day, Tara, and you go back to being the hopeless person you were before I married you.'

'Yes,' she muttered, 'hopeless.' Like Baba's, her face looked bruised.

'And you won't let me help you. I thought I had taught you a different life, a different way of living. Taught you to execute your will. Be strong. Face challenges. Be decisive. But no, the day you enter your old home, you are as weak-willed and helpless and defeatist as ever.' He stood up and looked down to see if his shoes were bright enough to reflect his face. Nothing less would do. Yes, yes. He shrugged his shoulders inside his shirtsleeves. 'What should I do with you? I ought to take you away immediately. Let us go and stay with my uncle in New Delhi.'

'No.' She shook her head. 'Leave me here.'

'You're not happy here,' he said, and the unexpectedness of these words made her look up at him, questioning. 'Look at your face – so sad, so worried.' He even came close to her and touched her cheek, very lightly, as if he could hardly bear the unpleasant contact but forced himself to do it out of compassion. 'If only you would come with me, I would show you how to be happy. How to be active and busy – and then you would be happy. If you came.'

But she shook her head. She felt she had followed him enough, it had been such an enormous strain, always pushing against her grain, it had drained her of too much strength, now she could only collapse, inevitably collapse.

Bakul had married her when she was eighteen. He knew her. He left her, saying 'Then I'll tell Uncle you are busy with your own family and will come another time,' and went out to wait for the car.

He passed Bim as he went through the drawing room. Bim was holding court there – seated on the divan with her legs drawn up under her – like Tara, she had not dressed yet and was still in her nightdress – and on the carpet below sat the students, a brightly coloured bunch of young girls in jeans and in *salwar-kameez*, laughing and eyeing each other and him as he went through. He raised his eyebrows at Bim and gave her a significant look as if to say '*This* – your history lesson?'

Bim nodded and laughed and wriggled her toes and waggled her pencil, completely at ease and without the least sense of guilt. 'No, no, you won't,' he heard her say as he went out onto the veranda, 'you won't get me started on the empress Razia – nor on the empress Nur Jehan. I refuse. We must be serious. We are going to discuss the war between Shivaji and Aurangzeb – no empresses.'

The girls groaned exaggeratedly. 'Please, miss,' he heard them beg as he sat down on a creaking cane chair to wait, 'please let's talk about something interesting, miss. You will enjoy it too, miss.'

'Enjoy? You rascals, I haven't asked you here to enjoy yourselves. Come on, Keya, please begin – I'm listening –' and then there was some semblance of order and of a tutorial going on that Bakul could almost recognise and approve. He wondered, placing one leg over the other reflectively, as he had sometimes wondered when he had first started coming to this house, as a young man who had just entered the foreign service and was in a position to look around for a suitable wife, if Bim were not, for all her plainness and brusqueness, the superior of the two sisters, if she had not those qualities – decision, firmness, resolve – that he admired and tried to instil in his wife who lacked them so deplorably. If only Bim had not that rather coarse laugh and way of sitting with her legs up . . . now Tara would never . . . and if her nose were not so large unlike Tara's which was small . . . and Tara was gentler, more tender . . . He sighed a bit, shifting his bottom on the broken rattan seat of the chair. Things were as they were and had to be made the most of, he always said. At least in this country, he sighed, and just then his uncle's car appeared at the gate, slowly turned in, its windshield flooded by the sun, and came up the drive to park beneath the bougainvilleas.

Bim did get Tara to smile before the morning was over, however. Tara was leaning against the veranda pillar, watching the parrots quarrel in the guava trees, listening for a sound from Baba's room, hoping to hear a record played, when Bim came out with her band of girls and suddenly shouted 'Ice-cream! Caryhom Ice-cream-wallah!' and, before Tara's startled eyes, a bicycle with a small painted van attached to it that had been rolling down the empty, blazing road, stopped and turned in at the gate with its Sikh driver beaming broadly at the laughing girls and their professor.

Seeing Tara, Bim called out 'Look at these babies, Tara. When they hear the Caryhom ice-cream man going by they just stop paying any attention to my lecture. I can't do anything till I've handed each of them a cone. I suppose strawberry cones are what you all want, you babies? Strawberry cones for all of them, *Sardar-ji*,' she ordered and stood laughing on the steps as she watched him fill the cones with large helpings of pink ice-cream and hand them to the girls who were giggling, Tara realised, as much at their professor as at this childish diversion.

Bim noticed nothing. Swinging her arms about, she saw to it that each girl got her cone and then had one of them, a pretty child dressed in *salwar-kameez* patterned with pink and green parrots, carry a dripping cone down the veranda to Tara. 'Tara,' she called, 'that's for you. *Sardar-ji* made it specially for you,' she laughed, smiling at the ice-cream man who had a slightly embarrassed look, Tara thought. Embarrassed herself, she took the slopping cone from the girl and licked it to please Bim, her tongue recoiling at the synthetic sweetness. 'Oh Bim, if my daughters were to see me now – or Bakul,' she murmured, as Bim walked past holding like a cornucopia a specially heaped and specially pink ice-cream cone into Baba's room. Tara stopped licking, stared, trying to probe the bamboo screen into the room where there had been silence and shadows all morning. She heard Bim's voice, loud and gay, and although Baba made no audible answer, she saw Bim come out without the cone and knew Baba was eating it, perhaps quite happily. There was something magnetic about the icy pink sweetness, the synthetic sweet pinkness, she reflected, licking.

Now Bim let out a shout and began to scold. One of the girls had tipped the remains of her cone onto the veranda steps for the dog to lick – she had seen him standing by, watching, his tongue lolling and leaking. 'You silly, don't you know dogs shouldn't eat anything sweet? His hair will fall out – he'll get worms – it'll be your fault – he'll be spoilt – he won't eat his bread and soup now.'

'Let him enjoy himself, miss,' said the girl, smirking at the others because they all knew perfectly well how pleased Bim was to see them spoil her dog.

Tara narrowed her eyes at the spectacle of Bim scolding her students and smiling with pleasure because of the attention they had paid her dog, who had now licked up all the ice-cream and was continuing to lick and lick the floor as if it might have absorbed some of the delicious stuff. Remembering how Bim used to scold her for not disciplining her little daughters and making them eat up everything on their plates or go to bed on time, she shook her head slightly.

But the ice-cream did have, she had to admit, a beneficial effect all round: in a little while, as the students began to leave the house, prettily covering their heads against the sun with coloured veils and squealing as the heat of the earth burnt through their slippers, the gramophone in Baba's room stirred and rumbled into life again. Tara was grateful for it. She wished Bakul could see them now – her family.

When Bakul did come, late in the afternoon, almost comatose from the heat and the heavy lunch he had eaten, to fall onto his bed and sleep, this passage of lightness was over, or overcome again by the spirit of the house.

Tara, upright in a chair, tried first to write a letter to her daughters, then decided it was too soon, she would wait till she had more to say to them, and put the letter away in her case and tried to read instead, a book from the drawing room bookshelf that had been there even when she was a child – Jawaharlal Nehru's *Letters To A Daughter* in a green cloth binding – and sitting on the stuffed chair, spongy and clammy to touch, she felt that heavy spirit come and weigh down her eyelids and the back of her neck so that she was pinned down under it, motionless.

It seemed to her that the dullness and the boredom of her childhood, her youth, were stored here in the room under the worn dusty red rugs, in the bloated brassware, amongst the dried grasses in the swollen vases, behind the yellowed photographs in the oval frames – everything, everything that she had so hated as a child and that was still preserved here as if this were the storeroom of some dull, uninviting provincial museum.

She stared sullenly, without lifting her head, at a water-colour above the plaster mantelpiece – red cannas painted with some watery fluid that had trickled weakly down the brown paper: who could have painted that? Why was it hung here? How could Bim bear to look at it for all of her life? Had she developed no taste of her own, no likings that made her wish to sweep the old house of all its rubbish and place in it things of her own choice? Tara thought with longing of the neat, china-white flat in Washington, its cleanliness, its floweriness. She wished she had the will to get to her feet and escape from this room – where to? Even the veranda would be better, with the pigeons cooing soothingly, expressing their individual genius for combining complaint and contentment in one tone, and the spiky bougainvilleas scraping the outer walls and scattering their papery magenta flowers in the hot, sulphur-yellow wind. She actually got up and went to the door and lifted the bamboo screen that hung there, but the blank white glare of afternoon slanted in and slashed at her with its flashing knives so that she quickly dropped the screen. It creaked into place, releasing a noseful of dust. On the wall a gecko clucked loudly and disapprovingly at this untoward disturbance. She went back to the chair. If she could sleep, she might forget where she was, but it was not possible to sleep with the sweat trickling down one's face in rivulets and the heat enclosing one in its ring of fire.

Bakul said one could rise above the climate, that one could ignore it if one filled one's mind with so many thoughts and activities that there was no room for it. 'Look at me,' he had said the winter that they froze in Moscow. 'I don't let the cold immobilize me, do I?' and she and the girls, swaddled in all their warm clothing and the quilts and blankets off their beds, had had to agree that he did not. And gradually he had trained her and made her into an active, organised woman who looked up her engagement book every morning, made plans and programmes for the day ahead and then walked her way through them to retire to her room at night, tired with the triumphant tiredness of the virtuous and the dutiful. Now the engagement book lay at the bottom of her trunk. Bim had said nothing of engagements and, really, she could not bear to have any in this heat. The day stretched out like a sheet of glass that reflected the sun – too bare, too exposed to be faced.

Out in the garden only the coppersmiths were awake, clinging to the tree-trunks, beating out their mechanical call – tonk-tonk-tonk. Tonk-tonk-tonk.

Here in the house it was not just the empty, hopeless atmosphere of childhood, but the very spirits of her parents that brooded on – here they still sat, crouched about the little green baize folding table that was now shoved into a corner with a pile of old *Illustrated Weeklies* and a brass pot full of red and yellow spotted canna lilies on it as if to hold it firmly down, keep it from opening up with a snap and spilling out those stacks of cards, those long note-books and thin pencils with which her parents had sat, day after day and year after year till their deaths, playing bridge with friends like themselves, mostly silent, heads bent so that the knobs in their necks protruded, soft stained hands shuffling the cards, now and then speaking those names and numbers that remained a mystery to the children who were not allowed within the room while a game was in progress, who had sometimes folded themselves into the dusty curtains and stood peeping out, wondering at this strange, all-absorbing occupation that kept their parents sucked down into the silent centre of a deep, shadowy vortex while they floated on the surface, staring down into the underworld, their eyes popping with incomprehension.

Raja used to swear that one day he would leap up onto the table in a lion-mask, brandishing a torch, and set fire to this paper-world of theirs, while Bim flashed her sewing scissors in the sunlight and declared she would creep in secretly at night and snip all the cards into bits. But Tara simply sucked her finger and retreated down the veranda to Aunt Mira's room where she could always tuck herself up in the plum-coloured quilt that smelt so comfortingly of the aged relation and her ginger cat, lay her head down beside that purring creature and feel such a warmth, such a softness of comfort and protection as not to feel the need to wreck her parents' occupation or divert their atttention. It would have frightened her a bit if they had come away, followed her and tried to communicate with her.

And now she stirred uneasily in her chair although it held her damply as if with suckers, almost afraid that they would rise from their seats, drop their cards on the table and come towards her with papery faces, softly shuffling fingers, smoky breath, and welcome her back, welcome her home.

Once her father had risen, padded quietly to her mother's bedroom behind that closed door, and Tara had slipped in behind him, folded herself silently into the faded curtain and watched. She had seen him lean over her mother's bed and quickly, smoothly press a little shining syringe into her mother's arm that lay crookedly on the blue cover, press it in very hard so that she tilted her head back with a quick gasp of shock, or pain – Tara saw her chin rising up into the air and the grey head sinking back into the pillow and heard a long, whimpering sigh like an air-bag minutely punctured so that Tara had fled, trembling, because she was sure she had seen her father kill her mother.

All her life Tara had experienced that fear – her father had killed her mother. Even after Aunt Mira and Bim and Raja had explained to her what it was he did, what he kept on doing daily, Tara could not rid herself of the feel of that original stab of suspicion. Sometimes, edging up close to her mother, she would study the flabby, floury skin punctured with a hundred minute needle-holes, and catch her breath in an effort not to cry out. Surely these were the signs of death, she felt, not of healing?

Now she stared fixedly at the door in the wall, varnished a bright hideous brown with the varnish swelling into blisters or cracking into spidery patterns in the heat, and felt the same morbid, uncontrollable fear of it opening and death stalking out in the form of a pair of dreadfully familiar ghosts that gave out a sound of paper and filled her nostrils with white insidious dust.

In the sleeping garden the coppersmiths beat on and on monotonously like mechanics at work on a metal sheet – tonk-tonk-tonk. Tonk-tonk-tonk.

To look at Bim one would not think she had lived through the same childhood, the same experiences as Tara. She led the way so briskly up the stairs on the outside of the house to the flat rooftop where, as children, they had flown kites and hidden secrets, that it was clear she feared no ghosts to meet her there. Now they leant upon the stucco balustrade and looked down at the garden patterned with the light and shade of early evening. The heat of the day and the heavy dust were being sluiced and washed away by the garden hose as the gardener trained it now on the jasmines, now on the palms, bringing out the green scent of watered earth and refreshed plants. Flocks of parrots came winging in, a lurid, shrieking green, to settle on the sunflowers and rip their black-seeded centres to bits, while mynahs hopped up and down on the lawn, quarrelling over insects. Bim's cat, jet-black, picked her way carefully between the puddles left by the gardener's generously splashing, spraying hose, and twitched her whiskers and went 'meh-meh-meh' with annoyance when the mynahs shrieked at the sight of her and came to swoop over and divebomb her till she retreated under the hedge. A pair of hoopoes promenaded sedately up and down the lawn, furling and unfurling the striped fans on their heads. A scent of spider lilies rose from the flowerpots massed on the veranda steps as soon as they were watered, like ladies newly bathed, powdered and scented for the evening.

On either side of their garden were more gardens, neighbours' houses, as still and faded and shabby as theirs, the gardens as overgrown and neglected and teeming with wild, uncontrolled life. From the roof-top they could see the pink and yellow and grey stucco walls, peeling and spotted, or an occasional *gol mohur* tree scarlet with summer blossom.

Outside the sagging garden gate the road led down to the Jumna river. It had shrunk now to a mere rivulet of mud that Tara could barely make out in the huge flat expanse of sand that stretched out to the furry yellow horizon like some sleeping lion, shabby and old. There were no boats on the river except for a flat-bottomed ferry boat that idled slowly back and forth. There was no sign of life beyond an occasional washerman picking his washing off the sand dunes and loading it onto his donkey, and a few hairless *pai* dogs that slunk about the mud flats, nosing about for a dead fish or a frog to devour. A fisherman strode out into the river, flung out his net with a wave of his wrists and then drew in an empty net.

Tara could tell it was empty because he did not bend to pick up anything. There was nothing. 'Imagine,' she said, with wonder, for she could not believe the long-remembered, always-remembered childhood had had a backdrop as drab as this, 'we used to *like* playing there – in that dust and mud. What could we have seen in it – in that muddy little trickle? Why, it's hardly a river – it's nothing, just nothing.'

'Now Tara, your travels have made you very snobbish,' Bim protested, but lazily, good-naturedly. She was leaning heavily on her elbows, letting her grey-streaked hair tumble in whatever bit of breeze came off the river up to them, and now she turned to lean back against the balustrade and look up at the sky that was no longer flat and white-hot but patterned and wrinkled with pale brush-strokes of blue and grey and mauve. A flock of white egrets rose from the river bed and stitched their way slowly and evenly across this faded cloth. 'Nothing?' she repeated Tara's judgement. 'The holy river Jumna? On whose banks Krishna played his flute and Radha danced?'

'Oh Bim, it is nothing of the sort,' Tara dared to say, sure she was being teased. 'It's a little trickle of mud with banks of dust on either side.'

'It's where my ashes will be thrown after I am dead and burnt,' Bim said unexpectedly and abruptly. 'It is where Mira-*masi*'s ashes were thrown. Then they go down into the sea.' Seeing Tara start and quiver, she added more lightly 'It's where we played as children – ran races on the dunes and dug holes to bury ourselves in and bullied the ferryman into giving us free rides to the melon fields. Don't you remember the melons baking in the hot sand and splitting them open and eating them all warm and red and pouring with pink juice?'

'That was you and Raja,' Tara reminded her. 'I never dared get into that boat, and of course Baba stayed at home. It was you and Raja who used to play there, Bim.'

'I and Raja,' Bim mused, continuing to look up at the sky till the egrets pierced through the soft cloth of it and disappeared into the dusk like so many needles lost. 'I and Raja,' she said, 'I and Raja.' Then 'And the white horse and Hyder Ali Sahib going for his evening ride?' she asked Tara almost roughly, trying to shake out of her some corroboration as if she were unsure if this image were real or only imagined. It had the making of a legend, with the merest seed of truth. 'Can you remember playing on the sand late in the evening and the white horse riding by, Hyder Ali Sahib up on it, high above us, and his peon running in front of him, shouting, and his dog behind him, barking?' She laughed quite excitedly, seeing it again, this half-remembered picture. 'We stood up to watch them go past and he wouldn't even look at us. The peon shouted to us to get out of the way. I think Hyder Ali Sahib used to think of himself as some kind of prince, a nawab. And Raja *loved* that.' Her eyes gleamed as much with malice as with remembrance. 'Raja stood up straight and stared and stared and I'm sure he longed to ride on a white horse with a dog to run behind him just as old Hyder Ali did. Hyder Ali Sahib was always Raja's ideal, wasn't he?' she ended up.

Her words had cut a deep furrow through Tara's forehead. She too pressed down on her elbows, feeling the balustrade cut into her flesh as she tried to remember. Did she really remember or was it only Bim's picture that she saw, in shades of white and black and scarlet, out there on the shadowy sand-bank? To cover up a confusion she failed to resolve, she said 'Yes, and d'you remember Raja marching up and down here on the roof, swinging his arms and reciting his poems to us while we sat here on the balustrade, swinging our legs and listening? I used to feel like crying, it was so beautiful – those poems about death, and love, and wine, and flames.'

'They weren't. They were terrible,' Bim said icily, tossing her head with a stubborn air, like a bad-tempered mare's. '*Terrible* verses he wrote.'

'Oh Bim,' Tara exclaimed in dismay, widening her eyes in horror at such sacrilege. It was a family dictum that Raja was a poet and wrote great poetry. Now Bim, his favourite sister, was denying this doctrine. What had happened?

'Of course it was, Tara – terrible, terrible,' Bim insisted. 'We're not fifteen and ten years old any more – you and I. Have you tried reading it recently? It's *nauseating*. Can you remember any two lines of it that wouldn't make you sick with embarrassment now?'

Tara was too astounded, and too stricken to speak. Throughout her childhood, she had always stood on the outside of that enclosed world of love and admiration in which Bim and Raja moved, watching them, sucking her finger, excluded. Now here was Bim, cruelly and wilfully smashing up that charmed world with her cynicism, her criticism. She stood dismayed.

Bim was fierce. She no longer leant on the balustrade, drooping with reminiscences. She walked up and down agitatedly, swinging her arms in agitation, as Raja had done when quoting poetry in those days when he was a poet, at least to them. 'If you'll just come to my room,' she said, suddenly stopping, 'I'll show you some of those poems – I think they must be still lying around although I don't know why I haven't torn them all up.'

'Of course you wouldn't!' Tara exclaimed.

'Why not?' Bim flung at her. 'Come and see, tell me if you think it worth keeping,' and she swept down the stairs with a martial step, looking back once to shout at Tara '*And*, apart from poetry recitals, Tara, this terrace is where I cut your hair for you and made you cry. What an uproar there was.' She gave her head a quick, jerky toss. 'And here you are, with your hair grown long again, and it's mine that's cut short. Only no one cared when I cut *mine*.'

Tara hung back. She had been perfectly content to pace the terrace in the faint breeze, watch the evening darken, wait for the stars to come out and talk about the old days. Even if it was about the haircut, painful as that had been. But Bim was clattering down the stone stairs, the bells of the pink-spired temple at the bend of the river were suddenly clanging loudly and discordantly, the sky had turned a deep green with a wide purple channel through it for the night to come flowing in, and there was nothing for it but to follow Bim down the stairs, into the house, now unbearably warm and stuffy after the freshness and cool of the terrace, and then into Bim's cluttered, untidy room.

It had been their father's office room and the furniture in it was still office furniture – steel cupboards to hold safes and files, metal slotted shelves piled with registers and books, and the roll-top desk towards which Bim marched as Tara hesitated unwillingly by the door. Throwing down the lid, Bim started pulling out papers from the pigeon-holes and opening drawers and rifling through files and tutorial papers and college registers. Out of this mass of paper she separated some sheets and held them out to Tara with an absent-minded air.

Tara, glancing down at them, saw that they were in Urdu, a

language she had not learnt. It was quite useless her holding these sheets in her hand and pretending to read the verses that Raja had once recited to them and that had thrilled her then with their Persian glamour. But Bim did not notice her predicament, she was still occupied with the contents of the rifled desk. Finally she found what she was looking for and handed that, too, to Tara with a grim set of her mouth that made Tara quake.

'What is this, Bim?' she asked, looking down and seeing it was in Raja's English handwriting.

'A letter Raja wrote – read it. Read it,' she repeated as Tara hesitated, and walked across to the window and stood there staring out silently, compelling Tara to read while she tensely waited.

Tara read – unwillingly, unbelievingly.

Raja had written it years ago, she saw, and tried to link the written date with some event in their family history that might provide it with a context.

> *You will have got our wire with the news of Hyder Ali Sahib's death. I know you will have been as saddened by it as we are. Perhaps you are also a bit worried about the future. But you must remember that when I left you, I promised I would always look after you, Bim. When Hyder Ali Sahib was ill and making out his will, Benazir herself spoke to him about the house and asked him to allow you to keep it at the same rent we used to pay him when father and mother were alive. He agreed – you know he never cared for money, only for friendship – and I want to assure you that now that he is dead and has left all his property to us, you may continue to have it at the same rent, I shall never think of raising it or of selling the house as long as you and Baba need it. If you have any worries, Bim, you have only to tell – Raja.*

It took Tara some minutes to think out all the implications of this letter. To begin with, she studied the date and tried to recall when Hyder Ali had died. Instead a series of pictures of the Hyder Ali family flickered in the half-dark of the room. There was Hyder Ali, once their neighbour and their landlord, as handsome and stately as a commissioned oil painting hung over a mantelpiece, all in silver and grey and scarlet as he had been on the white horse on which he rode along the river bank in the evenings while the children stood and watched. He had cultivated the best roses in Old Delhi and given parties to which poets and musicians came. Their parents were not amongst his friends. Then there was his daughter Benazir, a very young girl, plump and pretty, a veil thrown over her head as she hurried into the closed carriage that took her to school, and the Begum whom they seldom saw, she lived in the closed quarters of the house, but at Id sent them, and their other tenant-neighbours, rich sweets covered with fine silver foil on a tray decked with embroidered napkins. They had lived in the tall stucco house across the road, distinguished from all the others by its wealth of decorative touches like the coloured fanlight above the front door, the china tiles along the veranda walls and the coloured glass chandeliers and lamps. They had owned half the houses on that road. When they left Delhi during the partition riots of 1947, they sold most of these houses to their Hindu tenants for a song – all except for Bim's house which she did not try to buy and which he continued to let to her at the same rent as before. It was to this that Raja, his only son-in-law and inheritor of his considerable property, referred in his letter. It was a very old letter.

Still confused, she said slowly 'But, Bim, it's a very old letter – years old.'

'But I still have it,' Bim said sharply, staring out of the window as if she too saw pictures in the dark. 'I still keep it in my desk – to remind me. Whenever I begin to wish to see Raja again or wish he would come and see us, then I take out that letter and read it again. Oh, I can tell you, I could write him such an answer, he wouldn't forget it for many years either!' She gave a short laugh and ended it with a kind of a choke, saying 'You say I should come to Hyderabad with you for his daughter's wedding. How can I? How can I enter his house – my landlord's house? I, such a poor tenant? Because of me, he can't raise the rent or sell the house and make a profit – imagine that. The sacrifice!'

'Oh Bim,' Tara said helplessly. Whenever she saw a tangle, an emotional tangle of this kind, rise up before her, she wanted only to turn and flee into that neat, sanitary, disinfected land in which she lived with Bakul, with its set of rules and regulations, its neatness and orderliness. And seemliness too – seemliness. She sat down weakly on the edge of Bim's bed, putting the letter down on the bedside table beside a pile of history books. She turned the pages of Sir Mortimer Wheeler's *Early India and Pakistan* and thought how relevant such a title was to the situation in their family, their brother's marriage to Hyder Ali's daughter. She wished she dared lighten the atmosphere by suggesting this to Bim, but Bim stood with her back arched, martial and defiant. 'Why let this go on and on?' she sighed instead. 'Why not end it now by going to Moyna's wedding, and then forget it all?'

'I have ended it already,' Bim said stubbornly, 'by not going to see them and not having them here either. It is ended. But I don't forget, no.'

'I wouldn't ever have believed – no one would ever have believed that you and Raja who were so close – so close – could be against each other ever. It's just unbelievable, Bim, and so – unnecessary, too,' she ended in a wail.

'Yes?' said Bim with scorn, turning around to stare at her sister. 'I don't think so. I don't think it is unnecessary to take offence when you are insulted. What was he trying to say to me? Was he trying to make me thank him – go down on my knees and thank him for this house in which we all grew up? Was he trying to threaten me with eviction and warn me what might happen if I ever stopped praising him and admiring him?'

'Of course not, Bim. How silly. He simply didn't know quite what he was writing. I suppose he was in a state – his father-in-law having just died, and you know how he always felt about him – and then having to take over Benazir's family business and all that. He just didn't know what he was writing.'

'A poet – not knowing what he was writing?' Bim laughed sarcastically as she came and picked up the letter and put it back in the desk. It seemed to have a pigeon-hole all to itself as if it were a holy relic like fingernails or a crooked yellow tooth.

'Do tear it up,' cried Tara, jumping up. 'Don't put it back there to take out and look at and hold against Raja. Tear it up, Bim, throw it away,' she urged.

Bim put the lid up with a harsh set to her mouth. 'I will keep it. I must look at it and remind myself every now and then. Whenever you come here and ask why I don't go to Hyderabād and visit him and see my little nieces and nephews – well then, I feel I have to explain to you, prove to you . . .' She stammered a bit and faltered to a stop.

'*Why*, Bim?'

But Bim would not tell her why she needed this bitterness and insult and anger. She picked up an old grey hairbrush that had lost half its bristles and was so matted with tangles of hair that Tara shuddered at the sight of it, and began to brush her hair with short, hard strokes. 'Come, let's go and visit the Misras. They've been asking about you, they want to see you. Ask Bakul to come, too – he must be getting bored. And he knows the Misras. You *met* him at their house – I'd nearly forgotten,' she laughed, a bit distractedly.

Tara followed her out, relieved to be in the open again, out of the dense musty web of Bim's room, Bim's entanglements, and to see the evening light and the garden. A bush of green flowers beside the veranda shook out its night scent as they came out and covered them with its powdery billows. Badshah rushed up, whining with expectation.

The sound of a 1940s foxtrot on Baba's gramophone followed them down the drive to the gate as if a mechanical bird had replaced the koels and pigeons of daylight. Here Bim stopped and told Badshah firmly to sit. They stood watching, waiting for him to obey. He made protesting sounds, turned around in circles, pawed Bim's feet with his claws, even whined a bit under his breath. Finally he yawned in resignation and sank onto his haunches. Then they turned out of the gate and ceased to hear the tinny rattle of the wartime foxtrot.

Walking up the Misras' driveway, they could hear instead the sounds of the music and dance lessons that the Misra sisters gave in the evenings after their little nursery school had closed for the day, for it seemed that they never ceased to toil and the pursuit of a living was unending. Out on the dusty lawn cane chairs were set in a circle and here the Misra brothers sat taking their rest – which they also never ceased to do – dressed in summer clothes of fine muslin, drinking iced drinks and discussing the day which meant very little since the day for them had been as blank and unblemished as an empty glass.

They immediately rose to welcome their neighbours but Bim stood apart, feeling a half-malicious desire to go into the house and watch the two grey-haired, spectacled, middle-aged women – once married but both rejected by their husbands soon after their marriage – giving themselves up to demonstrations of ecstatic song and dance, the songs always Radha's in praise of Krishna, the dance always of Radha pining for Krishna. She hadn't the heart after all and instead of joining the men on the lawn, she went up the steps to the veranda where the old father half-sat, half-reclined against the bolsters on a wooden divan, a glass of soda water in his hand, looking out and listening to his sons and occasionally shouting a command at them that went unheard, then sadly, meditatively burping. Tara and Bakul sat down with the brothers on the lawn and talked and listened to the voices of pupils and teachers mournfully rising and falling down the scales played on a lugubrious harmonium and tried, while talking of Delhi and Washington, politics and travel, to imagine the improbable scene indoors. Eventually the little pupils came out, drooping and perspiring, and rushed off down the drive to the gate where their ayahs waited for them, chatting and chewing betel leaves. After a while, the teachers, too, emerged onto the veranda. They too drooped and perspired and were grey with fatigue. There was nothing remotely amusing about them.

'Bim, Bim, why must you sit here with Papa? Come into the garden and have a drink,' they cried at once, together.

But Bim would not listen. She tucked up her feet under her to make it plain she was not getting up. 'No, no, I want to listen to Uncle,' she said, not wishing to add that she had no liking for his sons' company. 'Uncle is telling me how he was sent to England to study law but somehow landed up in Burma and made a fortune instead. I want to hear the whole story. And you must go and meet Tara and Bakul. They've come.'

'Tara and Bakul?' cried the two sisters and, straightening their spectacles and smoothing down their hair and their saris, they rushed down into the garden while Bim stayed by the sick old man.

'But Uncle, is it a true story?' she teased him. 'I never know with you.'

'Can't you see the proof?' he asked, waving his glass of soda water so that it spilt and frothed and sizzled down his arm. 'Now if I had gone north and had to work in a cold climate, learnt to wear a tie and button a jacket and keep my shoes laced and polished, I would have returned a proper person, a disciplined man. Instead, as you see, I went east, in order to fulfil a *swami's* prophecy, and there I could make money without working, and had to undress to keep cool, and sleep all afternoon, and drink all evening – and so I came back with money and no discipline and no degree,' he laughed, deliberately spilling some more soda water as if in a gesture of fatalism.

'What, all to satisfy a *swami*?'

'Yes, yes, it is true, Bimla. My father used to go to this *swami-ji*, no great man, just one of those common little *swamis* who sit outside the railway station and catch those people who come from the village to make their fortunes in the city. "*Swami-ji, swami-ji*, will I have luck?" they ask, and he puts his hand on their heads in blessing and says "Yes, son, if you first put five rupees in my pocket." That sort of man. My father went to him to buy a blessing for me – I was leaving for England next day. My trunk was packed, my passage booked, my mother was already weeping. But perhaps my father didn't give the *swami-ji* enough money. He said "Your son go to England? To Vilayat? Certainly not. He will never go north. He will go east." "No, no," said my father, "his passage is already booked on a P & O boat, he is leaving for Bombay tomorrow to catch it, he is going to study law in a great college in England." But *swami-ji* only shook his head and refused to say another word. So, as my father was walking home, very slowly and thoughtfully, who should bump into him, outside the Kashmere Gate post office, but an old friend of his who had been in school with him and then gone to Burma to set up in the teak business. And this man, this scoundrel, may he perish – oh, I forgot! He perished long ago, Bimla, leaving me all his money – he clasped my father in his arms and said "You are like a brother to me. Your son is my son. Send him to me, let him work for me and I will make a man of him." And so my passage was cancelled, I gave up my studies and went east, to Burma.' He gulped down half a glass of soda water suddenly, thirstily. 'That *swami-ji*,' he burped.

'And do you think if the *swami-ji* had not made that prophecy, your father would not have accepted his friend's offer?' asked Bim, filled with curiosity.

'Who can tell?' groaned the old man, shifting about in search of a more comfortable position. 'Fate – they talk about Fate. What is it?' He struck his head dramatically. 'This fate?'

'What is it, uncle? Does it pain?' Bim asked because his face, normally as smooth and bland as butter, was furrowed and gleaming with sweat.

He sank back, sighing 'Nothing, nothing, Bimla, my daughter, it is only old age. Just fate and old age and none of us escapes from either. You won't. You don't know, you don't think – and then suddenly it is there, it has come. When it comes, you too will know.'

Bim laughed, helping herself to some of the betel leaves in the silver box at his side. As she smeared them with lime and sprinkled them with aniseed and cardamoms, she said 'You think one doesn't know pain when one is young, uncle? You should sit down some day with ninety examination papers to correct and try and make out ninety different kinds of handwriting, all illegible, and see that your class has presented you with ninety different versions of what you taught them – all wrong!' She laughed and rolled up the betel leaf and packed it into her mouth. 'That is what I have been doing all day and it has given me a fine pain, too.' She grasped her head theatrically and the old man laughed. Bim had always made him laugh, even when she was a little girl and did tricks on her bicycle going round the drive while his two daughters screamed 'Bim, you'll fall!'

'You work too hard,' he said. 'You don't know how to enjoy life. You and my two girls – you are too alike – you work and let the brothers enjoy. Look at my sons there –' he waved his arm at them, the muslin sleeve of his shirt falling back to reveal an amulet tied to his arm with a black thread running through the thick growth of white hair. 'Look at them – fat, lazy slobs, drinking whisky. Drinking whisky all day that their sisters have to pay for – did you ever hear of such a thing? In my day, our sisters used to tie coloured threads on our wrists on Rakhibandhan day, begging for our protection, and we gave them gifts and promised to protect them and take care of them, and even if it was only a custom, an annual festival, we at least meant it. When my sister's husband died, I brought her to live here with us. She has lived here for years, she and her children. Perhaps she is still here, I don't know, I haven't seen her,' he trailed off vaguely, then ended up with a forceful 'But *they* – they let their sisters do the same ceremony, and they just don't care what it means as long as they can get their whisky and have the time to sit on their backsides, drinking it. Useless rubbish, my sons. Everything they ever did has failed . . .'

'What, not the new business as well? The real estate business that Brij started? Has that failed already?'

'Of course,' cried the old man, almost with delight. 'Of course it has. Can it succeed when Brij, the manager, cannot go to the office because he thinks it is degrading and refuses to speak to his clients because they are Punjabis, from Pakistan, and don't belong to the old families of Delhi? What is one to do with a fool like that? Am I to kick him out of the house and flog him down the road to the office? And look at Mulk – our great musician – all he does is wave his hand in the air and look at the stars in the daytime sky, and sing. Sing! He only wants to sing. Why? For whom? Who asked him to sing? Nobody. He just wants to, that is all. He doesn't think anyone should ask him to work or earn money – they should only ask him to sing.'

Out on the lawn there was a burst of laughter.

'And what about the old business they ran – the ice factory and soda water business? They had a good manager to run that.'

'Good manager – ho, yes! Very good manager. Had them eating out of his hand. They thought he was an angel on earth – a *farishtha* – slaving for their sakes, to fill their coffers with gold – till one day they went to the office to open the coffer for some gold – they must have needed it for those Grant Road women they go to, those song-and-dance women – and they found it empty, and the money gone.'

'And the manager?'

'Gone! He took care of money – the money went – he went with it.' The old man roared, slapping his thigh so that a fold of his *dhoti* fell aside, revealing the grey-haired stretch of old, slack flesh. Straightening it casually, he added 'What did they think? Someone else will work so that they can eat?'

'I didn't know about that,' said Bim, concerned. She had thought the Misras had at least one secure business behind them, as her own family still had their father's insurance business that still existed quietly and unspectacularly without their aid and kept them housed and fed. If the manager made more money than he ought to, Bim did not grudge him that. She earned her own living to supplement that unearned income, and it was really only Baba who needed to be supported. But the Misra boys – fat, hairy brutes – why should others look after them? The poor Misra girls, so grey and bony and needle-faced, still prancing through their Radha-Krishna dances and impersonating lovelorn maidens in order to earn their living . . . Bim shook her head.

'Fools,' the old man was still muttering as he fumbled about, looking for something under the pillows and bolsters and not finding it. Bim knew it was the hookah he was no longer allowed to smoke. 'Ugh,' he cried, the corners of his mouth turned down as though he were about to cry, like a baby. 'Not even my hookah any more. The doctor has said no, and the girls listen to the doctor, not to their father. What it is to be a father, to live without a smoke, or drink . . .'

Out on the lawn they were laughing again, their laughter spiralling up, up in the dark, as light as smoke.

'Laugh, laugh,' said the old man. 'Yes, laugh now – before it is all up with you and you are like me – washed up. But never mind, never mind,' he said to Bim, straightening his head and folding his arms so that he looked composed again, like a piece of stone sculpture. 'When I was young, when I was their age – do you think I was any better?' He winked suddenly at the surprised Bim. 'Was *I* a saint?' he laughed. 'I can tell you, I was just as fat, as greedy, as stupid, as wicked as *any* of them,' he suddenly roared, flinging out an arm as if to push them out of his way in contempt. 'A boozer, a womaniser, a bankrupt – running after drink, women, money – that was all I did, just like them, *worse* than them, any of them . . .' he chuckled and now his head wobbled on his neck as if something had come loose. '*Much* worse than any of them,' he repeated with desperate pride.

Bim, red-faced in the dark shadows, let down her feet cautiously and searched for her slippers.

And here was Jaya coming up the steps to fetch her. 'Bim, come and join us,' she called. 'Tara is telling us about Washington – it is such fun – and Papa should eat his dinner and go to sleep. Papa, I'm sending the cook with your dinner –' and she rushed off towards the kitchen while Bim went down the steps into the garden. The old man had sunk back against the bolsters and shut his eyes. She even thought he might have fallen asleep, he was so still, but a little later she heard him call 'The pickle, Jaya – don't forget the black lemon pickle – let me have a little of it, will you?'

Out on the lawn the talk was more sober, more predictable in spite of the whisky that accompanied it. Someone brought Bim a tall glass that chattered with ice. Could it be from their factory, Bim wondered, sipping, stretching her bare feet in the grass and feeling its dry tickle.

'Bakul-*bhai*, tell me,' said the older brother, rolling the ice cubes around in his glass, 'as a diplomat in an Indian embassy, how do you explain the situation to foreigners? Now when the foreign press asks you, perhaps you just say "No comment", but when you meet friends at a party, and they ask you what is going on here – how can a Prime Minister behave as ours does – how can ministers get away with all they do here – what is being done about the problems of this country – who is going to solve them – how, why is it like this? – then what do you say to them, Bakul-*bhai*?'

Bim, who was lighting herself a cigarette, stopped to watch her brother-in-law cope with this interrogation. It was quite dark on the lawn and although a light had been switched on in the veranda so that the old father could see to eat his dinner, it only threw a pale rectangle of light across the beds of cannas close to the house, and did not illuminate Bakul's face. He kept them all waiting in silence as he considered and then began his measured and diplomatic reply.

Elegantly holding his cigarette in its holder at arm's length, Bakul told them in his ripest, roundest tones, 'What I feel is my duty, my vocation, when I am abroad, is to be my country's ambassador. All of us abroad are, in varying degrees, ambassadors. I refuse to talk about famine or drought or caste wars or – or political disputes. I refuse – I *refuse* to discuss such things. "No comment" is the answer if I am asked. I can discuss such things here, with you, but not with foreigners, not in a foreign land. There I am an ambassador and I choose to show them and inform them only of the best, the finest.'

'The Taj Mahal?' asked Bim, blowing out a spume of smoke that wavered in the darkness, and avoiding Tara's eye, watchful and wary.

'Yes, exactly,' said Bakul promptly. 'The Taj Mahal – the Bhagavad Gita – Indian philosophy – music – art – the great, immortal values of ancient India. But why talk of local politics, party disputes, election malpractices, Nehru, his daughter, his grandson – such matters as will soon pass into oblivion? *These* aren't important when compared with India, eternal India –'

'Yes, it does help to live abroad if you feel that way,' mused Bim, while her foot played with the hem of her sari and she looked carefully away from Tara who watched. 'If you lived here, and particularly if you served the Government here, I think you would be obliged to notice such things: you would see their importance. I'm not sure if you could ignore bribery and corruption, red-tapism, famine, caste warfare and all that. In fact, living here, working here, you might easily forget the Taj Mahal and the message of the Gita –'

'Never,' interrupted Bakul firmly, ripely. 'A part of me lives here, the deepest part of me, always –'

'Ah,' Bim in turn interrupted him. 'Then it is definitely important to live abroad. In all the comfort and luxury of the embassy, it must be much easier, *very* easy to concentrate on the Taj, or the Emperor Akbar. Over here I'm afraid you would be too busy queueing up for your rations and juggling with your budget, making ends meet –'

'Oh Bim,' Tara burst out in protest, 'you *do* exaggerate. I don't see you queueing up for your rations – or even for a *bus*!'

Bim burst out laughing, delighted at having provoked Tara, and agreed there was some exaggeration in what she said. This annoyed Bakul who had taken it all so perfectly seriously, and he tapped his cigarette holder on the arm of his chair with the air of a judge tapping a gavel at a meeting grown unruly.

Tara cast her eyes around, looking for an escape. But Bim had thrown back her head in laughter, all the men beside her were laughing. Then she leant forward, a cigarette in her mouth, and Bakul leant towards her to light it. Seeing the match flare, the cigarette catch fire with a little throb, Tara was pricked with the realisation that although it was she who was the pretty sister, had always been, so that in their youth the young men had come flocking about her like inquisitive, hopeful, sanguine bees in search of some nectar that they sniffed on the air, it was Bim who was attractive. Bim who, when young, had been too tall and square-shouldered to be thought pretty, now that she was grey – and a good deal grey, observed Tara – had arrived at an age when she could be called handsome. All the men seemed to acknowledge this and to respond. There was that little sensual quiver in the air as they laughed at what she said, and a kind of quiet triumph in the way in which she drew in her cheeks to make the cigarette catch fire and then threw herself back into her chair, giving her head a toss and holding the cigarette away so that a curl of smoke circled languidly about her hand. Tara thought how attractive a woman who smokes is: there is some link formed between the man who leans forward with a match and the woman who bends her head towards that light, as Bakul and Bim did.

Tara did not smoke and no one offered her a light. Or was it just that Tara, having married, had rescinded the right to flirt, while Bim, who had not married, had not rescinded? No, it was not, for Bim could not be said to flirt. Slapping hard at a mosquito that had lighted on her arm, she was saying to Manu who had offered to fetch a Flit-gun, 'That's too much of a bother – don't.' Bim never bothered.

The Misra brothers and sisters were not interested in the subtleties underlying such exchanges. One brother wanted to know 'What is the price of good whisky in Washington? Not that terrible thing called bourbon but scotch – can you get scotch?' and the sisters asked Tara where she had bought her chiffon sari and her leather bag, and for how much. Bim listened to Tara giving them shoppers' information glibly but a little too fast, making her sound unreliable. It amused Bim to see, through a haze of cigarette smoke, Tara's not quite assimilated cosmopolitanism that sat on her oddly, as if a child had dressed up in its mother's high-heeled shoes – taller, certainly, but wobbling. Then the sisters' heads drew closer still to Tara, their voices dropped an octave, and they murmured, one from the left and one from the right, 'But how much longer can you keep your girls abroad? Mustn't they come home to marry now?'

Tara cowered back in her basket chair. 'They are only sixteen and seventeen,' she said plaintively.

'Time to marry – better to marry – time, time,' they cried, and Tara rubbed her mosquito-bitten toe in the grass in pained embarrassment, and Bim, overhearing them, lifted her eyebrows in horror and turned to Mulk, the younger brother who was silent, for sympathy.

Mulk had already drunk more glasses of whisky than anyone could count and sat ignoring the company, beating one hand on his knee, singing in little snatches in his hoarse, cracked voice, swaying his head joyfully to music that was audible only to him. Even since she had last seen him, he seemed to have deteriorated – his jaws prickled with several days' growth of beard, he wore a shirt with several buttons missing and a sleeve irremediably stained with betel juice, the slippers on his unwashed feet needed mending. He rolled his eyes in their sockets like a dog howling at the moon and hummed to himself. '*Zindagi*, O *Zindagi*,' he sang, tunelessly, and refreshed himself with another gulp of whisky.

Then suddenly the scene split, with a tearing sound. It was only whisky pouring out of an overturned glass and Mulk struggling to get out of the canvas chair, too tight for his heavy frame. As they all stopped talking to stare at him, he gestured widely and shouted dramatically, 'Where is my *tabla*-player? My harmonium player? My accompanists? Where are they? *Chotu-mia! Bare-mia*!' Standing, swaying on his thick legs, he roared at the lighted house and the scurrying figures on the veranda.

'Shh, Mulk-*bhai*,' cried Jaya and Sarla, their faces shrinking into small dark knots. 'You will wake Papa. Why are you shouting? You know they aren't there.'

'Yes, I know they aren't there' he blasted them, turning around and staggering towards them so that Bim and Tara had to hastily draw up their feet or he would have tripped over them. 'I know who turned them out – you two – you two turned them out –'

'Mulk, Mulk,' murmured his brothers.

Suddenly Mulk was clutching his hands to his chest like two puffy little birds and his voice rose in shrill, grotesque mimicry. '"It is a waste of money. How can we afford to keep them? We have to feed ourselves. Tell them to go, they must go – go – go –"' and he pushed out the two birds so that they fluttered away and fell at his sides. 'That is all I hear from them – these two –'

'Mulk, Mulk,' rose the pacifying croon from the pigeons in the chairs.

Mulk swung around to face Bim and Tara and Bakul now. 'They have got rid of my musicians,' he nearly wept. 'Sent them away. How am I to sing without accompaniment?'

'Mulk-*bhai*, we only pointed out that we haven't the money to pay them and we could not keep feeding them on kebabs and pilaos and kormas as you expected us to. Is it our fault if they went away once we stopped serving such food?'

'Food! It wasn't food they wanted. You are insulting them. You are insulting my *guru*. He does not want food, or money. He wants respect. Regard. That is what we must pay to a *guru*. But you have no respect, no regard. You think only of money – money – money. That is what you think about, you two –'

'Mulk, Mul-lk.'

'They have minds full of money, *dirty* minds. They don t understand the artist, how the artist lives for his art. They don't know how it is only music –' here he clasped his chest with a moist, sweating paw – 'only music that keeps me alive. Not food. Not money. Music: what can it mean to those who only think of money? If I say "I must have accompaniment for my singing", they say "Oh there is no money!" If I say, "I want my friends to come tonight so I can sing for them, cook dinner for them please," they cry "Oh we have no money!" Do you need money to make music?' he roared, lifting his arm so that the torn sleeve showed his armpit and the bush of grey hair in it. He stood, swaying, with the arm uplifted, the torn sleeve drooping, as he faced his visitors. 'Do you?' he roared, and they could see spit flying from his mouth and spraying them where they sat, helpless. 'Tell me – do you?'

The visitors were frozen. The family seethed. Then the sisters cracked like old dry pods from which the black seeds of protest and indignation spilt, infertile. Money, they were both saying, where were they to find money to pay for concerts and dinners?

'Don't I give you money?' shouted Mulk, lowering his head and swaying it from side to side threateningly. 'Where is all the money I give you – hey? Tell me. Tell me. Where is that five hundred rupee note I gave you – hey? Where is it? Show it to me. I want to see it. I want it.'

He began to plunge his legs up and down in the grass like a beast going methodically out of control. One of the small bamboo tables was knocked down, a glass spilt. Now at last Bakul acted. Rising to his feet casually, elegantly, he took Mulk by the arm, murmured to him in his most discreet voice, began to lead him away towards the house. They heard Mulk crying something about 'My *guru* – his birthday – I want to give – they won't let me – for my *guru* –' and then some sobbing intakes of breath, gasps for reason and control, and then only the flow of Bakul's voice, slipping and spreading as smoothly and evenly as oil, and then silence in which they became aware of Badshah barking fiercely out on the road.

Bim rose at last, brushing her sari as if there were crumbs, saying 'Listen to Badshah – he's saying we must get back. Come, Tara, if we don't go home at once, the cook will fall asleep and we'll have no dinner and Baba will go to bed without any.'

Now the Misra sisters too were released from their shell-shocked postures and rose gratefully, chattering once more. 'But why don't you stay to dinner, Bim?' 'Tara, have pot luck with us. We can't throw a dinner party as we would have in the old days – but pot luck . . .' and the brothers shouted 'Let's call Baba. Tell him we'll have music that will make him forget that rubbish he listens to – we'll get Mulk to sing!' Strangely enough, and much to Bim's and Tara's astonishment, Brij and Manu began to laugh, thumping each other like schoolboys. One even wiped his eyes of tears as he repeated 'Get Mulk to sing – Mulk to sing for us –' as if it were a family joke that only needed to be mentioned to set them off uncontrollably.

The sisters, a little more circumspect, edged closer to Tara, saying 'Mulk gets that way when he has had too much to drink. He doesn't mean it – he will forget about it – we'll give him his dinner – and, oh stay for pot luck, Tara!'

But Bim would not listen. The last time she had accepted an invitation to 'pot luck' she had been distressed to see the two Misra sisters halving and sharing a *chapati* between them, and jars of pickles had had to be opened to make up for the lack of meat and vegetables. It would not do. 'No, that won't do,' she said firmly. 'Can you hear Badshah calling? Listen to that bark – he'll have all the neighbours up, and your father, too,' and she swept up the veranda to say good night to the old man who lay supine on the divan, his two white, knobbed feet sticking out at the end of the sheet that covered him, saw that he was asleep and then went down to herd Tara and Bakul down the drive.

The sisters came to the gate with them, lingering by the jasmine bush to pick some for Tara. Giving her a handful, Jaya said 'Oh, Tara, these flowers make me think of that picnic – so many years ago now – do you remember, too? It was springtime – the flowers in Lodi Gardens –'

'And bees!' cried Sarla suddenly, catching Tara by the wrist so that a few of the jasmines fell. 'How those bees attacked Bim – oh don't you remember?'

But Tara withdrew her hand, dropping the remaining jasmines as she did so. She shook her head, refusing to remember any more. Bim, smiling faintly, covered up her ears with her hands and said 'How that dog barks – he has a voice like a trumpet,' and led Tara and Bakul across the road to their own gate where Badshah waited.

As they crossed the dusty road, Bakul cast a look at the tall dark house behind the hedge and asked 'What has happened to the Hyder Alis' house? Doesn't anyone live there?'

'No. I mean, only a poor relation of theirs. He must have been a nuisance to Raja in Hyderabad so they sent him here as caretaker. He takes opium – he just lies around – and the house is falling down about his ears. No one's replaced a brick or painted a wall there for years.'

'Oh what a shame – it was a lovely house, you know, Bakul,' said Tara.

Badshah's barks grew so urgent they could not speak to each other any more.

Baba was already asleep on his bed in the veranda when the sisters slipped quietly past, only glancing to see him lying on his side, one leg stretched out and the other slightly bent at the knee as if he were running, half-flying through the sky, one hand folded under his chin and the other uncurled beside it, palm upwards and fingers curved in – a finely composed piece of sculpture in white. Marble. Or milk. Or less: a spider's web, faint and shadowy, or just some moonlight spilt across the bed. There was something unsubstantial about his long slimness in the light white clothes, such a total absence of being, of character, of clamouring traits and characteristics. He was no more and no less than a white flower or harmless garden spider, the sisters thought, as if, when he was born, his parents, late in their lives, had no vitality and no personality left to hand down to him, having given it away in thoughtless handfuls to the children born earlier. Lying there in the dark, dressed in white, breathing quite imperceptibly, he might have been a creature without blood in his veins, without flesh on his bones, the sisters thought as they tiptoed past him, down the steps to the lawn to stroll.

The whole neighbourhood was silent now, asleep. The sound of traffic on the highway was distant, smothered by dust and darkness. At last one became aware of the presence of stars, the scent of night-flowering plants. The sisters, sleepless, rustled through the grass, up and down beside the long hedge. The black cat, pacing sedately beside them to begin with, suddenly leapt up into the air, darted sideways and disappeared.

Hands behind her back as she paced, Bim murmured 'Do you know, for a long time after Mira-*masi* died – for a long, long time – I used to keep seeing her, just here by the hedge –'

'Bim,' Tara cried incredulously.

'Yes, yes, I used to *feel* I was seeing her – just out of the corner of my eye, never directly before me, you know – just slipping past this hedge here –' she put out her hand and touched the white-flowering *chandni* – 'quite white and naked, as she was when she – when she –'

'Then – at that time,' Tara helped, pained.

'– small, like a thin little dog, a white one, just slipping along quietly – I felt as if towards the well at the back – that well –'

'That the cow drowned in?'

'And she used to say she would drown herself in but because she didn't, because she died, after all, in bed, I felt she was still trying to get there. A person needs to choose his death. But if I turned my head very quickly – then she would vanish – just disappear into the hedge –' and Bim touched it again, to remember, and had the back of her hand scratched by a thorn and heard some small creature skitter away into the leaves. 'I felt like one of those Antarctic explorers T.S. Eliot wrote about in his notes to *The Waste Land*, to that verse, do you know it, Tara?

> *Who is the third who walks always beside you?*
> *When I count, there are only you and I together*
> *But when I look ahead up the white road*
> *There is always another one walking beside you*
> *Gliding wrapt in a brown mantle, hooded*
> *I do not know whether a man or a woman*
> *– But who is that on the other side of you?*

They were silent as they scraped through the catching grasses at their feet, and had their heads bowed, not looking. Tara gave a small sigh that she disguised as a yawn: she had listened so often to Bim and Raja quoting poetry – the two of them had always had so much poetry that they carried in their heads. As a little girl, tongue-tied and shy, too diffident to attempt reciting or even memorising a poem – there had been that wretched episode in school when she was made to stand up and recite 'The Boy Stood On the Burning Deck' and it was found she could not proceed beyond the title – Tara was always struck dumb with wonder at their ability to memorise and quote. It was another of those games they shared and she did not. She felt herself shrink into that small miserable wretch of twenty years ago, both admiring and resenting her tall, striding sister who was acquainted with Byron, with Iqbal, even with T.S. Eliot.

Bim was calmly unaware of any of her sister's agonies, past or present. 'Only I was not at any extremity like those explorers in the icy wastes who used to see ghost figures,' she continued. 'I was not frozen or hungry or mad. Or even quite alone. I had Baba. After you married, and Raja went to Hyderabad, and Mira-*masi* died, I still had Baba. And that summer I got my job at the college and felt so pleased to be earning my living –'

She stopped abruptly as though there were a stone in the grass that she had stumbled on. Tara walked on, distracted, till she noticed Bim was not with her, then stopped to look back, fearfully. But Bim did not revive her tirade against Raja although Tara had feared they were beginning to slip into it again.

'Really, I was not mad in the least,' said Bim, strolling on. 'So then I thought there might be something in what the Tibetans say about the dead – how their souls linger on on earth and don't really leave till the forty-ninth day when a big feast is given and the last prayers are said and a final farewell given to the departed. It takes forty-nine days, they say in their Bardol Thodol, to travel through the three Bardos of death and all their stages. I felt Mira-*masi* was lingering on, in the garden, not able to leave because she hadn't been seen through all the stages with the relevant prayers and ceremonies. But then, who is?' Bim said more loudly, tossing her head, 'except for the Buddhist monks and nuns who die peacefully in their monasteries in the Himalayas? *We* were anything but peaceful that summer.'

'Yes, *what* a summer,' Tara murmured.

'Isn't it strange how life won't *flow*, like a river, but moves in jumps, as if it were held back by locks that are opened now and then to let it jump forwards in a kind of flood? There are these long still stretches – nothing happens – each day is exactly like the other – plodding, uneventful – and then suddenly there is a crash – mighty deeds take place – momentous events – even if one doesn't know it at the time – and then life subsides again into the backwaters till the next push, the next flood? That summer was certainly one of them – the summer of '47 –'

'For everyone in India,' Tara reminded primly. 'For every Hindu and Muslim. In India and in Pakistan.'

Bim laughed. 'Sometimes you sound exactly like Bakul.'

Tara stopped, hurt. Bim had always had this faculty of cutting her short, hurting her, and not even knowing.

But this time, it seemed, she did know. She touched Tara's elbow lightly. 'Of course you must – occasionally – when you've been married so long,' she explained good-humouredly and even apologetically

'But wouldn't you agree?' Tara said coldly.

'Yes, yes, you are perfectly right, Tara – it was so for all of us – for the whole family, and for everyone we knew, here in this neighbourhood. Nineteen forty-seven. That summer. We could see the fires burning in the city every night –'

Tara shuddered. 'I hate to think about it.'

'Why? It was the great event of our lives – of our youth. What would our youth have been without it to round it off in such a definite and dramatic way?'

'I was glad when it was over,' Tara's voice trembled with the passion she was always obliged to conceal. 'I'm so glad it is over and we can never be young again.'

'Young?' said Bim wonderingly, and as they were now near the veranda, she sank down on the steps where the quisqualis creeper threw its bunches of inky shadow on the white-washed steps, and sat there hugging her knees. Tara leaned against the pillar beside her, staring out and up at the stars that seemed to be swinging lower and lower as the night grew stiller. They made her deeply uneasy – they seemed so many milestones to mark the long distances, the dark distances that stretched and stretched beyond human knowledge and beyond human imagination. She huddled against the pillar, hugging it with one arm, like a child.

'Youth?' said Bim, her head sinking as if with sleep, or sorrow. 'Yes, I am glad, too, it is over – I never wish it back. Terrible, what it does to one – what it did to us – and one is too young to know how to cope, how to deal with that first terrible flood of life. One just goes under – it sweeps one along – and how many years and years it is before one can stand up to it, make a stand against it –' she shook her head sleepily. 'I never wish it back. I would never be young again for anything.'

An invisible cricket by her feet at that moment began to weep inconsolably.

# II

The city was in flames that summer. Every night fires lit up the horizon beyond the city walls so that the sky was luridly tinted with festive flames of orange and pink, and now and then a column of white smoke would rise and stand solid as an obelisk in the dark. Bim, pacing up and down on the rooftop, would imagine she could hear the sound of shots and of cries and screams, but they lived so far outside the city, out in the Civil Lines where the gardens and bungalows were quiet and sheltered behind their hedges, that it was really rather improbable and she told herself she only imagined it. All she really heard was the ceaseless rattling of frogs in the mud of the Jumna and occasionally a tonga horse nervously dashing down the road.

Raja, who had been ill all that year and could not climb the stairs to the terrace with her, groaned with impatience till she came down to tell him what she had seen.

Finding him soaked with perspiration from tossing on his bed in that small airless room on a close summer night, she hurried to bring a wet sponge and wipe his face.

'What do you think is happening?' he moaned. 'Can't you ask the Misras to go and find out? Did you see a light in Hyder Ali's house? Where do you think Hyder Ali Sahib could have gone? How could he have gone without sending a message to anyone? Not even to me?'

'How could he, Raja? You know it is far too dangerous.'

'He could have trusted *me*,' Raja cried.

Bim wanted to remind him he was only a boy, still in college, and that their neighbour, the old and venerable and wealthy Hyder Ali, could hardly be expected to take him into his confidence, but she knew better than to upset him. The slightest upset made his temperature rise. She dipped the sponge in the enamel bowl in which blocks of ice clinked, and dabbed at his head again. Lifting his dark, wavy hair, she trailed the sponge across his white forehead and saw how waxen and sick his white face was, with a physical pang that made her twinge. His face had been heavy once, his lips pouting and self-indulgent: now all was bloodless, fine and drawn. He moved his head aside angrily and the cold drops fell on the pillow, soaking it.

'Go to his house and find out, Bim,' he begged.

'I told you – I've just been up on the roof to see. One can see right into the garden from there. There's no one there, not even a gardener. The house is dark, all the doors are shut. There's no one there. They must have planned it in advance, Raja – it all looks quite orderly, as if they had planned and organised it all in advance just as if they were going up to Simla for the summer.'

'They could have been taken away – dragged out and taken away –'

'Of course not' Bim snapped. 'In that case, we would all have come to know, all the neighbours would have heard. We would have seen the mob arriving, seen the lights and heard all the noise. The Hyder Alis could have called for help, we would all have gone to help. There was no sound. No one came. They've just gone.'

'How is it you didn't hear them go then?' Raja snapped, equally angry.

'Raja, they must have done it *quietly* so as not to let anyone know,' Bim said in exasperation. 'Now you must just wait till you hear from them – they are sure to send word as soon as it is safe.'

'Safe? For Muslims? Here in India? It will be safe after every Muslim has had his throat slit,' Raja said with great viciousness. He half-lifted himself from the bed and then threw himself violently back again. 'And here I am – too ill to even get up and help. And the only time in my life that I've ever been ill,' he added bitterly.

Bim was quiet, floating the sponge back and forth in the bowl with wrinkled, frozen fingertips. She felt her exasperation blotted out by wonder at Raja's ways of thinking and feeling, so different from anyone else's at that time or day. She could not help admiring what she saw as his heroism, his independent thinking and courage. Raja was truly the stuff of which heroes are made, she was convinced, and yet here he lay, ironically, too ill to play the hero he longed to and, she half-believed, was meant to be. She lifted her eyes to see his chest rising and falling far too fast and excitedly and the twitching of his hands on the bedsheet.

'If you're not quiet, Raja, I shall have to call the doctor,' she said mournfully, and got up from the cane stool beside his bed. 'Let me read to you – it will take your mind off – '

'No, it won't,' he said explosively. 'Nothing can take my mind off – but read anyway, read if you like,' he mumbled.

She went to the bookshelves that lined one wall of the room, straight to a volume of Byron's poems that she knew, by experience, were what captivated him soonest, most easily swept him away into a mood of pleasure and appreciation. She brought it to his bed and, sitting down on the cane stool again, opened it at random and began to read aloud:

> '*The Assyrian came down like a wolf on the fold,*

*And his cohorts were gleaming in purple and gold . . .'*

and Raja lay quiet, his hands gathered together on his chest, stilled by the splendour of this vision, transported by the strength and rhythm of the lines, and Bim gloated that she could lead him so simply into a world out of this sickness and anxiety and chaos that burnt around them and across the country that summer.

All summer she nursed him and read to him. Sitting on the stool by his bed, her hair falling straight and lank on either side of her dark face, her eyes lowered to the book on her lap, she murmured aloud the poems of Tennyson and Byron and Swinburne that she and Raja both loved.

*'Now sleeps the crimson petal, now the white,*
*Nor waves the cypress in the palace walk;*
*Nor winks the gold fin in the porphyry font;*
*The firefly wakens: waken thou with me.*

*Now droops the milkwhite peacock like a ghost,*
*And like a ghost she glimmers on to me.*

*Now lies the earth all Danaë to the stars*
*And all thy heart lies open unto me . . .'*

Silent for a while, looking up to see if Raja's eyes were open and staring up at the flies crawling across the ceiling, or closed as he listened, half in sleep, she turned to another book and read:

*From too much love of living,*
*From hope and fear set free,*
*We thank with brief thanksgiving*
*Whatever gods may be*
*That no man lives forever,*
*That dead men rise up never;*
*That even the weariest river*
*Winds somewhere safe to sea.*

That was one of Raja's favourite poems, one he used to recite to her when they were up on the terrace together, reluctant to come down into the house at twilight, trying to prolong the evening and the sense of freedom they had up there under the unlimited sky. But now he would not express his enthusiasm quite so frankly. Now he would sometimes grunt 'Hmm, very lovely to hear, but – too many words, all words, just words. Now any Urdu poet could put all that into one couplet, Bim, just one couplet,' and she would pause for him to quote from his beloved Urdu poetry, all of which sounded exactly alike to her only she would rather have cut out her tongue than said so to him. It was always, as far as she could make out, the cup, the wine, the star, the lamp, ashes and roses – always the same. But to him each couplet was a new-cut gem.

'*We have passed every day from morning to night in pain,*
*We have forever drunk tears of blood,*'

he would quote in an expiring voice and with a roll of his eyes that she found excessively romantic and embarrassing so that she simply nodded in agreement in order to keep from bursting out in protest.

'But you don't understand,' Raja groaned, clasping his hands on his chest. 'You don't know any Urdu, you can't understand.'

Raja had studied Urdu in school in those days before the Partition when students had a choice between Hindi and Urdu. It was a natural enough choice to make for the son of a Delhi family: Urdu had been the court language in the days of the Muslim and Moghul rulers and had persisted as the language of the learned and the cultivated. Hindi was not then considered a language of great pedigree; it had little to show for itself in its modern, clipped, workaday form, and its literature was all in ancient, extinct dialects. Raja, who read much and had a good ear, was aware of such differences.

'See,' he told his sisters when he came upon them, bent over their homework at the veranda table, laboriously writing out Hindi compositions on My Village or The Cow, 'you can't call this a language.' He made a scornful sound in his nose, holding up one of their Hindi copy-books as if it were an old sock. 'Look, its angles are all wrong. And this having to go back and cross every word as you finish writing it, it is an – an impediment. How can you think fluently when you have to keep going back and crossing? It impedes the flow of the – the composition,' he told them and they were thunderstruck by such intellectual revelations. 'Look,' he said again and wrote out a few lines in the Urdu script with a flourish that made them quiver with admiration.

Their neighbour and landlord, Hyder Ali, came to hear of the boy's interests. He himself had a substantial library housed in a curious tower-like protuberance built at one corner of his bungalow. Seeing Raja swinging on the garden gate as he was coming back from his evening ride along the banks of the Jumna, he stopped to invite him to visit his library. Raja, appalled at having been caught at the childish pastime of hanging on the creaking, swaying garden gate, dazzled by the impressive figure of the old gentleman with silvery hair, dressed in white riding clothes and seated upon the white horse that Raja had for years envied him, often climbing up the garden wall to watch it being fed and groomed in the stable at the back, quite overcome at being given an invitation that he had only dreamt of in secret, nodded his acceptance in dumbfounded silence at which the old landlord smiled.

He presented himself at the Hyder Alis' next day, was shown in by a suspicious servant, waved into the library by a preoccupied Hyder Ali in his office room, and let loose amongst the books and manuscripts that were to him as the treasures of Haroun al Raschid. He would sit there for hours, daily, turning over the more valuable of Hyder Ali's manuscripts under the watchful eye of an old clerk employed by the landlord to keep his books, an aged priest with the face of a white goat who glared, slit-eyed, through his wire-rimmed spectacles at this son of the heathen allowed by some dangerous whim of the rich landlord's to touch holy manuscripts he should not have come near. The air was so sharp, so pungent with the old man's distaste and suspicion that finally Raja would become physically uncomfortable and go home, often with several volumes of poetry lent him by the amused and generous Hyder Ali.

Aunt Mira seemed as perturbed as the old clerk by this strange friendship. Sitting on the veranda with her mending, she saw Raja come out of his room with an armful of books to return to Hyder Ali and warned him in an awkward mumble 'Raja, don't you think you go there a little too often? Are you sure you are not in their way?'

'But Hyder Ali Sahib invited me – he told me I could take all the books I wanted, as often as I liked.'

'That was generous of him. But perhaps he didn't mean *quite* so often, *quite* so many.'

'Why?' asked Raja stubbornly. He stood on the steps a minute, waiting for Aunt Mira to reply. When she did not, he went off with a disgusted look.

If Hyder Ali found his visits too frequent and the hours spent in his library too long, he neither said so nor even implied it by a look. He himself was either out on business or in his office room adjoining the library, going through his letters and files with a pair of clerks, for he was the owner of much property in Old Delhi and this seemed to entail an endless amount of paper work. Raja would hear him dictating to his clerks and the scratching of their pens while he himself sat cross-legged on a rug in the 'tower' or on a curly sofa upholstered in velvet and backed with painted tiles set in the ornately carved rosewood, reading and glorying in the beauty of the manuscripts and the poetry and in the extraordinary fact of his being here at all.

As he grew older and more sure of himself, he began to take part in Hyder Ali's family life, for they all grew accustomed to him so that the sharp watchfulness softened into baffled acceptance.

Coming out of the library, he would see Hyder Ali's wife and daughter sitting on a divan on the veranda, cutting up vegetables for pickles or embroidering their coloured veils, and accept a slice of guava held out by the Begum or stop to tell them of his parents' health or some gossip about the servants demanded of him. In the evenings, tired of his own noisy sisters and peculiar old aunt and still more peculiar little brother, he would wander across to the Hyder Ali's garden where there was always a gathering of friends at that hour, chairs and divans and bolsters arranged in a circle on the lawn, drinks and ice and betel leaves served on silver trays, and gentlemen discussing politics and quoting poetry. It was an almost shocking contrast to the shabbiness of their own house, its peculiarities that hurt Raja by embarrassing him as he grew up and began to compare them with other homes, other families. Raja naturally inclined towards society, company, applause; towards colour, song, charm. It amazed and enchanted him that in the Hyder Ali household such elements were a part of their lives, of their background. In his own home they were totally alien. He felt there could be no house as dismal as his own, as dusty and grimy and uncharming. Surely no other family could have as much illness contained in it as his, or so much oddity, so many things that could not be mentioned and had to be camouflaged or ignored. The restraints placed on him by such demands made him chafe – he was naturally one to burst out and overflow with enthusiasm or praise or excitement. These possibilities were enticingly held out to him at the Hyder Alis'.

Once he had outgrown his khaki school shorts and taken to fine white muslin shirts and pyjamas, he acquired sufficient self-confidence to join the circle of much older men on the lawn, and wisely sat listening rather than talking, saving up the talk for later when he would return home and tell Bim every detail, however casual or trivial, that glowed in his eyes with a special radiance related to everything that was Hyder Ali's.

Having angered everyone in his own family by coming home very late one night, long after their dinner time, he lay awake on his cot in the garden and gave Bim a whispered account of the glories of a party at the Hyder Alis'.

'There was a poet there tonight,' he whispered, too tense with excitement to sleep. 'A real poet, from Hyderabad, who is visiting them. He read out his poetry to us – it was wonderful – and Hyder Ali Sahib gave him a ring with a ruby in it.'

'Was it that good?' Bim murmured sleepily, exhausted by having waited up so late for Raja to come home and by Aunt Mira's tearful laments about his bad ways.

'Good – but I think I could write as good verse. And, you know, Hyder Ali Sahib asked me to recite, too.'

'Did you?'

'Yes, but not my own,' he said regretfully. 'They asked me to recite my favourite verses so I read them Iqbal's,' and he quoted to the uncomprehending Bim in proud, triumphant tones:

> '*Thou didst create night but I made the lamp.*
> *Thou didst create clay but I made the cup.*
> *Thou didst create the deserts, mountains and forests,*
> *I produced the orchards, gardens and groves.*
> *It is I who made the glass out of stone*
> *And it is I who turn a poison into an antidote.*'

The words were absorbed by the dusty night garden so brimful of sleep and quiet as to seem crowded and to press upon them with its weight. Then Bim asked ironically 'And did Hyder Ali Sahib give you a ring with a ruby in it too?'

Raja might have been offended if he had caught the irony in the low voice but all he heard were the voices of Hyder Ali's guests as they praised his excellent diction, his perfect pronunciation. The poet from Hyderabad had fondled his shoulder, saying 'He will go far, Hyder Ali Sahib. A mind that can appreciate Iqbal at such a tender age will surely go far.' Entirely missing the sycophancy behind the words, the gesture, Raja had glowed almost as if he had written the verses himself. Even Bim and the dark garden could not dampen his glow.

But he was affronted when, seeing him write frenziedly all one afternoon that they were locked into the house because of a dust-storm raging outside, she had asked 'Are you going to be an Urdu poet when you grow up, Raja?'

He felt that she ought to know that he was one already. But of course an ignorant younger sister could not see that. He gave her a bitter look through a haze of cigarette smoke. He had taken to smoking.

The summer his final school examination results came out, his parents were obliged to pay some attention to him. Raja would stand in their way as they went down the veranda steps to the car waiting to take them to the Roshonara Club for their daily game of bridge, or he would wait up for them in the veranda till they returned, late at night when the others were asleep.

'Why are you still awake?' his mother sighed disapprovingly as she drifted towards her bedroom, fatigued as always.

'Father, I have to give in my application form for college. You have to sign.'

'Give it to me,' his father grunted through the disintegrating flakes of a moist cigar. Then, peering at the form in the dim light that came through the open front door, he frowned 'But this is no college for you. It is a Jamia Millia form.'

'That is where I want to study. I went there to get a form.'

'You can't study there,' his father said, taking the cigar out of his mouth and spitting out a shred of tobacco. 'It is a college for Muslim boys.'

'No, anyone can go there who wants to specialise in Islamic studies.'

It was a phrase Raja liked to use. He had picked it up from Hyder Ali. It had impressed his sisters and his aunt. He gazed into his father's face in the hope of similarly impressing him.

But his father's face darkened by several shades and he stuttered in his curiously insipid and uninflected voice, 'Specialise in Islamic studies? What are you talking about, you dunce?'

'That is what I am going in for, father,' Raja said steadily, somehow managing to imply his pride in his unusual choice, and his steadfastness, and his scorn for this vague old man who could not understand.

'Rubbish,' said his father flatly. 'Bunkum,' he said, using one of his favourite phrases, and tore the form in two before marching off to his room.

It was a stormy summer. Bim and Tara would chew their lips and exchange puzzled looks as they stood listening behind the curtains while father and son argued hotly whenever they met which was only occasionally and briefly so that all the arguments they built up inside themselves in silence burst out with great explosiveness on those few occasions. In the meantime, Raja grew more and more sullen and unpredictable in his temper while their father appeared to retreat deeper into the shadows off-stage where he existed unseen by his children. Finally, late one night when Raja forced him to sit down after his return from the club, not brush him aside as he walked past quickly, his father explained. Perhaps he had played a good game at the club. Perhaps he had enjoyed his dinner there. He was puffing at his cigar with an air of calm self-confidence as he talked.

'If you had asked me a few years ago, I would have said yes at once: yes, all right.'

'How could I ask a few years ago? I've only finished school this year, in April.'

'I know, I know. I am not talking about you, about your school record.' He waved his cigar so that the thick odour of tobacco swept through the closed room like a damp rag. 'I'm talking about the political situation. Don't you know anything about it? Don't you know what a struggle is going on for Pakistan? How the Muslims are pressing the British to divide the country and give them half? There is going to be trouble, Raja – there are going to be riots and slaughter,' he said, dropping his voice cautiously. 'If you, a Hindu boy, are caught in Jamia Millia, the centre of Islamic studies – as you call it – you will be torn to bits, you will be burnt alive – '

'*Who* will do that to me?' asked Raja in astonishment, somewhat feigned for he knew of the political situation well enough from the evening gatherings in the Hyder Alis' garden. The men there talked freely, forgetting the young boy's presence, or his religion, and he listened, he was aware. Only he had never related such talk to his own plans or life. At that time he was still childish enough to consider it a kind of adults' game in which he was not allowed to take part. He was somewhat flattered that his father, of all people, appeared to consider him adult enough now. He was flattered enough to listen attentively.

'*Who* will do that to you? Muslims, for trying to join them when they don't want you and don't trust you, and Hindus, for deserting them and going over to the enemy. Hindus and Muslims alike will be out for your blood. It isn't safe, Raja, it isn't safe, son.'

Raja was thrilled by the idea and looked as bright-eyed as a child presented with a bright sword, but a thin, irritated voice whined from the bedroom 'What is it you are telling the boy?'

'Some facts,' shouted the father, suddenly determined, suddenly decisive, 'that he should know.' He had seen Raja's steadfastness waver and he jumped to take advantage: he was a practised bridge player.

Seeing this triumph, Raja shrunk visibly on the stool and became sullen again. He had not expected either quickness of response or reasoned opposition from the man who appeared to deal with both family and business by following a policy of neglect. Raja had known him only as someone leaving for the office or for the club, returning late and too tired for anything. He was startled by this unexpected aspect of his father, startled and put out.

His father saw his advantage with the shrewd, watchful eye of the card-player, and went on expounding his theme to the boy – superfluously, no more was really needed. When his wife called again, he went in to pacify her but took up the matter with Raja again the next day and the next. Now it was Raja who retreated, who avoided him and tried to wriggle out of these confrontations by staying close to Aunt Mira and his sisters. They were all astonished by the way the father began to turn up in their midst while they were having a quietly domestic tea, or bickering over their homework, and began to address Raja as though he were not one of them but one of the adults, a person with whom adult affairs could be discussed. Raja was silent now. He had not expected this. He had certainly expected his father to oppose him, but ineffectually and non-verbally, merely with arrogance and silence. Raja was not really prepared to reason or debate with his father. He was carried away by ideas, on wings of imagination, not by reason or analysis. Recognising his father's superior forces, he dispiritedly gave in and ceased to argue.

Their father's visits to their part of the house ceased, too. Once again he went through the day without addressing a word to them on his way out of it or into it. They knew him only as the master of the entrance and the exit.

And then their mother, for the first time in twenty years, missed an evening at the club, said she did not feel well and would stay in bed. That night she passed quietly into a coma so that when her husband returned from the club after an unsatisfactory game with an unaccustomed partner, he found her lying still and flaccid on her bed, quite beyond questioning him on his game.

The ambulance came. The children stumbled out of their beds to watch her being carried out like a parcel containing some dangerous material that had to be carefully handled.

Next day, Tara, possessed by a childish memory of trailing after her mother along the rose walk on a summer morning, clamoured to be taken to see her, but a trembling Aunt Mira held her in her arms as if to protect her from something so unsuitable, and their father told them bluntly that she was unconscious and there was no point in their visiting her.

Instead of going to the club, he went to the hospital every evening now. The children sat on the veranda steps waiting for him to come home with some news. While they waited, they told stories, read, played games, and forgot. Only the whiff of hospital disinfectants and anaesthetics that clung to his clothes when he returned, reminded them that he had been to the hospital and not to the club. His face looked even gloomier than when he had played a bad game at the bridge table and, looking at it, they did not want to question him after all. Instead they turned instinctively to Aunt Mira who smiled with grotesque unnaturalness into their troubled faces and made them laugh by dropping things, forgetting others and stumbling about the house like a sad comedian.

Their mother died without seeing any of them again. If she ever, for a minute, regained consciousness, it was only to murmur the names of familiar cards that seemed to drift through her mind with a dying rustle.

Since they were not taken to her funeral, it was a little difficult for the children to remember always that she was not at the club, playing cards, but dead. The difference was not as large as friends and neighbours supposed it to be and the children, exchanging looks of mutual guilt when the neighbours came and wept a few tears required by custom and commiserated and tried to console, tacitly agreed to keep their guilt a secret. The secret replaced their mother's presence in the house, a kind of ghostly surrogate which they never quite acknowledged and quite often forgot.

Raja went dispiritedly to Hindu College one day with one of the Misra boys summoned by his father to take him, since he was already a student of this college in Kashmere Gate picked by his father as suitable since he had studied there himself. When he came back, admission forms filled, subscriptions paid, a student enrolled in the English Literature course, he flung himself onto his bed and sulked for a week, refusing even to get up and go across to the Hyder Alis' in the evenings although the Begum herself, hearing of their mother's death, sent across a personal invitation.

'Father's gone to the club – get up, Raja. Come on. We're playing Seven Tiles in the garden – won't you play?' coaxed Bim from the doorway. She was afraid that he was not only brooding over his defeat in the matter of the Jamia Millia but over their mother's death, and could not bear the thought of his silent feelings.

He only snarled a reply and flung a book at her to drive her away. It was a little volume of Urdu poetry. Shocked, she bent to pick it up and dust it before quietly placing it on his bookshelf.

Raja started cycling to college with the Misra boys. This activity seemed to rouse him out of his sulks and, in spite of himself, he did begin to grow interested in college life and in his studies. He brought home volumes of Tennyson and Swinburne and lent them to Bim to read. No one in their family had studied literature before. Now she and Raja fell upon it with a kind of hunger, as if it were the missing element in their lives at last made available, and devoured it with an appetite, reading aloud to each other and memorising verses to quote aloud till Tara squirmed in misery and Aunt Mira's jaw swung from its hinges in admiration.

But English literature, newly come upon and radiant in its freshness, was not the only gate opened to Raja now. His father had been a student of the college long ago; it had been very different in his time, and he had no idea how politically aware the students now were, what a hotbed it was for political fanaticism, and how many politicians and fanatics from outside had successfully infiltrated it. The quickly-aroused and enthusiastic Raja was drawn into this feverish atmosphere by curiosity and by an adolescent need for a cause. The boys there saw an easy recruit but had no inkling that Raja's true and considered reaction to their fanatical Hindu beliefs would be one of outrage and opposition. They had not known, after all, about his admiration for Hyder Ali, for Urdu poetry, for the evening gatherings of poets and politicians in the garden. There was an immediate clash between them that roused each of them to greater, wilder enthusiasm for his particular cause. The atmosphere was so explosive, the air vibrated with threats and rumours of violence and enemity. Raja withdrew, began to be a bit cautious in what he said, assumed a cool air, watched, listened. He read mostly Lord Byron. Reading, he seemed to form a picture of himself, an image, that Bim, not his college acquaintances, was the first to recognise.

Bim remembered how, as small children, Raja had announced, so grandly, 'When I grow up, I shall be a hero,' making her instantly, with shining eyes, respond 'And I will be a heroine,' which had made Tara feel so miserable and excluded that she ran to Aunt Mira, whimpering 'Bim and Raja say they will be a hero and heroine. They laugh when I say I will be a mother,' and made Aunt Mira call the two of them for a scolding.

Bim remembered that when she heard Raja read aloud to her from Byron:

*'Place me on Sunium's marbled steep,*
*Where nothing, save the waves and I,*
*May hear our mutual murmurs sweep:*
*There, swan-like, let me sing and die:*
*A land of slaves shall ne'er be mine:*
*Dash down yon cup of Samian wine.'*

and tell her the story of Byron's fight for Greek independence and his death in Greece as a hero and poet. 'Like you,' Bim murmured, making Raja stare hard at her to see if she were mocking. She gazed back at him innocently. Then he gave a slight curl of his lip as if he were pleased, and she was both perturbed and annoyed at herself. She did not like it and she later wondered if it had put ideas into his head – dangerous, heady ones about his heroism, his poetry. He must have let the boys in college know this somehow because Bim overheard the Misra boys call him 'Lord Byron' and, at times, simply 'Lord'. It made her hot with anger and remorse at her own part in it.

Raja started going to the Hyder Alis' for those evening gatherings again. Aunt Mira was perturbed. She had heard their father talk, she had heard talk amongst the servants and the neighbours, that worried her. Her lips closed about a thread she was sucking to a fineness so that it would enter a needle's eye, she frowned and shook her head at him as he went leaping down the veranda steps and raced down the drive.

'Why, Mira-*masi*?' Bim asked, putting one hand on her knee, moved by her aunt's expression.

Her aunt sat helplessly sucking the thread that dangled from her lips like a fine tail. As she put up her hand to remove it, her hand trembled. 'He should not,' she said in a kind of whimper. 'It isn't safe.'

'They are our neighbours, Mira-*masi*' Bim exclaimed in surprise.

'But Muslims – it isn't safe,' her aunt whispered, trembling. 'Oh, Bim,' she said distractedly, 'won't you get me your father's brandy bottle from the sideboard? A drop – just a drop in my tea – I do need it – it might help – it isn't safe . . .' And Bim, astonished and also tickled by the idea, rushed to fetch the bottle from the dark and richly odoriferous recesses of the great gloomy sideboard in the dining room and tipped it over her aunt's tumbler of tea. 'More, Mira-*masi*, more?' she asked as the drops trickled in and Aunt Mira, pressing her fingers to her trembling lips, nodded: more, more, till the tumbler was full and then she seized it and drank it, watched open-mouthedly by her nieces. They heard the tumbler chatter against her false teeth and laughed. But 'No, it isn't safe,' she repeated with a hiccup, lowering the tumbler to the tea tray with a nervous clatter. 'Run and put the bottle back, Bim – it's not safe.'

Raja didn't care. He climbed over the gate and jumped into the road rather than laboriously open and shut it, then strolled into the Hyder Alis' garden, past the bushes of flowering jasmine and oleander, the rose beds and the fountain, slightly surprised to find the gathering much shrunk since he had last visited it. Many of the Hyder Alis' friends seemed to have vanished. Had they already gone to the Pakistan that was to be? Raja wondered. He was slightly stalled, too, when he felt the welcome at the Hyder Alis' not quite so warm, as gracious and effusive as before. He wondered if it could be because he had joined Hindu College and was studying English Literature instead of Urdu at Jamia Millia as Hyder Ali had advised him to do. But it was not Hyder Ali who was cool to him – in fact there was something gently loving in his gesture of placing his arm across the boy's shoulders as he came up, somehow making Raja think that Hyder Ali had no son, only a daughter – a curious thought, never spoken of, yet clearly felt. It was his friends who seemed to fall silent when he came and to ostentatiously change the subject of discussion. The awkwardness did not last. Glasses of whisky were passed around, some poetry quoted, and soon they forgot Raja, or Raja's Hindu presence, and picked up the subject they had dropped on seeing him – Pakistan, as ever Pakistan. Raja listened silently as they spoke of Jinnah, of Gandhi and Nehru, of Mountbatten and Attlee and Churchill, because he knew this was not a matter in which he should express an opinion, but he listened and he began to see Pakistan as they did – as a possibility, very close to them, palpable and real.

When the boys at Hindu College found that Raja was one Hindu who actually accepted the idea of Pakistan as feasible, they changed from charmed friends into dangerous enemies. Raja, whose home and family gave him an exceptionally closed and sheltered background, was slow to realise this. The boys had taken him to tea-shops and given him cigarettes and *samosas*, he had gone to cinema shows with them, sung songs with them as they cycled back at night. Now they were strangely and abruptly altered. When he spoke to them of Pakistan as something he quite accepted, they turned on him openly, called him a traitor, drowned out his piping efforts at reasonableness with the powerful arguments of fanatics. Some of them, his two or three closest friends, disclosed to him that they were members of terrorist societies; they told him they were not giving in cravenly to the partitioning of the country no matter what Gandhi said or Nehru did – they were going to fight to defend their country, their society, their religion. As they declaimed, they watched Raja carefully for signs of wavering, of weakening. They so much wanted him to join them. He was so desirable as a member of their cause in his idealistic enthusiasm, his graceful carriage, his incipient heroism. They wanted him. They pursued him. When he did not come to college, they came to see him at his house, after dark.

For Raja had fallen ill. His father and his aunt were convinced it was something to do with the atmosphere of that spring, the threatening, advancing violence in the air at one with the dust storms that gathered and broke, the koels that called frantically in the trees all day, the terrific heat that was already rising out of the parched, cracked yellow earth, and all the rumours that drifted in from the city like sand, or smoke. The doctor felt him over with the stethoscope, then ordered various tests to be carried out, saw the reports and said it was nothing so mental or emotional – the boy had become infected with tuberculosis.

'Tuberculosis?' Aunt Mira screamed, her voice slicing through

Bim like a cold knife. 'How can it be? The boy lives a healthy life – he drinks milk, eats eggs, eats meat . . .' she stammered, beginning to shred the end of her sari with her hands.

'No, no, it isn't always malnutrition that brings it on,' the doctor broke in irritably. 'He could have picked up a germ while drinking tea from a dirty cup, from using a soiled towel somewhere. Anywhere. But it is t.b.,' he insisted in the face of her incredulity.

Raja, too, was incredulous. He felt ill. He felt he couldn't get to his feet at all. To raise his head for a sip of water required a great effort and made a sharp pain leap and throb at his temples. But he was sure it was merely fatigue, anxiety, something to do with – what? He couldn't quite say – so much whirled through his head: Lord Byron, heroism, Pakistan, Jinnah, Gandhi, the boys at college, hissing at him from behind the gate-post, Hyder Ali sipping his whisky so slowly and reflectively in that group of poets and politicians in the garden across the road. It made him quite giddy, as if he were being whirled about in a dust-storm.

The whole family found it unacceptable that Raja was seriously ill. For a while they allowed the college boys to visit him, to sit about his bed, giving him news of refugee camps and killings, of looting and burning in the city, and pleading with him, in conspirators' voices, to join their society. They would not let him go.

'T.b?' they scoffed. 'The doctor's mad. A little heat fever. You'll soon be up. Then you can come with us. We'll show you where we hide our guns, and daggers, and where we meet to exercise and practise – '

They were sure Raja – so impetuous, so bold and dashing – would be fired by such talk. They cajoled him, they flattered. Aunt Mira even sent in lemonade for them to drink.

But met with blazing opposition from Raja. He was too weak to say much, too weak and dizzy, but when he thought of Hyder Ali, of Hyder Ali's library, of Hyder Ali's Begum and daughter quietly humming and chattering as they embroidered their veils together, and all those cool, calm evenings in their garden that had made his spirit rejoice by offering it all he craved, he felt giddy with rage at these boys and what they stood for.

Very near to tears in his weakness and frustration, he told them 'I'll tell the police that – I have only to phone the police to stop you –'

'You would never do that,' they gasped, taken aback. Then, more harshly, 'We'll see to it that you don't do that. We'll inform the police about *you*. You are more dangerous to India than we are – you're a traitor.'

That was what they must have done for soon a plainclothes

policeman began to hover about their gate, from six in the evening to six in the morning, too punctually to be anything but a plain-clothes policeman. Bim peered out through the bamboo screen at the door at him. At first she thought it might be someone planning a burglary. She watched while Raja dozed. When he woke, she told him. He realised at once that his terrorist friends had warned the police that he was a Muslim sympathiser. Perhaps they had made him out to be a Pakistani spy.

For a moment, he thrilled at the idea of his importance, his dangerousness. He saw himself as fighting for the Hyder Alis, brandishing a sword, keeping the mob at bay. The very thought made him break into a sweat. His clothes, his bed were soaked. Left weak and trembling, he confessed to Bim that he was afraid.

'What will they do if their house is attacked?' he muttered. 'Who will protect them? The police won't do it – they're afraid of the mob.'

Bim tried to reassure him but he wanted to talk, not listen to her. He talked of Hyder Ali, of the Begum, of their daughter, the young girl Benazir. He asked Bim questions about her but Bim hardly knew her at all – she was a good deal younger, still at school, a pretty child with a round porcelain face, always clinging close to her mother like a young pigeon that still needs to be nourished.

'She doesn't come to school any more,' Bim said, trying to find something to say. 'None of the Muslim girls come any more.'

'Her parents must be afraid to send her out of the house. I *wish* I could go and see her.'

'Go and see her?' Bim repeated, puzzled. 'Why?'

'I know I can't – the doctor says everyone is to keep away from me. Damn this t.b. Damn it – why must I have t.b. *now*?'

'The doctor says it could have been a tea-cup or a dirty towel – '

'A dirty towel? A tea-cup?' Raja cried, lifting his head from the pillow to glare at her. 'When I ought to be out in the streets – fighting the mobs – saving Hyder Ali and Benazir – '

'Oh God, Raja,' moaned Bim, running for the thermometer. 'Be quiet or your temperature will go up. It is all this worry – all this nonsense – '

'Nonsense!' he gasped at her, white and damp with rage. He wanted to roar at her, he was so outraged and so frustrated, but all he could manage was a gasp.

'It's making you worse,' Bim cried angrily, mopping his face with a sponge and going to get a change of nightshirt for him. 'How will you get better if you keep worrying about fighting in the streets? *What* fighting in the streets?'

'Don't you *see* – there is going to be fighting in the streets, people like Hyder Ali Sahib are going to be driven out, their property will be burnt and looted, the government is helpless, they're not preventing – preventing – ' but now tears of weakness rose in his throat, flooding it, and he closed his mouth and turned his head from side to side like a dog tied to a tight leash.

His situation was Romantic in the extreme, Bim could see as she sponged his face and helped him struggle out of one muslin shirt and into another – his heavy, limp body as she lifted it as spent and sapped as a bled fish, and the city of Delhi burning down about them. He hoped, like Byron, to go to the rescue of those in peril. Instead, like Byron, he lay ill, dying. Bim was sure he was dying. Her eyes streamed with tears as she buttoned up his shirt. 'Shall I read to you, Raja?' she asked with a brave gulp.

'Shall I read to you, Raja?'

Sometimes he nodded yes, sometimes he shook his head no.

'No. Won't you go up on the roof again, Bim, and see what's happening?'

'Here, on Bela Road?' Bim asked in surprise, letting the book fall from her lap in surprise.

'At the Hyder Alis' of course,' Raja explained with an irritated twitch. 'Go up and see.'

Sometimes Bim grumbled but went, dragging her feet because she was tired and knew nothing was happening either on Bela Road or in the Hyder Alis' garden, or in the Misras' compound, or anywhere closer than the horizon where the city walls smouldered and smoked by day and blazed by night.

Sometimes she was glad to leave the stuffy, airless sickroom with its stale, disinfected odours and Raja's low spirits and her own headache, to stroll on the terrace for a while and see the river birds descending from the sky to settle on the sand dunes for the night with harsh, alarmed cries, or hang over the balustrade and search the quiet leafy gardens and walled compounds for some sign of life, or action, that she could report to Raja. A bicycle wobbled drunkenly out of the servants' quarters at the back of the house and past the guava trees. A washerman was going in at the Misras' gate with a neatly tied bundle of white washing on his head. A dog barked in the Hyder Alis' garden. That was all. It was nothing.

One day, less than nothing.

'The house seems empty,' she told Raja bluntly as she came down. 'I think they've gone.'

'Who?'

'The Hyder Alis, of course,' she said irritably, going straight to the dressing table where the medicines were lined up, for his evening dose.

'Gone where?'

'I don't know, Raja, I only went up on the terrace to see. The house is dark, and everything seems shut.'

'But then – but then – go and find out,' he cried in a kind of muffled scream. 'Go and find out!'

Bim gave him a dark look from over the brimming medicine spoon. 'I will if you swallow this and stop screaming.'

'I'm not screaming – I'm shouting!' He gulped down the medicine and the hysteria in his voice with an effort. 'But go. Go.'

'I *wish* there was someone else who would go,' Bim could not keep from saying as she swept out. 'There is never anybody except me.'

There was no one except Bim. Everything was left to her. Aunt Mira was strangely absent. To begin with, she used to come stumbling into Raja's room and try ineffectually to tidy his books and medicines with shaking hands and ask tentatively about his meals, his temperature. Or she would huddle up in a cane chair on the veranda, just outside his door, saying to Bim 'Call me when you need me. I'll wait here for Tara.'

Tara was always out now. Since their mother's death, and Raja's illness, she had taken to going to the Misras' every evening and often they would take her to the cinema, to Connaught Place to shop, or to the Roshonara Club to play badminton and drink lemonade. They would bring her back in the family car quite punctually at whatever hour Aunt Mira had stipulated. Only now Aunt Mira seldom managed to stay up so long. For a while she would sit hunched on the cane chair, inspecting with narrowed eyes her cheesy, blue-nailed hands through which thick veins twisted like green worms, then begin to shiver and to mutter to herself as Bim watched her out of the corner of her eye from Raja's bedside, and then she would be seen – and heard – to go stumbling down the veranda to her own room and vanish into her bed. Bim was perturbed but far too busy with Raja to think much about Aunt Mira. Sometimes, when she went into the dining room for dinner and found neither Tara nor her aunt at the table, their plates turned upside down and waiting on the tablecloth, she frowned and went down to Aunt Mira's room to implore her to come and eat a little. The meals on the table did not look appealing but they had to be eaten all the same, Bim thought. But Aunt Mira, huddling under her blanket – why a blanket in the middle of summer? It was crazy – shook her head and smiled with her lower lip hanging loosely and gleaming wet in the dark. There was a strange smell in the closed, stuffy room. Bim wrinkled up her nose. She went and sat on the veranda, waiting up for Tara in place of her aunt.

Baba sat there, on the veranda steps, beside a pot of petunias that flowered now in the dark with a kind of lunar luminosity, giving out a maidenly white scent that made one soon feel cooler, calmer. Baba's presence, too, was so much less than a presence, that it could not intrude or chafe. He did not turn to Bim or speak. He had his handful of pebbles that Aunt Mira had given him years ago and with which he played perpetually so that they were quite smooth and round from use. Everyone in the household knew the sound they made as he scattered them across the tiles with a little, quiet unfolding gesture of his hand, then gathered them up again with that curiously remote and peaceful smile on his thin face. It was the sound of the house, as much as the contented muttering of the pigeons in the veranda. It gave time a continuity and regularity that the ticking of a clock in the hall might convey in other homes. Bim was at times grateful for it and at times irritated beyond endurance by it, just as one might be by the perpetual sameness of clock hands.

'Tara's late,' Bim said to him, to herself, sighing.

Baba smiled vaguely but not quite in her direction and jiggled the pebbles in his fist for a moment before he let them fall again. Bim had to set her jaw firmly to keep from rebuking him for the clatter. Leaning back in her broken basket chair, she kept her eyes on the gate at the end of the drive, worriedly. The street lamp shone on it without illuminating it, it was so dim and the air so dusty. She knew Tara could come to no harm – harm was beyond Tara's childish capacity. Yet she was uneasy for unease was in the air like a swarm of germs, an incipient disease. The empty house across the road breathed it at them. Its emptiness and darkness was a warning, a threat perhaps.

Bim wondered at Tara going again and again to visit the Misra sisters. All through their school years they had chafed at this too close relationship with girls they considered dull and conservative. But they were neighbours and so had had to cycle to school together – it was considered safer for four girls to bicycle together than for two groups of two girls – and sometimes do their homework together in the evenings or crawl through the hedge between the two gardens to borrow a book or get some sewing done by the many and useful aunts in the Misra household. Yet they had always regarded – or at least Bim had – the Misra girls as too boring to be cultivated. They had also been more than a little nervous of the Misra boys who had been merely rough and loud-mouthed as children but, when they grew older, with bristly jaws and swelling thighs and bellies, ran their eyes over the girls in a smiling, appraising way that made them shiver as horses do when flies settle. When Bim finished with school and went to college, she was relieved that the Misra girls did not follow; they stayed home to help their mother and aunts with the housekeeping and await marriages to be arranged for them. Then Tara took to visiting them on her own, almost every evening. 'D'you think I could have mother's bracelet to wear, Bim?' she would ask before leaving, or 'Can I have your white Lucknow sari just for today, Bim? They're taking me to the club.'

When Tara did appear in the pool of green, insect-fretted light at the gate, she was not alone. Bim had known, in those bones that jarred every time Baba threw his pebbles across the tiles, that she would have someone with her when she came. Here he was.

'This is Bakul,' Tara told her in an almost inaudible murmur, turning their mother's bracelet about her wrist, round and round and round. 'The Misras – the Misras – ' she stammered, 'took us to the Roshonara Club. There was a dance.'

While she stammered and Bakul tried gallantly to help with some more polished and assured phrases that he slipped in with a self-assurance that filled in the gaps left by Tara and even propped up the little that she managed to say, coolly and powerfully, Aunt Mira came out of her room to stare. 'This is my aunt,' whispered Tara, dropping her eyes so as not to have to see the way Aunt Mira's mouth twitched and a nerve jumped in her cheek, making her left eye flicker, and Bakul said at once 'I came to ask if Tara may come to a party at my house tomorrow. My sisters are giving a party and the Misra girls are coming. They could bring Tara with them – with your permission.' He actually made a little bow when he said this, and aunt and sister regarded him with astonishment that made the aunt's face twitch and flicker and jerk and the sister's face solidify into stone. They might have stared in this fashion if a young prince had ridden up on horseback to sweep Tara up onto the saddle and away. This wonderfully good-looking, well-groomed, well-spoken young man who had arrived on their doorstep with Tara was just such an apparition to them – unexpected, unsought, and yet exactly what they would have sought for Tara, expected for Tara if they had sought, or expected. Suddenly they did.

'Yes, she may go,' Bim said slowly. 'Can't she, Mira-*masi*?' she demanded of her aunt.

Aunt Mira, nodding frantically, looked for a moment or two as if she would come sweeping across the veranda and fall upon Bakul, hold him fast for her niece before he had time to flee. Instead, to Tara's relief, she teetered upon her toes, swung around and dived back into her room, leaving Bim to give Bakul sober directions about when to send Tara home. After Bakul had promised and left, she went in to see Aunt Mira for a moment and was so engrossed in this new prospect with which Tara had presented them that she didn't notice, or remark on, her aunt hastily pouring a drink into her tumbler from a familiar looking bottle on her cupboard shelf, and only said 'Mira-*masi*, do you think he will want to marry Tara?'

'Yes,' said Aunt Mira with a loud hiccup. 'Yes, yes, I do,' and she dipped her face into the tumbler and drank, agitatedly, as if to hide from the intolerable prospect.

The prospect was entirely Bim's to survey.

Their father had died suddenly. On his way back from the club one night, the car had bumped slightly against the curb of a traffic roundabout on a deserted street on the Ridge. The slight bump had caused the door to fly open and the father to be flung out. He was dead, of a broken neck, when the driver stopped the car and ran out to him. There was no damage to the car at all. It could scarcely be called an accident, so minor was it in appearance, and harmless, but of course that was the only label that fitted, and it was fatal. Dressed in his usual dark suit for the club, with a white handkerchief and a cigar in his breast pocket, he seemed prepared for death as if it were an evening at the club.

Few of the people, mostly club members and bridge players, who came to condole, realised how little difference his death made to the household – they were so accustomed to his absence that it was but a small transition from the temporary to the permanent.

Also, he left so little behind. A wardrobe full of very dark and sombre suits and very white and crisp shirts, a shelf ranged with shoes – all old but polished to the glow of wood, walnut, mahogany or black lacquer – and a desk piled with office files: that was all. He had even just come to the end of his stock of cigars, as if he had prepared for his accidental end. There was not one left for his son to try if he wanted, or to give his room a familiar whiff that might linger.

For a while all that disturbed the children was the continuous presence of the car in the garage – it made them uneasy. They were simply not used to seeing it so much at home. When would it leave – for the club? for the office? Why did it not go? The driver, a surly man who seldom spoke a word, sat on his haunches by the garage door, sometimes smoking and staring over the caps of his knees, and sometimes just staring. Made nervous by their perpetual presence in the back yard, Bim told Raja they must decide on what to do about it. Raja simply telephoned a garage owner, whose son he knew at college, and sold him the car at the very first price he offered. It was taken off to the garage the very next day, leaving the driver still sitting on his haunches by the garage door, looking more surly and more vacant than before.

For a while Bim dreaded seeing the car on the road, passing her by on her way to college. She knew she would strain to see the familiar figures in it, and knew it would be a blow to find unfamiliar ones instead. But she did not. The car was too old and too large to be in demand any more, and it simply rotted in the junk yard behind the garage – Bim often saw it from the No. 9 bus window – till only a rusted skeleton was left.

The driver, after waiting a while as if in expectation of the car being returned to him, finally got to his feet and began to help the gardener by mending his hose pipe and oiling his shears while Bim wondered what to do. Then this problem, too, was resolved quite simply and accidentally: the gardener was called home to his village since his elder brother had died and he was required to work on the farm, and the driver moved in to take his place. That was all.

The garage door remained shut on the cobwebs, the oil stains and the empty tin cans.

The effect of this death in the family then, was pecuniary only, for the father had been, if nothing else, a provider.

When his junior partner at the insurance firm came to call on the family after the cremation – attended largely by the office staff and bridge players distinguished by their age, apparel and complexion – even Raja got himself out of bed and came to the drawing room in his pyjamas. The drawing room was as still and petrified as in their parents' lifetime – the card table ready in the corner, the brass pot filled with spotted cannas from the garden, the thick red curtains and red carpets and red rexine sofas all emitting a faint pall of dust that seemed to stifle anyone who entered as if it were a vault containing the mortal remains of the departed.

Raja was feverish – he had been to the cremation at the height of the afternoon to light his father's funeral pyre: it was what he had to do – and he spoke rapidly, gesturing with his hands which had grown very long and thin and artistic after so many months of fever.

'No, I don't care what my father has written in his will – I don't want to be a partner. I won't have anything to do with it – I'm not a businessman – I'm –'

'Raja,' Bim burst out in agitation, 'do *think* –'

'Bim, I know what I'm saying,' he snapped at her, tossing back the hair that had grown so long and lanky from his moist forehead. 'I know what I'm doing. Baba can take whatever position father meant for me –'

'Baba? What are you talking about? You know Baba,' Bim cried out in disbelief. 'You are making fun of him, very cruelly, Raja, if you want to send him to the office –'

'No, no, no, that is not necessary at all,' the young man from the office soothed her, perching on the edge of the sofa like a teetering pigeon and making not dissimilar sounds of solace. 'Not necessary at all. You know, your father himself was not at all concerned with the day-to-day administration – he left it all to me and to the staff. We can manage all that. All we need is the name, the signature – the name must remain, for the firm, that is all.'

'Oh, is that all?' said Bim, and Raja looked at her in triumph.

'You see,' he told her, 'that is all. Don't you think Baba can manage that much? Just signing papers?'

'No, he can't,' Bim said more sharply. 'But *you* can.'

'Nonsense. I'll speak to Baba – I'll explain to him. He can go to the office for an hour or two – and then – Mr Sharma will help him. Don't baby him, Bim, you treat him like a baby –'

'What else can I do?' she flared up, furious with Raja for talking so carelessly, with such cynical thoughtlessness, and furious with Mr Sharma for listening.

'Let him grow up, let him take a little responsibility. Give him a simple task or two to perform. See if he can't manage.'

'And if he can't – what then?'

'Then,' said Mr Sharma, giving a little bounce on the sofa to attract their attention and distract them from their quarrel, 'then I shall manage. I can bring the files here to the house for you to see –'

'You do that, Mr Sharma,' Raja said hurriedly. 'Yes, you do that. What a good idea. And Baba and I will sign whatever you ask us to –'

'Raja,' Bim warned him again; her face looked thin and elderly with warning.

Mr Sharma smiled at her reassuringly. 'It is what your father did also in these last years. It is all he did. The work was left to the clerks and myself. We will manage – you will have no worries.'

'Then that's all right,' Raja said with relief and stood up to go back to bed while Mr Sharma hurried away, explaining he had to get back before the curfew.

When Bim went in to take Raja's temperature and see that he was quiet again, he said 'It's nothing to worry about, see, Bim. These aren't the things to worry about in life.'

'No?' she said shortly as she shook down the thermometer with a professional air. 'What do *you* worry about then?'

'Oh Bim, Bim,' he said, dramatically gesturing towards the door that opened out into the thick, dusty twilight. 'Look there – look,' he said, 'the city's burning down. Delhi is being destroyed. The whole country is split up and everyone's become a refugee. Our friends have been driven away, perhaps killed. And you ask me to worry about a few cheques and files in father's office.'

'No, that's only for me to worry about,' said Bim, as dour as her father, as their house, popping the thermometer into his mouth. 'That, and the rent to be paid on the house, and five, six, seven people to be fed every day, and Tara to be married off, and Baba to be taken care of for the rest of his life, and you to be got well again – and I don't know what else.'

Raja sputtered a bit and the thermometer wobbled between his lips so that she had to snap 'Don't talk.'

That day Bim was so disturbed, so little reassured by Raja's argument, that when the doctor came to visit him in the evening, she did not simply shove the temperature chart at him and ask for a new prescription but actually invited him to sit down with her on the veranda before he left.

'How much longer do you think it will be before he begins to get better?' she asked him.

The doctor, a soft-spoken and awkward young Bengali sent them by their father's partner and not unlike him – they both went to the Ramakrishna Mission for the lectures and the hymn singing – was so taken aback by her unusual invitation to sit down and talk that his knees gave way and he collapsed onto the creaking cane sofa weakly, then took a few minutes to understand what she had asked him and to notice that her face was drawn and colourless and that her lank, untidy hair had a distinct streak of grey in it, just over her left ear. It seemed to him at least twenty years too early for such an occurrence, and he was shocked. In his family the women washed their hair with *shikakai* solution and oiled it with coconut oil every morning so that at forty, at fifty even, their hair was black and glossy as a newly-opened tin of shoe polish. His mouth was a little open as he stared.

Then, in a concerned voice, he urged, 'You mustn't worry so much, Miss Das. It is a very mild attack of t.b. These days we can control t.b. with drugs, quite effectively, yes. The drugs, combined with good nursing and good diet, will cure him, yes. Only it will take time, yes. One has to have patience also –'

'How much time?' Bim persisted. 'You know, my father –' she began, then stopped short, wondering how she had let herself go to such an extent. The young doctor's face, his posture – clutching the bag set on his knees neatly placed together but every now and then giving an uncontrollable twitch or jerk – were the face and the posture of all nonentities, people seen in a bus queue, bending over a table in a tea-shop, huddled in a suburban train, at desks in cluttered offices or at counters in crowded shops: anxious, fretting, conscious of failing, of not managing, and trying only not to let it show. He had nothing to give her. Why did she ask?

'I know, I know,' the young doctor stammered urgently, shyly. 'He has passed away. I am so – so sorry. I came to the – the ceremony. You did not see me. I was with Mr Sharma –'

'I know,' Bim broke in abruptly, untruthfully. 'Will you have a cup of tea?'

'Yes,' gasped the young man, as much to his own surprise as to Bim's.

Bim went down the veranda and called 'Mira-*masi*, send some tea for the doctor, will you? Tell Janaki to make tea for the doctor.' Aunt Mira gave an agitated cry in her room and Bim came back to the circle of cane chairs and sat down.

'I see, I see it all,' Dr Biswas hurried on, staring hard at his shoes, making the most of this unusual burst of courage while it lasted. 'There are great problems. Your father – the house – the family – Raja's illness – it is all too much for a young lady. Raja must recover, he must take his father's place –'

Bim gave a laugh, or a snort. An ugly sound that stopped him short. In the sudden silence they heard a handful of pebbles fall with a clatter on the veranda steps, making them aware, too, of Baba's presence. The doctor had not mentioned Baba. Now they both breathed heavily, adding Baba to his list.

'Father's place?' Bim mocked, and then stopped: she would not reveal more. The hedges round the garden grew high – to hide, to conceal. She would not cut them short, or reveal. She got up impatiently, restlessly, and went down to the kitchen to call Janaki herself, knowing that Aunt Mira had done nothing about the tea. Janaki gave her a surly look from the yellow smoke she was stirring up out of the coal fire. Bim glared back. Eventually the tea appeared on a brass tray that had not been polished for years.

The doctor's bag fell down as he rose with a jerk to accept the cup of tea. He held the cup in one hand, picked up the bag with the other, spilling tea as he did so. Then there was the need to keep his knees together. To be positive and reassuring. To calm himself, he stirred and stirred the tea with a loud spoon. Then he looked up at Bim with timid respect. 'I see how it is,' he said, wanting her also to see that he saw. 'I see what a difficult position – I mean, for you – the problems –'

'No, no, what problems,' blustered Bim, wanting to clear him out now, be on her own again. 'Baba,' she shouted, 'd'you want tea? Sugar?'

'I think I may reassure you on one point at least – Raja *will* get well.'

Bim gave him a quick look to see if he was being honest, or only kind. He had a very honest face, she decided, painfully honest, like a peeled vegetable. But it was also kind, dreadfully kind. She sighed 'Are you sure? You don't think we will have to send him to hospital, or to a sanatorium?'

Dr Biswas stirred and stirred his tea with a crazy clatter, frowning with concentration, making the spoon spin round and round the cup like some mechanism gone out of control. Then he stopped it with his little finger very abruptly so that the tea sloshed over the rim into the saucer. 'Let us say,' he said, staring at the puddle of spilt tea, 'that it is not necessary *now* because there has been no deterioration. If the position remains stable, then once the cool weather starts, I feel his health will begin to pick up, he will regain his strength. He should show improvement in the winter. If *not* – if *not*,' he repeated, with renewed agitation making the teaspoon tremble, the cup wobble, the puddle slop, 'then, at the end of the winter, when it is no longer cold, we might send him to a sanatorium – in Kasauli, or Dagshai. *But*', he added desperately, tearing his mind away from such a possibility and looking up at her with remorse, 'I have no doubt, *no* doubt, it will *not* be necessary, he will improve –'

But Bim, although she nodded, looked doubtful again, and unsure. Having failed in his effort to reassure her, Dr Biswas raised the cup to his mouth at last and drank the cold tea in one gulp while the cup dripped down onto his knees, and then rose to leave, realising he had not given her what she needed, had not been up to it. As usual, he had not been up to it. The look of failure overcame the look of anxiety.

When Tara came home with Bakul, she found Bim alone in the veranda, her face so grey and old that the glow went out of Tara's and she, too, became subdued.

Bakul did not notice and sat down to chat with the sisters with that bland oil of self-confidence smoothing his voice and giving it a kind of calculated ease that made Tara gaze at him with maidenly admiration and made Bim look away into the shadowy garden in boredom. It was the opposite of poor Dr Biswas's tone: then why did they equally bore her, she wondered as she watched Aunt Mira's cat stealing past the flowerpots, stalking something in the tall grass that edged the ill-kept lawn. A cloud of mosquitoes followed her, hovering over her flattened head and the two pointed ears, like a filmy parasol. Bim watched her, her chin cupped in her hand. She was the only thing that moved in the stiff, desiccated garden which, at that time, lay between two gardeners, in transition.

Bakul had just said something that she had failed to hear – the cat had at that instance pounced on a stalk of grass and a purple moth had fluttered up out of reach, exquisitely in time.

'Bim,' Tara said, perturbed by such absent-mindedness, 'Bakul's posting has just come through.'

Was that what he had said? Bim turned to look at them, smiling at each other.

'Tell her, Bakul,' Tara urged, now that Bim's attention was drawn to them even if her look were tired and not interested enough to really do Bakul justice.

'I have been told to proceed to Ceylon,' Bakul told her, somewhat smugly, she thought. 'Of course it isn't the country of my choice, but it's to be only while I am in training. After a year, I expect to be sent to the West since I specialised in European languages and asked for a posting in Western Europe. That was my first preference – not Ceylon.'

'Ceylon?' Bim responded at last, slowly and quite dreamily, Tara thought, as if it aroused romantic, scented pictures in her mind as it did in Tara's. But all she said was 'That will be interesting.'

'Exactly. That is what I told Tara,' he said gaily, still not noticing Bim's abstraction, her preoccupation. He smiled at Tara sitting beside her sister and tensely watching her, watching him, and Tara smiled back. Bim gazed at them, at their happiness, as if she were seeing it through a gauze screen, vaguely, not clearly.

'Bakul,' she said with sudden crispness, 'what is happening?'

'Happening?' he asked, turning his handsome profile to look directly at her. 'But I was expecting it any day – it is the foreign service after all – I had told Tara –'

'No, no, no. I mean, in New Delhi.'

'In New Delhi?'

'Yes, yes,' she said impatiently. 'I mean – about Independence – about Pakistan –'

'Oh,' he said. 'Well, we are all waiting – for the date to be set – for partition, for independence. It will come any day now.'

'And then?'

'And then there will be trouble,' he said simply, not liking to dramatize a situation that he himself feared. 'But you needn't worry. All steps are being taken to carry out partition smoothly, we hope safely. Refugee camps are being formed. Special trains are being arranged. The police, the army – all are alerted. Anyway, you will be quite safe here, outside the city walls. There won't be riots here, and the Muslims who live here –'

'Yes, exactly – I'm worried about them. So is Raja. Our neighbours, you know, the Hyder Alis, they have disappeared.'

'Most of them have already left. They have acted quickly, wisely. The Hyder Alis must have done that.'

'But they must still be in the country, somewhere. What will happen to them?'

'They will have police protection. They can go to the refugee camps. It is all arranged.'

Bim shook her head and was silent while Bakul went on about measures taken by the government, about Mountbatten's goodwill and integrity, about Nehru's idealism and integrity, about Jinnah and Pakistan – but Bim felt she was listening to banal newspaper articles being read aloud and she brushed her hand across her forehead and got up. 'I'll go and tell Raja what you say,' she said. 'He keeps asking for news – he's anxious about the Hyder Alis.'

Bakul instantly got up. 'You must tell him there is no need,' he said. 'Please tell him I will go back and make enquiries about them and will see to it personally that they are not harmed.'

'We don't even know where they are,' Bim said, giving him an ironical look as she walked away, and Bakul looked puzzled for a moment. He wondered if he had been snubbed – Bim did have such discouraging ways. He was a very junior servant in the foreign service, it was true. In fact, he was still in training. He did not really know what was to be done. Still, he did like everyone to think he did.

So he sat down again beside Tara and picked up her hand and squeezed it lightly. To Tara he could speak in a different tone. From Tara he got a different response. He smiled at her fondly, like an indulgent father. She smiled back gratefully – she had not had an indulgent father, after all. She wore a white *chameli* flower in her hair. She was very like it herself. He told her so.

'I must take you with me, Tara,' he said softly. 'This place is bad for you – so much sickness, so many worries. You are too young for all this. I must take you away.'

There was rioting all through the country and slaughter on both sides of the new border when a letter came from Hyder Ali. Bim ran into the room when Raja called, loudly and excitedly. 'Raja, don't roar,' she panted, 'it's bad for you. Dr Biswas said –'

'Bim,' he shouted, sitting up in bed, with his hair grown long and wild about his flushed face. 'Look, a letter from Hyder Ali Sahib!'

She gave a shiver as at a touch of ice. Raja's anxiety had transferred itself to her, kept her awake nights: both had wondered if the Hyder Alis were not dead, murdered while trying to escape to Pakistan.

'Where are they, Raja?'

'In Hyderabad – quite safe. In Hyder Ali Sahib's home – his mother lives there, and his sister. They're all safe. He says there is no trouble in Hyderabad. They are in hiding, but they are safe and well, and they even found a friend to post this letter to me. Bim,' he said joyfully, 'wasn't it good of Hyder Ali Sahib to write to me? To *me*? He even says Benazir sends her best wishes.' He handed Bim the letter to share the joy of it with her. She sat on the edge of his bed, reading, and laughing with relief, relief as much for his sake as for theirs.

It seemed the evening light that came in that day was softer, milder, not so lurid. They listened to the mynahs chattering on the lawn, to Baba playing with his pebbles on the steps, and looked at each other in relief and joy. Raja, sitting upright in bed, looked as if he were going to get well.

'I wonder how they did the journey – he doesn't say.'

'Of course not – he can't – it's not safe to. Only I wish he had told me – he could have trusted me –'

'How could he, Raja? With a plainclothes policeman posted at our gate? And the sort of friends you picked up at college?'

'They weren't my friends – they were traitors. And he should have known I was never one of them.'

'He knew – that's why he has written to you.'

'Look, Bim, he has asked me to look up the house – see what has happened to it. Will you do that for me?'

'Of course,' said Bim, springing up. 'Has he left anything there? Does he want me to see if they're safe?' and when Raja said there were no instructions, nothing specific, she went instantly, calling to Baba to put his pebbles away and come with her. They crossed the road together, her hand on his elbow, to the house that had stood silent and dark across from them for weeks now.

Lifting the catch of the gate and letting it down again as they entered the garden, Baba turned as if to go back, then drew closer to Bim and although she gave him a little encouraging push, she was affected by his unwillingness nevertheless. It was as if they had walked into a cobweb – they could feel it on their faces, a clinging, slightly moist net which they brushed at with ineffectual fingers.

The house was so strangely unlit and deserted as it had never been for as long as they had known it – like a body whose life and warmth they were accustomed to and took for granted, now grown cold and stiff and faded. It looked accusing, too, as if it held them responsible. The envied roses still bloomed in the formal beds of precise geometrical shapes but their petals lay scattered and unswept: even the gardeners had gone. Ripe fruit had fallen to the ground beneath the trees along the drive, ripe mangoes and guavas, and lay there rotting, touched by a few birds and then left, mutilated. A long-tailed hornbill swooped out of the tall jacaranda tree by the porch and gave a harsh, croaking cry as it rattled through the air into the trees by the drive, making Baba raise his arm to protect his face, and duck. But Bim held his hand and led him on.

The fanlight above the door, glowing in the orange evening light, deceived them for an instant into thinking there was a light on in the hall. But when they pushed open the door by its painted porcelain handle and went in, the bulb inside the pendulous glass globe was unlit and there was nothing there but a hatstand with its many extended hooks, empty, and a wilting potted plant.

All the rooms were unnaturally enlarged by emptiness for all the small objects of ornament and comfort had been taken away and only the large pieces of furniture left, ornate and heavily carved sofas and marble-topped tables that, stripped of cushions and vases and silver boxes and coloured glassware, sulked and looked as accusing as abandoned husbands in the gloom. The squares and oblongs on the walls from which pictures had been removed were marked by brown rims of grime.

They walked down the tiled passages, opening frosted glass-paned doors to the left and right, peering in, half-expecting to find someone left behind – perhaps an old sick aunt with embroidery spools heaped on her lap and fluttering a ghostly fan, or the kittens Benazir used to play with and cuddle. But there was no one there. A mirror on the wall flashed a blank, empty glare at them – the heathen, unwanted. At the library door Bim hesitated with her hand on the glass knob, wanting intensely to go in and see this room that Raja had for years regarded as his own retreat, his spiritual home, and somehow not daring to violate what he had kept scrupulously private. Would the books still be there? she wondered. She walked past without looking to see – some day Raja could come here about them.

Only in Benazir's room there was still a childish, girlish debris strewn across the heavy, carved bed – bits of ribbon and lace, pictures cut out of illustrated magazines, a little velvet bag with gold tassels. Bim curled her lip: Benazir was untidy, she noted, a spoilt only child. 'Can't I take them with me?' she seemed to hear the pouting voice. 'Oh why can't I?' Contemptuously, Bim tried to sweep everything into a heap, tidy up.

Baba had been silent all through this ghostly tour, keeping close to her except when she made some small, nervous comment, when he gave a start and jumped away from her. Now he pointed his finger and made a little desperate sound like a bell that won't ring when pressed. Bim looked. 'What?' she asked, 'that?' Baba nodded, and she went with him to a corner where an old-fashioned His Master's Voice gramophone stood on a small three-legged table, on the lower shelf of which were stacked the records Benazir and her friends had listened to, in the afternoons when her father was out and her mother asleep and not likely to hear the profane sounds so unlike the music the family enjoyed under the drawing room chandelier or in the flowering summer garden. Bim shuffled through them out of curiosity – it amused her to think of a scholar poet's daughter listening to these American foxtrots and quicksteps that the World War and the American GIs and British Tommies had brought to India. What would Raja think of her taste?

'Come, let's go,' said Bim, turning away. 'Let's go and look in the servants' quarters – there may be someone there.' But Baba would not go. He stood there fingering the smooth shining metal gadgetry in the green box, his long fingers closing about the curved silver horn, admiringly, lovingly. 'Come, Baba, come,' Bim said several times, more and more impatiently, but he was smiling to himself, quite deaf and unresponsive in the enclosed bubble of his dream, till she said angrily 'Then I'm going alone,' whereupon he reluctantly let down the lid, closing the box with a gentle creak, and followed her, dragging his foot and looking whipped so that she said in exasperation 'If you want it, I suppose there's nothing to stop you taking it. But first let's go and see if there's anyone outside, at the back, whom we can ask.' He raised his chin and gave her a shy, fearful look of hope then and followed her more willingly.

As they entered the dark, cavernous kitchen at the back, packed full of the smell of coal and smoke, and stained and blotched with the signs of many feasts and much drudgery, they heard a whine. They opened cupboards and looked into coal holes but could find nothing. Then they opened the door onto the back veranda and there, behind the woodbox, found the dog that whined so pathetically, in such a shrunken, faded voice. It was Hyder Ali's dog, they had not been able to take her with them. Exceptionally sweet and gentle of face, with long, drooping ears and hopeful, tearful eyes that gazed at the visitors in fear, she thumped her long tail in tentative greeting.

'It's Begum,' cried Bim in an outburst of relief at seeing something alive in this deserted house. She patted the overcome creature in pity and reassurance while Baba knelt on the ground, fondling her, clasping her dribbling mouth to his chest in gentle protectiveness. 'We'll have to take her back with us or she'll starve,' Bim said, and Baba lowered his face to the dog's brow and kissed it in gratitude.

Their voices and the ecstatic whining of the half-starved creature did flush someone out of the servants' quarters. At first they were only aware of someone peeping out from the cracks of a heavily barred wooden door but obviously their features and their behaviour were not intimidating to the owner of the eyes for after a moment the door creaked open and one of Hyder Ali's old servants, the groom who had looked after Hyder Ali's white mare, came sidling out. He salaamed extravagantly as Bim cried out in surprise, then whispered 'Please don't speak so loudly. People may come. They may call the police. I will be taken to jail –'

'Why?' asked Bim, puzzled. She hated the way the man cringed although the cringing of the dog had only aroused compassion. 'What have you done?' she asked coldly. 'You haven't murdered the Hyder Ali family, have you?'

The poor man nearly screamed in terror and his eyes flashed to the left and to the right as if he expected the police to fall out of the guava trees or bound out of the well. 'They will take me to jail and question me,' he hissed. 'They will torture me till I speak. That is what they do – I have heard.'

'But why? What information have you got?'

'None, none at all,' whined the man, striking his head. 'Hyder Ali Sahib packed and left so quietly – his friends came to help, sent them cars to take them to the station, and armed guards too. But they did not tell me where they were going. The police will want to know. They will ask. They will think I helped them to escape –'

'Escape?' Bim said scornfully. 'What do you mean, escape? They have every right to leave their house in Delhi and go and live in their house in Hyderabad. If they took their belongings with them, well, they were *their* belongings, it's not theft.'

'Ah, but they were Muslims,' wailed the old man, doubling up in front of her and swaying nearly to the ground. 'We should not have allowed them to go.'

'You had better go away,' Bim told him in disgust. 'You had better go to your village. Did Hyder Ali Sahib leave you any money?'

'Yes, yes, Hyder Ali Sahib was always good to me – Muslim though he was. May God keep him – his God and ours. But how can I travel? These are bad times, murderers and thugs are everywhere, and if I meet anyone who knew I worked for Muslims, I will be –' he drew his finger across his throat and rolled his eyes.

'Then you had better come to our house. Janaki will give you a bed – you can stay till it is safe for you to go home.' Then, when he looked as if he would really grovel at her feet, she said sharply 'And where is Hyder Ali Sahib's horse?'

He straightened up then and babbled quickly 'Oh, Hyder Ali Sahib gave her away to Lala Ram Narain who helped them to pack and leave. He tried to send Begum also, but Begum would not leave the compound – she lay on the ground and would not let anyone touch her. She tried to bite me – see.' He began to roll up his sleeve to show them.

'Then Begum must come with us,' said Bim and whistled to the dog who crawled after them on bent legs as they walked round to the front of the house, the old man hobbling after them, his sleeve rolled back and his arm still extended as if to show them the bite, or to beg. When Bim went up the steps to the front door to make sure it was shut, Baba suddenly darted past her and disappeared into the house. She stopped to wait for him, wondering at the unusual decisiveness of his movements, and in a little while he came out, staggering under the weight of the gramophone that he carried in his arms, carefully balancing the stack of records on top of it.

'Oh Baba,' she grumbled, helping him by taking the records off and carrying them for him. 'Do you have to have this stupid old thing? I don't suppose it matters,' she added as she saw Baba's face fall. 'Benazir can always write and ask for it when she wants it. Come, Begum, come,' she called encouragingly to the dog who hung back at the gate, not quite knowing how to act, equally reluctant to abandon her home and to give up these newly-found protectors. Finally she followed them across the road and into their own garden, growing more animated and more upright as she realised she was welcome here.

Raja was waiting for them on the veranda. Bim ran forward, crying 'Raja, why didn't you wait in bed? Go to bed at once. I'll come and tell you all about it as soon as I've found a quarter for Bhakta here and some food for Begum – they're all we found in the house. It's quite empty. And oh, this gramophone.'

'Benazir's gramophone,' Raja said in astonishment at the sight of Baba so carefully and proudly carrying in his treasure. 'And records – she used to play those records when her friends came. I used to see them dancing together in her room on my way to the library.'

'She won't mind Baba having it, will she? You can write and tell her about it. But go to bed now, and I'll go and ask Mira-*masi* what to do about Bhakta, and the poor dog –'

'That's what I wanted to tell you, Bim,' Raja said, soberly. 'You'd better go and see Mira-*masi*, she doesn't seem very well.'

'No?' said Bim in surprise, stopping short on her way to the kitchen, and then turned and flew down the veranda to her aunt's room, fear thudding hard at her side.

Raja had bolted the door on the outside. Drawing back the bolt, Bim threw open the door, then quickly shut it behind her so that no one should come in, for Aunt Mira was in a disgraceful state, a state no one should see her in. She had clawed off her clothes from her body so that her blouse hung in strips from the little shrivelled flaps of her blue-veined breasts and her sari trailed behind her on the floor as she lurched about the room in a kind of halting dance, her feet getting tangled in the torn muslin that lay everywhere, her one hand jerking at her side while the other held onto a glass of what smelt unmistakably like raw, undiluted liquor. Yes, there was the brandy bottle, nearly empty, on the floor by her bed. Bim rushed towards her aunt with her arms outstretched to catch her and enclose her and hold her, but Aunt Mira stepped aside as lightly as a nimble old goat and, making a comical face at Bim's dismay, sang out in a quavering trill:

'*Said the night-in-gale to the ro-o-ose*,'

when her feet caught in a loop of trailing muslin, she stumbled and knocked over the bottle that fell with a clatter and spilt out its reeking liquid. Seeing it leak and spread about her feet, soaking the shed clothes, Aunt Mira stopped in mid-song, clutched her throat, gave a little choked cry and sank onto her bed, whimpering soggily. Her cat, sitting on the edge with her paws tucked neatly together as if into a white muff, watched her with huge eyes of amber slit with black – shocked and disdainful.

Next door, in Baba's room, a strange rasping roar started out of the stillness, grew louder like a train approaching through a tunnel, and emerged, not in a whistle, but in a woman's voice smokily wailing:

'*Underneath the lamp-post . . .*'

Life spread in a pool around her, low and bright, lapping at her feet, but then quickly, treacherously rising to her ankles, to her knees. She had to get out of it. She had to lift herself out before it rose to her waist, to her armpits. If only they had not wrapped her in those long swaddlings as if she was a baby, or a mummy – these long strips that went round and round her, slipping over her eyes, crossing over her nose, making her breath stop so that she had to gasp and clutch and tear –

Not to panic, not to panic, she whispered to herself. It is a pool, it must not spread. Gather it, contain it. Here, in this bottle. A tall, fine bottle. She had it by its neck, her fingers went round it – almost around it, not quite – but she could, could grasp it – just. She would contain it. Pour it into a glass. See, how it trickled in, colourless, but she could feel it, smell it: it was real, she had not imagined it. When she lowered her mouth to the rim, it leapt up to meet her, went scorching up her nostrils and burning down her throat, leaving it raw and bleeding. She drew back in fright, her eyes leapt quickly in and out of their red sockets.

That was the way life was: it lay so quiet, so still that you put your fingers out to touch it, stroke it. Then it leapt up and struck you full in the face so that you spun about and spun about, gasping. The flames leapt up all around, rising by inches every minute, rising in rings.

At first they had been only little flames, so pretty in the dark. So many candles at a celebration, a festival. She would hear their voices ringing, as pure as glass, or flame. Raja and Bim, tall and straight and true, their voices ringing out: 'I will be a hero,' one had called out from the pure white peak of a candle flame, and the other had echoed back, as in a song, 'And I will be a heroine.' But then they had shot up into such tall, towering flames, crackling and spitting, making her shut her eyes and cower. Down at her knees the little Tara whimpered '*Masi*, they say I'm silly. *Masi*, they called me a fool.' The child's fingers stuck to her, waxy and white, and the flames crackled up above them, taller and fiercer every minute. When she put out her hands to stop them, the flames pricked her like pins, drawing out beads of blood so that she dropped her hands with a cry and backed away from them. This made them jump higher. They grew taller and taller.

They cast huge shadows on the walls around her. White walls, livid shadows, lurching from side to side. 'Bim and Raja,' she called desperately, 'stop it, stop it!' But the shadows did not listen. The shadows lurched towards her, and the flames leapt higher to meet them. Flames and shadows of flames, they advanced on each other, they merged with each other and she was caught between them, helpless as a splinter, a scrap of paper.

She could not manage them, she could not cope – they were too big for her, too hot and fierce and frightening. It was no good petting, consoling – they did not listen. They made such harsh, piercing sounds in her ears. She wished they would stop, it hurt so, it was torture. She pulled her white hair about her face, shielding herself. And some soft cloth to stop up her ears, her nose, shut herself up, hide from them. They prowled about, searching her out, menacing her. She moaned in fright. She needed protection. She wanted help. She reached out for the hand that would help her, protect her . . .

. . . Here it was. Here, in this tall, slim coolness just by her hand, at the tips of her fingers. If she got her fingers around it, its slender pale glassiness, and then drew it closer, close to her mouth, she could close her lips about it and suck, suck little, little sips, with little, little juicy sounds, and it would be so sweet, so sweet again, just as when they were little babies, little babies for her to feed, herself a little baby sucking, sucking at the little trickle of juice that came hurrying in, sliding in . . .

And she sucked and laughed and sucked and cried.

There was much for Dr Biswas to do in their house. That summer he was summoned almost every day, if not to subdue Aunt Mira and put her somehow to sleep so that she could not get at the bottle or scream and fight for it, then for Raja whose temperature remained obstinately at the same point, giving him a flushed, unnatural colour and at times raising his spirits to dangerous heights, then plunging them into the deepest gloom, neither of them governable by Bim who rushed from one room to the other in an effort to cope, always to the sound of Baba's records grinding out on the gramophone one cabaret tune after the other, relentlessly gay, unquenchably merry.

'How can you bear it?' Dr Biswas once asked her as she stood leaning briefly against a veranda pillar, waiting for him to come out of Aunt Mira's room while trombones shrieked and saxophones howled in Baba's room, making poor Begum, who lay at Bim's feet on the top step, raise her head and gaze into Bim's face like a sick child pleading for comfort.

Bim shrugged, too tired to explain how her mind was occupied with far worse problems so that it barely registered the sounds that had become so essential to the calm rhythm and silent contentment of Baba's existence.

'You do care for music, don't you?' persisted Dr Biswas who was always very reluctant to leave although he got no encouragement and hardly any attention from her.

'Do I?' wondered Bim. 'I don't know – I seldom hear any – apart from that –' she jerked her chin slightly.

'But Miss Das, you should, you must,' he pleaded seriously. 'Music is one of the greatest joys we can have on earth. If one has that pleasure, then one can bear almost anything in life.'

Bim at last paid him the little attention that he craved. 'Yes?' she asked in slow surprise. 'Does it mean that much to you?'

His eyes shone as he stood there, dark and awkward, his bag in one hand, smelling like a pharmacy. 'It is almost the only pleasure I have,' he assured her. 'Without it, life would be too drab – it would be only drudgery. Miss Das,' he added quickly, clutching his bag to him, 'will you come with me to a concert on Sunday, by the Delhi Music Society in the Freemasons' Hall? They are giving a performance of Brahms and Schubert, and they really play quite well, they are not professionals, they are amateurs, but not bad – and for two hours one hears these beautiful sounds,' he rushed on, sweating, 'and one forgets everything – everything.'

Bim studied him as if he were a curiosity in a museum. But all she said was 'Sunday? No, quite impossible, doctor. I can't leave the house –' she waved her hand in a sweeping gesture, taking in one, two, three bedrooms all opening out onto the veranda where they stood, and containing their one, two, three patients. Suddenly she was struck by the humour of it – it seemed so immensely funny: her standing here with the doctor, guarding these three doors with the three patients behind them, and the doctor inviting her to a concert of eighteenth-century European music in the middle of the riot-torn city – so that she began to laugh and laugh. Collapsing against the pillar, she hung her head and rang like a bell with laughter, quite uncontrollably, making the doctor smile uneasily and then murmur good-bye and slide off sideways in a hurry.

She was still grinning to herself when Bakul brought Tara home. Tara smiled at her with the same small apprehensive smile the doctor's face had had, and then slipped up the steps and went towards her room, almost guiltily. Bakul stopped beside Bim on the steps, lighting himself a cigarette. 'You find life amusing, Bim, do you?' he asked.

She placed her elbows on the balustrade, her chin on her hands, and looked down on him with her usual sardonic look. 'Amusing isn't exactly the word, but interesting – interesting enough.'

He sucked at his cigarette, regarding her, his eyes openly admiring her. Suddenly he took the cigarette from his lips and exclaimed 'Bim, why do you have grey hair already? You're much too young for that!'

'Grey hair? Where? I don't!' She stood up straight, feeling her hair, tugging out bits to stare at down her nose. 'You're making fun of me.'

'No, I'm not. Look, here,' he said, and touched the hair at her temple with his fingers, drawing it softly down her brow to her ear. She took the strand from him, brought it before her eyes and frowned at it.

'Yes,' she said flatly, even a little proudly, perhaps. 'It is grey. I didn't know.'

'You have too many worries,' he said.

Bim did not reply. She had already had that kind of conversation a few minutes ago and was bored with it. Bakul did always bore her:

it was his smoothness of manner; there was no roughness that could catch the interest, snag it.

But he would not bore her today. 'Bim,' he said again with unusual suddenness, 'would it add to your worries or would it lessen them if Tara married me?'

'What?' She was startled. She had still been regarding the grey hair between her fingers. Now she let it go so that it hung by her ear like a bit of pale ribbon. 'Oh. Oh, I see. You want to marry Tara. Yes, I thought you did. I think she wants to marry you too.'

'Yes, she says she does but wanted me to speak to you first.'

'Oh, did she?' laughed Bim. 'I'm head of the family now, am I? You think so, so I must be.' She shrugged, looking plain again. 'I don't think you need to ask anyone – except Tara. Modern times. Modern India. Independent India.'

Bakul turned aside. He never liked Bim when she spoke in this manner. He liked nothing abrupt, staccato. He held out the cigarette at a slight angle from him and looked down at the dog stretched out on the step by his foot, studying a flea that crawled past her nose and his toe. 'I can speak to Raja, of course, if you think I should.'

'No, don't worry him,' she said sharply.

'I don't like you having all the worries of the family.'

'You are lessening them, aren't you, by taking Tara off my hands?'

'Will I? Or is she a help to you? In that case, I won't press her now – not till later when Raja is well and Baba settled and your aunt –'

'You'll be grey-haired yourself if you wait that long,' Bim interrupted, flatly. 'There's no need to wait. Do marry – quickly. But what about your parents?'

'They know Tara. They love her. And since I am to go to Ceylon shortly, they will agree to an early marriage.'

'An early marriage – that is exactly what I'd like for Tara,' Bim said. 'It will suit her. And she will suit you. Blessings, blessings,' she called lightly, and began to laugh again as she saw Tara, half-hidden behind the bamboo screen at her door, listening, waiting.

Bakul was happier now that she laughed. He waved his cigarette in the air gaily, looking lighthearted and absurdly debonair. 'I'll have to buy you a bottle of Blacko for your hair, Bim,' he teased. 'I won't have you coming grey-haired to my wedding. Can't have such an elderly sister-in-law, I can't. You'll have to dye your hair for the wedding, Bim,' and they laughed together, she tugging at the grey strand in her hair and he drawing elegant designs in the air with his cigarette.

The dog suddenly pounced upon the flea.

With Tara married and gone, Aunt Mira more and more confined to her room and secret access to the bottle and less and less sober or controlled, Baba happily watching the records turn on Benazir's old green gramophone, Bim and Raja were thrown together for company and comfort even more than at any time of their lives.

Raja was calmer now that he had regular news of the Hyder Ali family and was left alone by the college terrorists who were too occupied in arson, looting and murder in the city to come out to the quiet suburbs and persuade an erstwhile comrade made useless by illness and poetic ideas of heroism and loyalty. He spent more time in reading aloud to Bim as she sat by his bed or, when he felt well enough to be propped up, in writing Urdu verse of his own. This caused him much mental anguish and he would read out every line to Bim as he wrote it, easily grow discouraged and crumple up the papers and fling them on the floor for her to clear away. She was made shy by these verses – something in her cringed at a kind of heavy sentimentality of expression that was alien to her and also, she felt, to him, except when he chose to express himself in Urdu so that she regretted its effect on him while at the same time her admiration for him was too great to allow her to even admit it to herself. Instead, she suggested in a low voice 'Why not take up a more original subject for your new poem? You know – just for the sake of – originality,' and that was enough to make him tug at his hair and roar with despair.

Bim began to wish Raja would not discuss his poetry with her. Why did he not read it to Dr Biswas, she suggested suddenly, quite surprised by the idea herself. Surely Biswas' soul was a sensitive one and would be more responsive than her own unpoetic one. 'He plays the violin, you know,' she informed Raja. 'He told me.'

'Ugh. I can imagine what it must sound like – the kind of thing that makes Begum raise her face to the sky and howl,' laughed Raja, fondling the dog's muzzle that she liked to lay on Bim's foot or on the edge of his bed when she sat with them. 'Can't you just imagine?' Raja pretended to sweep a bow across some violin strings. 'O wine and ro-oses, O mo-on and sta-ars' he wailed, and Bim laughed.

'He plays Mozart, Raja, and Brahms, so he couldn't be so hopeless!'

'Have you ever heard him? No? Then what makes you think he could ever be a musician? He just hasn't the guts.'

'He has soul, Raja – soul.'

'Soul!' Raja exclaimed. 'Who hasn't soul? It's guts you need – like Iqbal had. Now Iqbal said:

*'O painter divine, Thy painting is still imperfect*
*Lying in ambush for mankind are the vagabond, the exploiter and the monk.*
*In Thy universe the old order still continueth."'*

Nevertheless Bim suggested to Dr Biswas that he bring his violin with him one day and play for them but this embarrassed him so much that he became quite agitated. Dropping his bag, spilling his stethoscope, he fumbled about on the floor, picked them up, mumbling 'Oh no. Impossible. You won't – I can't – you don't really – it won't – no, no, no. I can't play. Miss Das, instead – I will be so honoured – will you come – can you – a concert – you will hear – it will be – I would like –'

She was so exasperated by his spinsterish nerves that she swooped down on the stethoscope that had fallen again and shoved it at him, saying angrily 'All right, I'll come,' which made him snap his mouth shut in astonishment so that he looked like a fish that had snapped up a hook by accident.

Raja lay back against his pillows and laughed and laughed. 'That did for him', he laughed as Dr Biswas hurried away down the drive. 'Oh you really put the lid on him this time, Bim. That was great. Like seeing a man knocked down in the first round. You should have been a lady wrestler, Bim – you're great. Terrific. But poor Biswas. Poor Mozart. *Ach, so Mozart*!' he wailed in tremolo, clasping his hands under his chin, and Bim, shamefaced, laughed.

'Mozart,' said Dr Biswas with great earnestness, leaning forwards with his elbows on the table on either side of a glass of beer, 'when I first heard Mozart, Miss Das, I closed my eyes, and it was as if my whole past vanished, just rolled away from me – the country of my birth, my ancestors, my family, everything – and I arrived in a new world. It was a new world, a shining new world. I felt that when I heard Mozart for the first time – not when I stepped off the boat at Hamburg, or saw strange white faces and heard the strange language, or drank my first glass of beer – no. These experiences were nothing by comparison. After that there was nothing in my life – only Mozart.'

'Only Mozart, hmm?' repeated Bim, thoughtfully smoking her first cigarette. It was a more complicated process than she had guessed and required more than a little attention. Also, Dr Biswas perplexed her. She could hardly believe her ears heard right.

'That was the beginning. Then the whole world of music unfolded for me. It was lucky I went to Germany, you know, Miss Das. It is what makes the German nation great – this love, no, not just love, but a belief that music is essential, a part of one's daily life, like bread or water. Or wine. In every small village you could hear music of the highest standard, and in Berlin – ah, it was magnificent!' His eyes flashed behind his spectacles, quite electrically.

'I wonder you still had time for medicine once you were so taken up with music,' said Bim, rolling the taste of tobacco on her tongue, finding it familiar, like something she had tasted before. When? And what?

'Oh, I never slept at all, in those years. No, no – there was medicine, there was music, there was the German language to be learnt, there was no time for sleep. I think I was delirious in those years. I used to walk down the broad avenues, and look at the cherry trees in bloom, and smell the lime blossom, and hear music at every street café, in every park – and, really, I was delirious. I was floating in the air in those days – floating!' He laughed and his hand trembled as he poured himself some more beer and drank. He had already had a great deal, Bim felt.

Bim stirred restlessly on the faded velvet sofa. The velvet curtains hanging beside her were so dusty, she felt she would sneeze. She felt they had been sitting here in this almost empty hall of velvet and gilt and blank-faced waiters for a very long time.

'You don't believe me,' he said, his eyes fading. 'I can hardly believe it myself any more. When I came back to India – to my mother and my sister and my practice here – it vanished so completely, nothing was left. It was – gone.'

'But you do still play the violin, you said.'

'Yes. Yes, I do. That is only an attempt to keep something of what I had in Germany in my student years – I had so much there, I was so *rich* then! Now I feel very poor, useless. I touch my violin and try to make sounds to remind me of that time. I take lessons from the first violinist of the Delhi Music Society orchestra, and I play to myself and inflict my playing on my mother who is an old-fashioned Bengali lady and likes only Tagore's songs and suffers in silence because she loves me. I am her only son.'

'She lives with you?'

'Yes, we have a flat in Darya Ganj. My sister married and went to live in Calcutta so now I am an only child. It is a great responsibility, being an only child of a loving mother,' he sighed, his face darkening visibly.

'I wouldn't know,' said Bim, stubbing out her cigarette in the square white ashtray and immediately reaching for another one from the pack Dr Biswas had placed on the table. 'I didn't have one.'

Dr Biswas looked at her vaguely, as if he had not heard, his thoughts were on another continent and moved to a different tune. Just then the band returned from the retiring room, tiredly mounted the small stage at the far end of the hall, picked up their instruments and then, turning on professional smiles as if at the lift of a puppeteer's strings, began to play a medley of Strauss waltzes. The waltzes spun and staggered from table to table like exhausted bees. Dr Biswas's head drooped.

'Yes,' he sighed, 'that is what we have here – the band in Davico's playing "medleys" as we drink tea.'

'I have finished,' said Bim, having quite lost interest in Dr Biswas's story which was not quite as interesting as it might have been, and also in the unaccustomed setting of Davico's restaurant which had entertained her for a while in the beginning – the arched doorways with the red velvet curtains, the thick pile carpet smeared with icecream and smelling of cigarette ash, the plates of meringues and cups of vanilla icecream balanced by graceful waiters, the long windows that looked out onto the leafy trees in the centre of Connaught Place, the red buses that trundled loudly by in the dust, the violet dusk falling out of the murky sky onto the home-going crowds from shops and offices all around, and the sweet treacle of music that the band spread over it all, slowing everything down till it seemed stuck. 'Now we *must* go,' she urged, 'I've never left Raja alone for so long, or Mira-*masi*.' They had been to the concert at Freemasons' Hall before coming to Davico's.

He stood up at once, apologetically saying 'But that is why I brought you out – oh yes, for the pleasure of taking you to hear this little orchestra, but also to give you a change. You can't always be at home, nursing your family – you will fall ill yourself.'

Bim laughed with more scorn than humour. She had no patience with weakness, she thought, none. 'I could have been a nurse – or a matron – in a plague hospital. I can handle it all.'

'Have you really thought of nursing?' Dr Biswas asked, hurrying after her down the mirror-lined passage and the marble stairs to the dusty, crowded street below.

'It is all I do,' she snapped at him.

'Of course, of course,' he stammered, flushing. 'I meant – but we must go round this corner to the No. 9 bus stop. I must get you home before the curfew. I meant – have you considered it as a profession? You do it so – so excellently.'

'No,' she assured him. 'What I think I shall do – I mean when Raja is well again and I have the time – I think I'll go back to college and finish my history course that I dropped when my aunt too fell ill, and when I get my degree – I might teach,' she ended up in a rush, the idea having just come to her as in a natural sequence of affairs.

He was all admiration. In the bus going home, while Bim gazed out of the window at the violet globes of the street lamps casting their harsh light on the passers-by below, at the shops being lighted up and filled with after-office crowds, at the pavement stalls with their paper and plastic and tin goods, and the beggars and their individual and flamboyant ways of attracting attention and small change, he talked again of his student days, of his professors who had invited him home for fruit wine and biscuits, and his landlady who had brought up seven children on her own, her husband being a cripple, and how inspiring it had all been and how much he owed them all, how they had made him what he was.

'Yes,' said Bim turning to him briefly, 'You are lucky, Dr Biswas.'

'Lucky?' He stopped short in his patter of reminiscence. 'How am I lucky, do you think?'

'You have known such glories – such joys.'

'Ah,' he said, and folded his arms across his chest and looked gloomy. 'Yes.'

He did not speak again, only shook his head stubbornly when she asked him not to bother to see her home. The bus lumbered on past the city walls and the massed jungle of rag-and-tin huts that had grown beneath them, housing the millions of refugees who were struggling in across the new border. Here there was no light except for the dull glow of small cooking fires, blotted out by smoke and dust and twilight. They swarmed and crawled with a kind of crippled, subterranean life that made Bim feel that the city would never recover from this horror, that it would be changed irremediably, that it was already changed, no longer the city she had been born in. She set her jaw and stared into its shadowy thickness, wretched with its wretchedness.

Dr Biswas' lips, too, were pinched together, although his silence had a different reason, she felt. Silently, he accompanied her all the way to her bus stop and then walked down Bela Road to her gate. There he stood, with the insects frizzling in the green light cast by the street lamp onto the gate and the bougainvillea, while Begum barked hysterically from the veranda. 'Miss Das,' he said, clasping the catch of the gate, 'Miss Das, I want to tell you – thank you for having given me such – such pleasure. It was the most beautiful evening I have had since coming back to India. I wish that you – '

'Now,' laughed Bim, uncomfortably, 'you are prompting me to say the things I should be saying to you. I am the one to say thank you, surely.'

'No,' he cried in anguish, gripping the catch so that Begum, thwarted, howled more piteously. 'You don't know – you can't possibly know what it has meant to me. Only, please do come with me again – '

'Oh, I don't know,' cried Bim in a panic, and pushed at the gate so that he had to let go of the catch to save his fingers. Hurrying through, she shut the gate between them. 'It's really not right for me to have been out for so long – with Raja ill – and my aunt – you know my aunt – '

'Yes, yes, but you can't be a slave to them. I can't be a slave to my mother. We must be ourselves. We must go out, have a little rest, some refreshment. Miss Das,' he gulped, 'come and meet my mother, please.'

This was worse than anything she had feared. Growing darkly red, she said hastily 'Yes, but I must run – I must see if Raja – and my aunt – you know my aunt – and Begum is barking. Begum, stop!'

Dashing up the drive to the veranda, she quietened Begum with a quick pat on the head and then flew up the steps to where Raja was sitting in the dark, watching. She sank down on a basket chair beside him, put her face into her hands and grimaced as hideously as she knew how while Raja laughed.

'Did he play you the vi-oh-lin, Bim?' Raja demanded. 'Diddly-dum, diddly-dum? No? Then did he sing you a Tagore song?' When she raised her face and shook her head, smiling, he placed one hand on his heart and quavered 'O mango flower, fall into my lap! O lamp, flicker in the dark!' which made her laugh and protest 'Oh Raja, you don't know a word of Bengali. You've never read Tagore.'

'I don't have to know Bengali – all you do is pronounce 's' as 'sh' and roll the vowels like round, sweet *rossogollas* in your mouth,' he said airily. 'O mango flower . . . Has he asked you to meet his mother? Has his mother sent you her home-made *rossogollas*, Bim?'

But now Bim stopped laughing. Crossly, she got up to go to her room. As she went, followed by Begum, she heard Raja sigh dramatically '*Ach, so Mozart*!'

It was a long time before Dr Biswas could persuade her to come out again. It was true that Raja improved steadily now that the cold weather had come, with dew on the lawn early in the mornings and beds of coloured flowers blooming in the sunshine, and he could sit out in the garden, wrapped in Bim's *pashmina* shawl, eating oranges and nuts and alternating between reading letters from the Hyder Ali family and composing Urdu verses for them. He looked unusually bulky and compact, and when he removed the shawl or his thick pullover, both brother and sister were startled to find that the bulk adhered to him, not to the woollen garments. They stared at each other in disbelief. It was all the rest, and the milk and the butter, they saw, and shook their heads in amazement.

Still, Bim had her hands full with Aunt Mira. She had made good her promise to herself and gone back to college to complete the course in history, and she had also picked up a hint dropped by Dr Biswas and gone to help in a clinic for women in the Kingsway Camp for refugees. It was close to the University and she could go there after the lectures and help hand out vitamin drops to pregnant women and mix powdered milk for the babies, but it took up all afternoon and she came home after dusk and regretted it for when she was out of the house there was no one to keep an eye on Aunt Mira who grew rapidly more difficult.

To begin with, Raja and Bim had told each other Aunt Mira was going through the bottles left in the sideboard by their father. But as time went on and Aunt Mira spent fewer hours in sobriety and slipped off to her room more frequently – guiltily and desperately – coming out only rarely and then stumbling and brushing her hands constantly over her face as if she felt a cobweb growing across it, her tongue slipping thickly from one bit of nonsense to another as if from one cup of drink to another, they had to admit those few bottles could not still be providing her. She was getting her supply of liquor from somewhere. Bim had taken over the household accounts from her a long time ago and old Janaki did not appear to be charging more than usual. It could not be her connivance that kept Aunt Mira floating and splashing in drink. Who was it then?

'I suspect that old Bhakta I brought across from the Hyder Alis, Raja,' Bim said, striking her head in dismay as they heard Aunt Mira drop a glass in her room and shriek as it shattered. 'He gives me such an insolent look when I glare at him for sitting idle outside the kitchen all day, just waiting for Janaki to bring him his meals – as if he had a secret that made him superior to me. I'm sure it's him.'

'How can you say that when you have no proof?' Raja answered. He could bear no criticism of anything or anyone who had to do with the Hyder Ali family.

'No proof – just instinct,' said Bim, and rushing off to clean the mess in Aunt Mira's room, found that she had cut her hands and was crying and bleeding all over the bed, more over the spilt drink and the splintered glass than over the strips of blood that hung from her spidery grey fingers in scarlet webs and which she barely noticed in her lament. It was Bim who cried over them.

Dr Biswas came and handled Aunt Mira with such gentleness and compassion that, watching him from the foot of the bed, Bim softened to see him wrap bandages around Aunt Mira's childish wrists and hear him give her such kindly, good-humoured advice that Aunt Mira lay back on her pillows and weakly glowed with pleasure and gratitude like a very small dim bulb with a fine, weak filament. Bim realised with a pang that she had not seen such a happy look on the old lady's face since before the troubles of last summer began. Holding onto her aunt's small-boned and cold feet, she saw now what her aunt had suffered through their parents' deaths, through Raja's illness, Tara's going away and the perpetual sorrow over Baba. It was all scored over her face, about her quivering mouth and watery eyes, and Bim had not cared to see it. Now she was lying back calmly on her pillows, smiling at the young doctor, smiling guilelessly and purely as a baby relieved from discomfort. Clasping those knuckled ankles, Bim wished she could remain such a baby in a cot, innocent and malleable.

Seeing out Dr Biswas, she said, quite humbly, yes, she would come to tea with his mother next week.

She was soaked, clammy wet cloths bound her. They had bound her. She had thought they were bandaging her wounds, stemming the blood, but actually they had bound her so that she could not get free, could not get her hands free and reach out. Swaddled and bound, she was suffocating in this mass of cloth. If she could only tear it off, or tear herself out – then she could reach out and touch, trembling, and grab. But they would not let her. They would come and stand over her and press her down into this soft, cottony mass, deep down. Sleep baby, sleep, they sang to her. She had sung to them in their cots, rocking them gently. But they were not gentle to her – sleep baby sleep, they roared at her, and kicked the side of her cot. They had grown so loud, so big. They were bigger than her, they loomed over her and threatened her if they saw her wriggle one finger out of the cotton bandaging towards the tall shining bottle in the dark. She had held out the bottle to them, held it to their lips and chuckled to see them drink. But they threatened her and pushed her back into the grey suffocating cell and denied her.

A drudge in her cell, sealed into her chamber. A grey chamber, woven shut. Here she lived, here she crawled, dragging her heavy wings behind her. Crawled from cell to cell, feeding the fat white larvae that lived in the cells and swelled on the nourishment she brought them. The cells swarmed with them, with their little tight white glistening lives. And she slaved and toiled, her long wings dragging. The air was filled with the angry buzzing of the queen bee. It bored through her ears and zoomed through the greyness like a lurid meteor, making her shut her eyes and burrow down into her cell, into her cotton swaddling, hiding. When it receded, she peeped out with flickering eyes. Where was the bottle? Where was its laughing, sparkling gleam in the dark, winking at her, beckoning to her? They had hidden it.

If she could only reach out and fetch it, then draw it close to her mouth – she whimpered with want. Just a sip, she whimpered, it was time for a drop. Time for milk. The children must have their milk – and leave a little for me, please, just a drop.

But there was no milk, the cow had died, drowned in the well. In that well, deep and stony and still, in which all must drown to die. The navel of the world it was, secret and hidden in thick folds of grass, from which they all emerged and to which they must return, crawling on their hands and knees.

She crawled towards it, dragging the cotton wings. When she reached the edge, she would peer in, then lower her head and go tumbling down, and at some point, at some time, strike the shining surface and break through to the dark and secret drink. She opened her mouth to drink. She whimpered for that drink.

The tea party was of course a mistake and Bim scowled and cursed herself for having softened and let herself in for what was a humiliation and a disaster for everyone concerned.

Had Mrs Biswas dressed for it? Bim had never seen anyone so dressed. So bathed, so powdered. She seemed to be dusted all over with flour. Perhaps she had fallen into a flour bin, like a large bun. But she smelt so powerfully of synthetic flowers, it must be powder after all. And her white sari crackled with starch, like a biscuit. And her hair gleamed with coconut oil, and flecks of gold glinted at the lobes of her ears and in the ringed folds of her neck. Altogether a piece of confectionery, thought Bim.

She was given a platter with all the goodies already heaped on it – neatly counted out, so many biscuits, so many pieces of *mithai*, so many fritters and a spoonful of chutney. Similar plates with exactly the same number of goodies were handed to Dr Biswas, one kept by her. They ate.

A china cabinet against the wall watched them. It stood on four legs and housed little plaster figures from Germany – a miniature beer mug, Hansel and Gretel skipping in a meadow, a squirrel dressed in a daisy chain. There were Indian dolls, less travelled but more worn, tinsel garlands flaking off onto red organdie saris and gold turbans. There were clay toys in cane baskets – yellow bananas, green chillies. A parrot. A cow. A plastic baby. And they all stared at Bim munching her way through the goodies. Dr Biswas stared at his brown shoes, so highly polished. He ate nothing.

His mother sighed. 'Eat a little, Shona,' she coaxed in a discontented mutter like a pigeon's. He did not and she took the plate away from him with a sigh, limped to the table to put it down. Earlier she had not limped: it was his not eating that brought on her limp. Now she cast a suspicious look at Bim who still ate, who ate on and on, blaming her.

Why blame me? thought Bim, her mouth full of syrup.

But then the old lady sat down, sighing, to complain. It was not her son and his poor appetite she complained of: she began with her husband who was dead, and went on to her arthritis which was painful and for which there was no cure – *he* said there was no cure – and ended up with the servant boy who had run away that very morning on being told there was a visitor coming to tea. Lazy, that was the trouble. Too lazy. And you? she questioned, her small eyes like raisins in the large soft bun of her face. How many servants? What do they do? What do you pay them?

'Ma,' Dr Biswas gasped, pressing down with all his weight on his toes so that the new shoes shrieked.

The little raisin eyes gave him a quick sharp look. Then the puffy white hand waved him away. 'He – he is the only one who knows what work is,' she went on. Work, work, nothing but work. Did any man ever work so hard? He was killing himself.

Sitting back on the sofa with the pink-flowered cushion behind her, she talked and talked – quite often in Bengali which gave Bim time to glance at Dr Biswas with some curiosity, wondering how she could have overlooked so many virtues, such glorious and unique qualities. His mother made it seem he was Apollo in disguise. His degrees in medicine – his dedication to his profession – the love his patients felt for him. And his music, too. Here the mother clasped her hands together, wrung them almost as if in despair. 'Play your violin,' she even said, 'for Miss Das. I don't understand all this Western music he plays, but perhaps you can. You are a college girl? What degree?'

Bim's mouth was full of crumbs. They were even more difficult to get through than the syrup. While she coughed and choked, the mother went on, about the violin, the music. What was it all about – could the college girl explain? 'I don't understand. He wants someone who understands – '

'Ma,' Dr Biswas broke in hastily, perspiring even. 'Perhaps Miss Das would like to hear you sing. Mother sings Tagore's songs, Miss Das – she has a trained voice. Would you like to hear?'

Now Bim began to feel annoyed. Let them play and sing to each other as much as they liked, she felt, why must I listen to them too? I listen to enough as it is, from everyone. Putting down her plate with several of the goodies still untouched – unfortunately they were the very ones Mrs Biswas had spent all morning cooking, but how was Bim to know that? – she listened to mother and son arguing more and more heatedly, the old lady on the brink of tears, determined to sacrifice herself for his sake, he somewhat maliciously as if to punish her for this embarrassing scene. Then Bim decided it was enough, and rose to her feet, saying brusquely 'I must get home before dark.'

Unfortunately, just as she stood up and said that, Mrs Biswas had relented and agreed, in Bengali, to fetch her harmonium and sing. Bim had of course not understood. Now here was Bim saying she would not stay, she would go. It was very unfortunate. Very rude and impolite and intolerable.

Setting her lips together, Mrs Biswas said, after a moment of silence, 'Of course you must go. It is getting dark.'

Dr Biswas, on his feet, swaying a bit as if struck with disaster, had no alternative now that she had been dismissed but to see her out. Then, casting a look over his shoulder at his mother as she shuffled about the small, drab room, collecting the scattered cups and plates and looking over all the uneaten goodies, he hurried down the stairs after Bim.

'I'll go back alone,' she said, her voice rising too high. 'Really, I *want* to, I'd *like* to.'

'You don't know what you are saying. It's not safe, these days, after dark, for a woman, alone.'

'Of course it's safe,' she said scornfully. 'Anyway, quite safe for a woman like *me*.'

He hunched his shoulders, taking the blow in silence, but would not give up and came clattering down the many flights of stairs after her onto the street. 'I would feel ashamed of myself,' he mumbled, as he caught up with her by the park railing across the road from his block of flats. 'I would never forgive myself,' he went on, hurrying past a cripple who sat propped up against the railings, holding out a begging bowl silently, and walked at her side.

She gave her shoulders an impatient twitch and walked on very fast past a drycleaner's shop, a tea shop and a stationery shop to the main street and the bus stop. How much his mother's son he was, she said to herself: he had inherited her gift for loading the weight of his self-sacrifices onto others.

The main street of Darya Ganj did look strangely empty and rather menacing in the early winter dusk, she had to admit. The few people they passed hurried by, unnaturally engrossed, and some shopkeepers were pulling down their shutters although it was surely still too early to be closing. Only around one tea shop was there a group of people and the sound of a news broadcast on the radio turned up above the babble.

'What do you think . . .' she began to ask when she nearly stumbled over a cobbler who had chosen to sit in a dark corner with his tool box and broken sandals spread before him. The man was saying almost as if to himself: 'Gandhi-*ji* is dead. Murdered, they say. Who would murder a good man, a saint?' He was shaking his head and swaying as he repeated the words in a monotone and Bim and Dr Biswas walked past him, barely taking note of his mutter when the words struck them and they stopped short to stare at each other and then at the cobbler.

'What – ' cried Dr Biswas, 'what did you say?'

His voice was so high-pitched, so hysterical, that the cobbler stopped mumbling to himself and looked up at them. Then he waved his hand towards the group of people around the tea-shop, listening to the radio. 'Go and hear for yourself,' he said. 'Gandhi-*ji* is dead. Murdered, they say . . .' and he began to sway from side to side in ritual mourning again.

Dr Biswas tore away towards the tea shop, Bim flying along behind him when she saw her bus come lumbering up and in a panic veered away from Dr Biswas and leapt onto the bus instead.

Hearing the bus screech to a halt by the curb, Dr Biswas too stopped and looked around wildly. 'Bimla,' he shouted, 'Bimla,' and waved to her to stop. She leant out from the crowd on the step, waving back, and saw him abandoned, scraps of paper blowing about his feet, the lamplight striking onto and ricocheting off the bald spot on his head. Then she disappeared into the bus and forgot him completely: she thought only of rushing to Raja with the news.

She heard him coughing as she rushed into his room. He was lying in bed under his thick winter quilt with Begum at his feet as limp as a rug. Both stiffened to hear her race in.

'Raja,' she shouted, 'Mahatma Gandhi's been killed. Murdered. He's dead.'

Raja gave a violent jerk and shot out of bed, the heavy quilt sliding to one side and falling to the floor, rolled up like a corpse. Raja's hair stood on end. Begum's began to bristle, too. 'You must be mad,' he shouted at her. 'You're crazy.'

'I tell you – everyone in the city knows – everybody in the bus was talking – where's the radio? Turn it on – let's listen.'

Raja hurried to the radio on his bookshelf and fiddled with the knobs in a kind of desperation. 'Bim,' he said, almost sobbing, 'there'll be more riots – killing – they'll slaughter every Muslim they can find – anywhere.'

'God no, not again, not again,' whispered Bim, but then the crackling of the radio sorted itself out and resolved into formal music, wailing miserably. A woman's voice was singing the *Ram Dhun* mournfully. Raja and Bim stood by, cracking their knuckles, waiting for a news announcement. When it came, they sank onto Raja's bed with relief to hear it was not a Muslim but a Hindu who had killed the Mahatma.

'Thank God,' Raja cried out, pulling up the quilt off the floor and hugging it to him almost violently. 'Thank God. I thought of the Hyder Alis – what they would have to go through – '

Bim glanced at him and his expression made her look away in embarrassment. It was as if the skin had been drawn off his face, leaving it peeled and bare. 'What do you think will happen now?' she murmured, turning to pat Begum who was calmed by her low voice and came to lay her muzzle on her lap, looking for reassurance.

'I think now perhaps Indians will forget Pakistan for a bit. Perhaps they will turn to their own problems at last. I don't know – at a time like this – it must be all chaos, Bim, chaos.'

They spent the evening listening to the news broadcasts, heard Nehru weep, were reduced to silence and shivering, then to irritation by the mournful dirges that were being sung continuously, sat together worried and relieved, shocked and thoughtful.

At last Raja said 'And your tea-party, Bim? How was it? Has Mrs Biswas approved of you as her daughter-in-law?'

That made Bim leap to her feet, switch on the light and start bustling about as if electrified. 'Daughter-in-law?' she spluttered. 'Dr Biswas's mother – just don't talk to me about her – about them – I hope I never have to see Dr Biswas again – he gives me the creeps – he's – he's just – '

'Oh Bim, don't be so hard on him – poor violinist, poor musician. *So Mozart – ach so Mozart*,' sang Raja, laughing, clasping his hands under his chin and making a sad clown face to make Bim laugh. And Bim laughed.

She always told herself that was the last time she saw him, the day that Mahatma Gandhi was shot. But it was not true – there was one more time, one that she never admitted and tried never to remember.

It had been at the end of spring. Raja had not needed the doctor since the winter – he was so much better, his temperature down to normal, getting stronger, puffing out with a thick padding of fat, as he sat in the sun, nibbling at nuts, tossing the shells to the squirrels that stole out of the trees and crept across the lawn to his feet to pick them up and scuttle back amongst the leaves. But as the weather grew warmer, the air seemed swollen with heat again, the garden was filled with drying, flying leaves, sand sprang out of the dunes by the river and blew all day long through the house and the garden, covering every leaf and every table and book and paper with grey grit, and Raja grew restless. He put away his verses, his books of poetry that he had found sufficient all winter, and paced up and down the long veranda, complaining about the heat and the dust, and 'Why isn't the drive ever swept up? Look at the leaves and the papers flying about. Can't you do something about this house, Bim? It grows dirtier and shabbier every day – like the house of the dead. Are we all dead? Don't you care any more? Don't you care about anything?' and he paced up and down, glowering, and Bim refused to pay attention to such petty complaints. But she knew it was not the dust or the untidiness of the place that was upsetting Raja, she knew he had begun to think beyond his illness, beyond his body, to the outer world and was restless to set out into it.

On a day late in spring, the koel began to call in the trees and went on and on ringing its obstreperous bell through that day of flying leaves and dust and summer heat that thrummed and vibrated like an electric line coiled around them. Bim was preparing for an exam – she sat before her books with her elbows glued to the sticky desk-top, trying to ignore Raja who paced up and down, interrupting and annoying her by mocking at the absurdity of her ambitions and putting forth ridiculous schemes for his own future that she could not bring herself to take seriously or encourage. She knew he was on the boil with impatience, longing to burst out, reach out to life and friends and movement, and that was at the bottom of all his grousing and grumbling, his unfair attacks on her and baiting of her, like a fire smouldering under a pot. Still, it was hard to tolerate.

'Oh Raja,' she sighed finally, bitterly, 'go back to bed, will you?'

This made him furious. His face bloated with temper as with angry gas and he stopped to lean on a chair-back with such pressure that the wood flinched and squeaked. 'I will not go to bed,' he hissed, spit flying. 'I will go – go to – to Hyderabad. Hyder Ali Sahib has asked me to come. He has plenty of work – I will work for him. I – I will – go today – today I will catch the train – I won't stop here, with you, another day. It's enough – enough – ' and he let go of the chair and spread out his arms as if to push everything out of his way.

Bim tried to stay calm. She merely tapped her pencil against her teeth and found it better not to look at his face – she had not suspected it capable of such ugliness. She looked critically at the sand accumulating on the desk, on her books, flying in and settling in grey, gritty flecks on the white surfaces.

Raja left the room but was not quiet. He could be heard striding about in his room, dragging out boxes and trunks, throwing things into them with all his strength so that there was a rumbling and shaking of danger. Danger. That roused Bim and made her go to his door and try to pacify him and bring him back to normalcy. Hearing them, a distraught Aunt Mira crawled out of her room and watched Raja pack with appalled eyes, pressing her trembling fingers to her lips. Bim tried to persuade her to go back to her room. She wept. In exasperation, Raja gave up packing and flung himself down onto his bed. To tell the truth, he was exhausted and could feel his temperature rising. It was heavy as lead but it rose, as inexorably as the mercury in a thermometer. The heat enclosed the house and all of them in it, sulphur-yellow in colour and tinged, like an egg-yolk, with blood. Aunt Mira locked herself into her room. Raja slept – or smouldered, and Bim watched, watched.

At three o'clock when the heat of the day had risen to its violent, brick-red peak above the house, threatening it, a door slid open – audaciously, dangerously – and out darted a naked white figure, screeching and prancing, streaked through the room, out onto the veranda and then fled pell-mell down the steps into the sun.

Bim, who had spent the afternoon stretched out on a sofa in the hall in between her brother's and her aunt's room, not quite certain what to expect from either, gave a violent start when she saw what she took to be a noontime ghost slipping through the room, then sprang to her feet and rushed after her.

Aunt Mira was naked, whipping herself around and around in the driveway, screeching as she whipped and spun till she fell into the gravel and rolled there in agony, crying 'Oh God – the rats, the rats! Rats, lizards, snakes – they are eating me – oh, they are eating me –' and her frantic hands tore the creatures from her throat, dragged them out of her hair. Then she doubled up and rolled and howled. When Bim flung herself at her and held her down with her arm, weeping and crying for Raja and Baba and Janaki to come, it was old Bhakta who heard and came running with knees bent. The aunt raged and bit their wrists and thrashed her legs, crying 'They're eating – eating – eating my *hands*,' and tried to fling off her fingers. Finally someone fetched a blanket and threw it on top of her and Bim rolled her up in it, picking up the shreds and soft blobs of grey flesh that leaked from the spindly body, the little empty balloons of skin and flesh, smelling and mouldy with age, from off the gravel and sand, that clung on in bits and shards, rolled them up into the blanket and carried her in like a corpse.

Then Dr Biswas came: that was all that Raja had been able to do from his bed – he had telephoned the doctor. Just one injection and the old woman lay still, slipping neatly as a little tube into heavy, sad sleep, not stirring when Bim lifted and turned and dressed her. The doctor helped. Together they tucked her out of sight – the little sad wisp of grey pubic hair like a bedraggled rat's tail, the empty slack pouches of her ancient breasts, the bits and scraps of her – then sat on either side of her bed, each holding one bird-boned wrist, the doctor to confirm the pulse, Bim to plead for forgiveness for the indignity of it all and for a return to her old, comforting self. Finally he spoke. 'I'll give you a bottle, Bimla, of brandy. When she wakes up, give her this much,' and he got up stiffly, brought out a bottle from his bag and poured some into a tumbler. Bim gasped at the amount and began to protest but he said 'She must have it. Or she'll go mad. Every three hours, give her some. After some time, you can water it. Water it more and more. Make it a long, watery drink that she can sip slowly by the hour. You will have to do this yourself – keep the bottle with you – or you will have to put her into hospital for some very drastic treatment that will kill her.' Bim hung her head and would not speak. So he got up to pack his bag and leave, saying 'I'll just go and see Raja for a few minutes.' At the door he paused for a moment, looked back at Bim mournfully. 'Now I understand everything,' he said with a deep sigh.

'What?' asked Bim, not very interested. She was more conscious of her aunt's pulse beating like a bird's under her finger – less than a bird, beating like the pulse of an embryo in a fine-shelled egg – only the merest flutter that she had to strain to feel and keep between her thumb and finger, safe.

'Now I understand why you do not wish to marry. You have dedicated your life to others – to your sick brother and your aged aunt and your little brother who will be dependent on you all his life. You have sacrificed your own life for them.'

Bim's mouth fell open with astonishment at this horrendous speech so solemnly, so leadenly spoken as if engraved on steel for posterity. Then, to her relief, Dr Biswas left and she was alone with her aunt. Looking down, she found she had dropped the thin wrist from her hand in shock, and now she pressed her hands together as if she wished to break, to wreck something. She even hissed slightly in her rage and frustration – at being so misunderstood, so totally misread, then gulped a little with laughter at such grotesque misunderstanding, and her tangled emotions twisted her face and shook her, shook the thought of Biswas out of her. Later, she never acknowledged, even to herself, that this ridiculous scene had ever taken place.

That was the beginning of the aunt's death for no one really expected her to recover. It was the long slow journey begun in earnest, and Bim sat reading, reading. She read the *Thodol Bardol* which she found, to her surprise, amongst her aunt's few books, and she read Lawrence's *Ship of Death*, moving her lips to silent words, wishing she dared speak them aloud:

*Now launch the small ship, now as the body dies*
*and life departs, launch out, the fragile soul*
*in the fragile ship of courage, the ark of faith*
*with its store of food and little cooking pans*
*and change of clothes,*
*upon the flood's black waste*
*upon the waters of the end*
*upon the sea of death, where still we sail*
*darkly, for we cannot steer, and have no port.*

and wished, almost, that she could herself lower herself into that dark tunnel and slip along behind the passage made for her by the older, the dying woman.

*Have you built your ship of death, O have you?*
*O build your ship of death, for you will need it,*

she murmured, almost aloud, but Aunt Mira did not hear. She lay quite still now, shrinking and shrivelling, till she almost ceased to be human, became bird instead, an old bird with its feathers plucked, its bones jutting out from under the blue-tinged skin, too antique, too crushed to move. Now Bim kept the brandy bottle in the cupboard and measured out the drink for her. She became a baby, crying and whimpering for the bottle if it was not there, her lips making little sucking sounds in hungry anticipation. Sometimes she trembled so much she could not drink from the glass, only spilt it all, and then Bim had to spoon it into her mouth and she would suck and suck the spoon as if it were a teat, blissfully, her little buried eyes shining with joy. She began to foul the bed. Bim engaged the gardener's wife to help her clean and wash. The woman was strong and lifted and washed and turned with vigour, but liked to talk. She would even try to force the aunt to eat a little of the rice and *dal* Janaki sent for her, but it seemed to hurt her to eat. She did it so unwillingly and pathetically that Bim, out of pity, sent the woman away with the dishes and gave her to drink instead.

Only on one night did she rouse herself out of the stupor that Bim had thought permanent, and then she tore at her clothes as if they were a net, tore at invisible things that seemed attached to her throat and fingers and hair, even screamed 'Let me go – let me jump into the well – *let* me!' She screamed that intermittently all through the night, like an owl, or a nightjar starting out of the silence, waking Bim. She seemed obsessed by the idea of the well – the hidden, scummy pool in which the bride-like cow they had once had, had drowned, and to which she seemed drawn. Bim held her wrists all night, wondering why of all things in this house and garden it was the well she wanted, to drown in that green scum that had never shown a ripple in its blackened crust since the cow's death. Even as children they had not gone very close to it ever: they had dared each other to throw pebbles in it but only Raja had accepted the dare, even Bim had lied and pretended but not actually gone. Now it seemed to encroach on the aunt's enclosing darkness like a dark flood and she seemed helpless to resist it – on the contrary, hopelessly attracted by it.

Trying to distract her, quieten her, Bim brought her a glassful of drink and helped her to sip it. While drinking, her head slipped to one side, the glass spilt across her chin, dribbled down her neck into her nightie, and she died, not hideously by drowning, but quietly in her bed, pleasantly overcome by fumes of alcohol. Yet it was as if she had drowned for Bim dreamt night after night of her bloated white body floating naked on the surface of the well. Even when drinking her morning tea, she had only to look into the tea-cup to see her aunt's drowned face in it, her fine-spun silver hair spread out like Ophelia's, floating in the tea. She would turn very pale and leave the tea cold in the white cup. Aunt Mira had not drowned, she told herself over and over again – not drowned, just died.

Bim and Janaki and the gardener's wife washed her clean and Bim fetched her only silk sari out of her trunk, the white silk that had a broad border of crimson and gold and that Aunt Mira had never worn while she lived, and they dressed her in it like a doll at a wedding, an idol on an altar. Janaki even lit some sticks of incense because of the smell in the room that shamed the family. Then the neighbours came and lifted the string cot on which she lay and carried it out of the house: it was as light as a leaf or a piece of paper.

Raja rose from his bed and accompanied Bim to the cremation ground. He lit the pyre with a torch and they stood watching, with perspiration streaming in sheets from their faces, the heat tremble and vibrate in the brilliant light of the summer afternoon like wings, or theosophical phantoms, till it was reduced to a mound of white ash on the silver sand beside the river. The earthen pot containing the ash was handed to Bim still warm, and she walked with Raja to the river's edge to lower it into the water and watch it bob for a while, a wreath of red roses around it, till the grey current caught it and swirled it away and it sank. A washerman, knee-deep in water, straightened up and watched, too. A donkey brayed. A lapwing cried. The river ran. They went home.

Yet for a long time Bim continued to see her, was certain that she saw her: the shrunken little body naked, trailing a torn shred of a nightie, a wisp of pubic hair, as she slipped surreptitiously along the hedge, head bent low as if she hoped no one would notice her as she hurried towards the well. Bim would catch her breath and shut her eyes before opening them again to stare wildly at the hedge and find only the tassels of the malaviscus dangling there, like leering red tongues, and nothing else. She thought of what she had read in Raja's copy of *The Waste Land*:

> '*Who is the third who walks always beside you?*
> *When I count there are only you and I together*
> *But when I look ahead up the white road*
> *There is always another one walking beside you*
> *Gliding wrapt in a brown mantle, hooded*
> *I do not know whether a man or a woman*
> *– But who is that on the other side of you?*'

At the end, she found a note to say that these lines were suggested by an account of an Antarctic expedition: 'The explorers at the extremity of their strength, had the constant delusion that there was one more member than could actually be counted.'

Bim caught her lip in her teeth in understanding when she read that, although she could not see the connection between explorers of the Antarctic and her little drunken aunt, but she was sure now that she was that extra person, that small shadow thrown by a subliminal ghost that existed in the corner of the eye. She wondered if she were losing her mind but then she ceased to see this vision, it receded gradually and then went altogether. Perhaps, as the Tibetans believed, the soul had lingered on earth for a while till it was finally fetched away on its long journey. The ship of death, O ship of death, Bim chanted to keep herself calm, calm.

She kept calm while Raja packed his bags, put away all his things, telling her that now he would go to Hyderabad. Looking up at her as she watched silently, he shouted 'I have to go. Now I can go. I have to begin my life some time, don't I? You don't want me to spend all my life down in this hole, do you? You don't think I can go on living just to keep my brother and sister company, do you?'

'I never said a word,' said Bim coldly.

'You don't have to. It's written all over your face. Just go, go, take your face away. Don't sit there staring. Don't stop me.'

'I won't stop you.'

'I'm going.'

'Go,' said Bim.

When the tonga arrived to take his things to the station and Bhakta was loading his bags onto it, each bag making the tonga dip down so that the horse had to spread its legs to steady itself, he spoke to Bim again. 'Bim, I'll come back,' he said. 'I'm leaving all my books and papers with you. Look after them till I come back.'

'Why should you come back?' Bim asked stonily.

'Bim, don't be so *hard*. You know I must come back – to look after you and Baba. I can't leave you alone.'

She started to say something but then only shrugged slightly and bent to hold Begum back as Raja swung himself onto the tonga, when Bhakta suddenly jumped onto the tonga step, clung to it, pleaded with Raja to take him, too, to Hyderabad, back to Hyder Ali Sahib, and then crouched down at Raja's feet, and went with him. Begum whined and quivered as the tonga driver raised his whip over his head and got the ribbed yellow nag started with a lurch. Bim stood petting her, quieting her, and when the tonga had lumbered out of the gate, she became aware of Baba coming out of his room as the gramophone ceased to rattle out the jolly rattle of Nelson Eddy singing 'The Donkey Serenade', and quietly settling down to play with his pebbles on the veranda tiles.

Bim sank down onto the steps beside him, sat there in a slumped way, both tired and relieved, her arms hanging limply over her knees and her head drooping. She watched Baba's pebbles scatter and fall, then his long fingers reach out to gather them together again, and began to talk, more to herself than to him.

'So now there are just you and I left, Baba,' she muttered. 'Does the house seem empty to you? Everyone's gone, except you and I. They won't come back. We'll be alone now. But we don't have to worry about anyone now – Tara or Raja or Mira-*masi*. We needn't worry now that they're all gone. We're just by ourselves and there's nothing to worry about. You're not afraid, are you? There's no need to be afraid. It's as if we were children again – sitting on the veranda, waiting for father and mother, when it's growing dark and it's bedtime. Really, it'll be just the way it was when we were children.' She yawned hugely, her eyes starting out of her head and her cheek bones straining at her stretched skin. 'It wasn't so bad then,' she mumbled, shaking her head sleepily, 'was it? No. When we were children – '

But she didn't say any more. She laid her head on her lap and seemed nearly asleep.

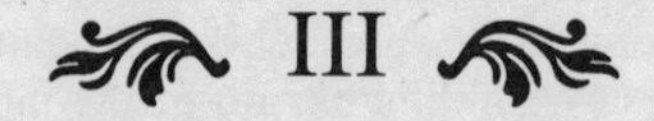

# III

Every morning, when the dew still lay fresh on the grass, the mother followed the doctor's orders and strolled up and down the rose walk at the far end of the garden. To Tara it was a long grassy tunnel between two beds of roses. Her father was supposed to have planted them. The gardener was ordered to take care of them. But neither the father nor the gardener knew roses: they put in cuttings and watched them come up, either small, weakly crimson ones or shaggy sick-pink ones, nothing else. Tara sighed, thinking of the sight that met her eyes whenever she peered through the wrought iron gate at their neighbour Hyder Ali Sahib's house, at the round, square, rectangular, triangular and star-shaped beds filled with roses like scoops of vanilla ice cream, pink ones like the flounced skirts of English dolls, silky yellow ones that had the same smell as the tea her mother drank, and crimson ones that others called 'black' and which she always studied with narrowed eyes, wondering why she could not see the blackness but only the rich velvety crimson of their waxen petals . . . Why could they not have such roses, too? Still, this early in the morning, even these negligible pink and crimson buttons gave off a cool, fresh scent. They should have pleased the mother and Tara cried continually 'Look, Mama, look,' but she seemed to notice nothing, to be absorbed in other worlds, as invisible to Tara as the black of the red roses.

Usually the mother did not take exercise. She either sat up at the card table, playing, or lay very still on her bed, with a suffering face tilted upwards in warning so that Tara did not dare approach. Even now she kept her distance. She paced slowly, obediently, her arms folded, her chin sunk into her neck, as if considering a hand of cards, while Tara, in her nightie, skipped and danced after her, her bare feet making tracks through the misty dew on the grass.

Suddenly she stopped with a shout: she had spied something under the rose bushes – a gleam of pearly white. Perhaps a jewel, a ring: Tara was always expecting to find treasure, to make her fortune, discover herself a princess. She stooped to part the leaves that hid it and saw the pale, whorled orb of a stopped snail. For a while she stayed on her knees, crushed with disappointment, then lifted it onto a leaf and immediately delight gushed up as in a newly mined well at seeing the small creature unfold, tentatively protrude its antennae and begin to slide forward on a stream of slime. 'Look,

Mama, look what I've found,' she cried, darting forwards, and of course it tumbled off the leaf and when the mother turned to look, there was Tara staring at the slimy leaf, then searching for the lost creature in the mud. Wrinkling her nose, the mother walked on, brooding. She had not chosen to walk here: the doctor had told her to; it was good for her, he had said. If one became pregnant so late in life – and yes, there were strands of grey thickening and spreading in her hair above her ears – and that, too, when one was so severely diabetic, one would have to be careful. She would have to take walks. Sullenly, she walked, frowning to hear the chattering of the mynah birds in the mulberry trees, wincing at Tara's sudden scream of delight and discovery followed by wails of distress and disappointment. Tara was still the baby of the family. She did not know her days were numbered, that she was soon to lose all her privileges and be removed to a distance, disregarded, as another made its appearance into their lives. That was life – a snail found, a pearl lost. Always, life was that.

The new baby was the prettiest of all, everyone declared, when they came to see him lying in his crib, so delicately pink, so divinely quiet. Even Tara, ordered to keep away, edged closer to where he lay sleeping and hung over the edge of the cot, wide-eyed and breathing heavily at the miracle of this tiny live thing, whole and complete and alive and yet able to fit, like a child's toy, into the crook of an arm, or onto a knee, folded into his shawl, so quietly content as if he did not wish to emerge any more than the snail from its shell.

No one could help noticing how slow he was to learn such baby skills as turning over, sitting up, smiling in response, talking, standing or walking. It all seemed to take an age with him. He seemed to have no desire to reach out and take anything. It was as if his parents, too aged, had given birth to a child without vitality or will – all that had gone into the other, earlier children and there had been none left for this last, late one. He would lie on his back, gazing at the light that rippled the ceiling, or propped up on someone's lap, and stare at the ants that crawled industriously by, not even reaching out a finger to them. His mother soon tired of carrying him about, feeding him milky foods with a silver spoon, washing and powdering him. She became restless, spoke of her bridge four; 'My bridge is suffering,' she complained. There was the ayah of course, Tara's ayah made nurse again, but she could only be made to work twelve hours a day, or sixteen, or eighteen, not more. She could not stay awake for twenty-four. For some time the mother tried to train her to but it was impossible – she was a stupid woman and would not learn. She would fall asleep with the child in her arms and the mother never knew how often he rolled off her lap onto the floor because he protested so gently, his cries did not disturb her as she sat playing cards with her friends in the drawing room. But the ayah spoke to her, told her it was time the child sat up, and stood, and talked. She said she could not bear the burden single-handed any more: he had grown too large and too heavy.

Then Aunt Mira was sent for. Aunt Mira was not exactly an aunt, she was a cousin of the mother's, a poor relation who had been widowed at the age of fifteen and had lived with her husband's family ever since as maid of all work, growing shabbier and skinnier and seedier with the years. By then there were more daughters-in-law in the house, younger, stronger and abler, and she was no longer indispensable. So when the mother wrote, asking her to come and stay with them, she was allowed to leave their house and come. Good riddance, they had even said. Aunt Mira had been frequently ill, had aged young, was growing dotty and bald. Useless, but another household might find some use for her, as the worn article, thrown away by one, is picked up and employed by another.

'She is coming to look after you children,' their mother told them. 'You have become too much for me – you are all so noisy and naughty. She will discipline you. And look after your brother. I don't know what is wrong with him – he should be walking by now and doing things for himself. She will keep him in her room and look after him. And you will have to learn to be quiet.'

Led to expect some fierce disciplinarian, a kind of female general equipped with tools of punishment, they stood hiding behind the veranda pillars and peeping to see her when she arrived, and were both relieved and disappointed by her appearance. She was a poor relation, they could see that by the way she was greeted by their mother and the way in which she returned the greeting – tremulously, gratefully. Her luggage was all in bits and pieces, bedding rolls and tin trunks, like the servants', no better. Yet, when she was shown into her room – 'Show Mira-*masi* her room, children' – and opened the green-painted tin trunk, they found it was crammed with presents for them. As they stood around in a ring, sucking their fingers or scratching their necks, she drew out the things she had been making for them ever since she had received their mother's summons – there were paper hats trimmed with parrot feathers, little slippers of felt and velvet for Tara's dolls, a scrapbook of wedding and birthday cards for Bim, lions and giraffes made out of sticks and straw for Raja. She took more and more stuff out of that battered trunk and they came closer, kneeling beside her, sitting cross-legged by her trunk, quickly growing accustomed to the scarecrow-like appearance that had caused them both disgust and reassurance at first appearance, growing accustomed to the unfortunately protruding teeth and collar-bones, the thin wispy hair drawn over the white scalp into an untidy blob, the myopic eyes that seemed to blink and twitch perpetually with nervousness, and were quite enthralled – no one had ever *made* them things before, no one had ever had the time. 'I'm just going to the club, I'm waiting for the car,' the mother had said irritably when approached, and the ayah would lift her arms out of the wash-tub, dripping, to threaten them as she shouted 'If you bother me, I'll thrash you,' while no one had even considered approaching anyone so unapproachable as the father.

Now they had an aunt, handed to them like a discarded household appliance they might find of use. They exchanged deep, understanding looks with each other: they had understood their power over her, they had seen she was buying, or begging for their tolerance and patronage. They were not beyond, even at that age, feeling the superiority of their position and of extending their gratitude from that elevated position of power. Perhaps Aunt Mira felt all this, too. But it did not seem to matter to her. She said 'I saw green mangoes on those trees outside. Can you make mango sherbet?' They shook their heads, dumbly, wondering if she had been ordered to teach them cooking. But she only said, gleefully sucking in her breath, 'I'll make it for you if you fetch me a basket of mangoes from your garden,' and with a yell they streamed out as in wild celebration at this new season in their lives, a season of presents and green mangoes and companionship. She went to the kitchen with all of them dancing behind her, to watch while she cut and sliced and chopped and stirred, and let them taste in little sips from a spoon. The cook watched stonily for a while, then grudgingly gave up the cooking spoon and even began to help.

When they left the kitchen, Tara clasped her aunt's knees, not caring if the shabby sari smelt somewhat of onions and cooking fat, and asked 'Have you come to look after us? Or are you to look after Baba only?'

'I am to look after Baba,' Aunt Mira agreed, 'but I would like to play with *you*.' It was not said ingratiatingly. It seemed to Tara that her aunt's darting eyes and trembling fingers were searching for friends and she was happy to have them. Hope and trust instantly springing up like grass inside her, Tara squeezed the creaking knees and said '*I'll* play with you.'

Aunt Mira even played with Baba, teaching him games no one else had tried to play with him, thinking him too hopelessly backward.

To begin with, she stopped feeding him those milky sops from the tip of a silver spoon. Instead, she cut up small pieces of bread and let him pick them up and put them in his mouth himself. His sisters and his brother, who had not seen him perform this skill before, stood by, entranced, applauding him. Then she showed him how to slip a button into a buttonhole. They got a great deal of amusement out of that, too. Eventually he could do up his buttons himself and then would stand basking in their congratulations like a duck in a shower of rain. Visitors could hardly believe their eyes when they saw him sitting on the veranda and playing a game of marbles with Aunt Mira – how his fingers got round the rolling globes of glass, how he manipulated them and rolled them back to her: it was a miracle. Baba would lift his head timidly – pale, shining – then drop it in shy triumph. On winter evenings Aunt Mira would place him on her bed, tucked up in her plum-coloured quilt, and play a game of bagatelle with him on Raja's old board with its row of heavy lead balls and small baton with which to strike them and send them rambling down a long chute to wander about the board, amidst the nailed enclosures and the lead pits, till they rolled into one or the other or, as mostly happened in Aunt Mira's case, returned to the bottom of the board without running up any marks at all. Then they were gathered up and rolled back into the chute for the next player. Bim and Tara would keep the score and hug their knees with delight when Baba won.

Only their efforts to make him talk failed. He would say one word at a time, if pressed, but seemed happier not to and could not be made to repeat a whole line. Gradually, as his family learnt how to anticipate his few needs and how to respond, they ceased to notice his silence – his manner of communication seemed full and rich enough to them: he no more needed to converse than Aunt Mira's cat did.

Not only Baba but animals, too, followed in her wake as she scurried busily through the household. One day a small kitten took to mewing desperately under the veranda. A saucer of milk was set out for it, surreptitiously, a watch kept on the parents's door to make sure they did not suddenly emerge and catch them at it. The kitten had no such qualms and in no time was slipping up the steps and rolling about the veranda, catching its tail or scampering after a wasp, and soon it was wrapped up in Aunt Mira's quilt where it grew larger and larger and eyed them commandingly with its yellow eyes, more mistress than Aunt Mira.

Then Aunt Mira summoned courage to speak out on a matter that had been bothering her. Slipping into their mother's room, she described how she had often watched the milkman fill up the milk can at the garden tap before coming up the drive to the kitchen door to ladle out the watered milk into the saucepan held out by the cook. 'It is more blue than white,' Aunt Mira's voice cracked into splinters with indignation, 'and there's no cream at all. It is as if the children were drinking water. They get no nourishment. It can't go on.'

The mother seemed as displeased with Aunt Mira as with the milkman, or possibly more. 'Then what do you suggest?' she asked sourly as if to put a stop to the distasteful conversation and get on with the inserting of ear-rings into the waiting ear-lobes.

'It would be best to have a cow,' Aunt Mira said excitedly, and the children at the door jumped in surprise and joy at the unexpected boldness of her imagination. 'The gardener could look after it. He could bring it to the door and I could watch it being milked myself every morning. We would have pure milk for the children.'

The mother looked at her as if she were mad. A cow? A cow to give them milk? She shook her head in amazement, but now the ayah came up and loudly supported the aunt, and then the cook. It seemed the milkman was a rogue, had swindled them all, they did not wish to have anything to do with him. Faced with a rebellion of this size, the mother capitulated and the cow arrived, led in by the gardener on a rope to be examined and admired like a new bride even if she had her calf with her.

There was something bride-like about her white face, her placid eyes and somewhat sullen expression. The children fondled her pink, opaque ears that let in the light and glowed shell-pink in the sun. Tara laid her face against the folds of her neck, milky white and warm. She smelt sweetly of straw, and cud. She was housed in a shed. For a week, she was treated like a bride, fed on the tenderest of grass and newest of shoots. Her milk was the subject of ecstatic admiration: how it frothed into the pan, how thick the cream that rose on it. She stood in the garden, under the jacaranda tree, the lilac flowers showering down on her as at a wedding.

It was spring. The nights grew warmer. The gardener left her out instead of putting her in the shed at night. In the dark, while everyone slept, she broke the rope that tethered her and wandered through the garden like a white ghost, her hooves silent in the grass. She blundered her way through the carvanda hedge at the back of the house, and tumbled into the well and drowned in a welter of sounds that no one heard.

The well then contained death as it once had contained merely water, frogs and harmless floating things. The horror of that death by drowning lived in the area behind the carvanda hedge like a mad relation, a family scandal or a hereditary illness waiting to re-emerge. It was a blot, a black and stinking blot.

The parents were furious at this disastrous expenditure, the gardener guilty and therefore sulky, and the children shocked. Most horrifying of all, the calf pined and died. It kept Aunt Mira awake in the night and nightly she saw the white cow die in the black well.

Aunt Mira was younger than their mother although she looked so much older. She had been twelve years old when she married and was a virgin when she was widowed – her young student husband, having left to study in England immediately after their wedding, caught a cold in the rain one winter night, and died. She was left stranded with his family and they blamed her bitterly for his death: it was her unfortunate horoscope that had brought it about, they said. She should be made to pay for her guilt. Guiltily, she scrubbed and washed and cooked for them. At night she massaged her mother-in-law's legs and nursed wakeful babies and stitched trousseaux for her sisters-in-law. Of course she aged. Not only was her hair white but she was nearly bald. At least that saved her from being used by her brothers-in-law who would have put the widow to a different use had she been more appetising. Since she was not, they eyed her unpleasing person sullenly and made jokes loudly enough for her to overhear. There was laughter, till they grew bored. She stayed with them so long that she became boring. They suspected her of being a parasite. It was time she was turned out. She was turned out. Another household could find some use for her: cracked pot, torn rag, picked bone.

The children wondered why she always wore white. The mother explained, smoothing down her own ripe, flushed silks, that white was the widow's colour. 'But now she is not a widow, now she lives with *us*,' said Raja, and the girls asked if she had not had any wedding finery. Oh yes, she said without resentment, she had had some but had given it all away to her sisters-in-law when they married, to fill out their dowries. She added, with regret, that she wished she had been allowed to keep some for her nieces. The girls, too, regretted this and looked through the green tin trunk once again for some remnant of her wedding, of her improbable married life. And there was one: a stripe of crimson and gold edging an untouched Benares silk sari. Since it was white, she had been allowed to retain it, and now it was yellowed like old ivory. The strip of crimson and gold made it impossible for her to wear: taboo. It was wrapped carefully in tissue and laid away like some precious relic. The girls would try and persuade her to wear it once when her Theosophist friends took her out to a meeting or arranged a tea for a visiting Friend, but she always shook her head nervously and refused, superstitiously afraid. The girls fondled it, buried their faces in it, sniffed at its old, musky scent that they preferred to their mother's French perfumes: it seemed more human. After all, it contained Aunt Mira's past, and the might-have-been future, as floating and elusive as the musk itself. But she would not touch it. When they became insistent, she said, laughing, 'All right, when I die, you may dress me in it for the funeral pyre,' then immediately looked guilty and repentant at the shock that swept across their faces.

Aunt Mira, though widowed, could not be said to be abandoned. She was searched out, even, by those whom misery attracted just as it nauseated others. As she was such a useful slave, she might be a useful convert, these thought, and burrowing into the suspicious family like persistent wood-borers, they found her out and carried her off to the Theosophy Lodge for meetings, lectures and teas. Aunt Mira shook at the possibilities, at the stormy wastes she glimpsed there, and the cyclones and avalanches and apparitions that swept through it. While she shivered and dithered, the dead man's family disapproved, disapproved. Removed from them, she dithered again – should she? could she now? Raja and Bim urged her on, excited, giggling – it was as good as opening up a cupboard full of ghosts, they felt, shivering in delighted anticipation. They fully expected poltergeists to arrive by air, three-legged tables to rise to the ceiling, strange messages to be imparted. But Aunt Mira was too weak. She had to be dragged to meetings, she was so afraid of them, and soon found excuses for not going. So they sent her books. She had little time for reading. Yet she seemed to imbibe something from their uncut pages and closed covers, and grew more vague, absent-minded – 'ectoplasmic,' Raja said.

To Tara, she was nothing of the sort: she was solid as a bed, she smelt of cooking and was made of knitting. Tara could wrap herself up in her as in an old soft shawl. This Tara needed for she had lost most at Baba's birth and the turning of the entire family from her to the new baby. Wrapped in the folds of Aunt Mira's white cotton sari, or into her loosely knitted grey shawl, or the plump billows of the plum-coloured quilt in winter, she became baby again, breathing in her aunt's smell, finding in it a deep, musty comfort. On summer nights she lay on the pallet closest to her aunt's string bed out on the lawn where they slept in a row of cots under the stars. Then Aunt Mira would tell them stories: 'Once there was a king and a queen. The queen said to her pet parrot, Go to the king and tell him I want the red ruby that the king cobra keeps hidden under its hood . . .' and Tara, who believed ardently in jewels, gave a wriggle of pleasure. Aunt Mira's voice murmured on and on, following all the loops and turns of the story as skilfully as water flowing down its necessary channel, till the car's headlights lit up the gate-posts with its green flood of phosphorescence and came sliding up the drive, bringing their parents home from the club. Then they would hastily lie down flat and stiff as a row of corpses, pretending to be fast asleep. When the parents had gone in to change and to sleep on their own veranda at the other end of the house, Tara would whisper urgently, 'And then, Mira-*masi*? And then?' and the voice would continue, in an even lower register, 'And the cobra said, I will give you my ruby if the Queen sends me the princess dressed in a gold wedding sari and holding the Queen's pet parrot on her finger . . .' and the stars blurred and the jasmines shook out the powdery frills and flounces of their night scent till sleep came out of the dark hedges to devour them.

Sunny winter mornings had the same quality of perfection. Then the quilts would all be carried out and laid onto a string cot in the sun to air and Tara and Baba would roll themselves into them till they went pink from the heat of the cotton stuffing and the sun. Aunt Mira would sit on her cane stool, the knitting needles going clack-clack while she knitted their school sweaters, and now and then turned the brown and white pottery jars filled with pickles that lined the veranda so that each side of the jars got the sun in turn. When she was not looking, they would lift the lids off the jars and fish out bits with their fingers to eat, but it always made them sneeze and their eyes water so that Aunt Mira would know what they had been up to and scold, in a low voice so as not to be heard by their mother who sat playing cards with her friends on the veranda amongst the massed pots of chrysanthemums, pink and egg-yellow and bronze, fretted and shaggy and spicy. The cat stalked the butterflies that fluttered two by two over the flower-beds, as packed and coloured as a paint-box, but Aunt Mira was quick and never let her catch them.

Quick, nervy and jumpy – yet to the children she was as constant as a staff, a tree that can be counted on not to pull up its roots and shift in the night. She was the tree that grew in the centre of their lives and in whose shade they lived. Strange, when she was not their mother and did not rule the household. She really had not the qualities required by a mother or a wife. Even the children did not believe she had. Looking at her, they could not blame the husband for going away to England and dying. Aunt Mira would not have made a wife. What does make a wife? Why, they felt, a wife is someone like their mother who raised her eyes when the father rose from the table and dropped them when he sat down; who spent long hours at a dressing-table before a mirror, amongst jars and bottles that smelt sweet and into which she dipped questing fingers and drew out the ingredients of a wife – sweet-smelling but soon rancid; who commanded servants and chastised children and was obeyed like a queen. Aunt Mira had none of these attributes. Stick-like, she whipped her sari about her, jammed a few long steel pins into the little knot of hair on her head, and was dressed in an instant, ready to fly. She neither commanded nor chastised, and was certainly never obeyed. She was not soft or scented or sensual. She was bony and angular, wrinkled and desiccated – like a stick, or an ancient tree to which they adhered.

They grew around her knees, stubby and strong, some as high as her waist, some rising to her shoulders. She felt their limbs, brown and knobby with muscle, hot with the life force. They crowded about her so that they formed a ring, a protective railing about her. Now no one could approach, no threat, no menace. Their arms were tight around her, keeping her for themselves. They owned her and yes, she wanted to be owned. She owned them too, and they needed to be owned. Their opposing needs seemed to mingle and meet at the very roots, inside the soil in which they grew.

Touching them, dressing them, lifting them, drawing them to her, she felt how their life streams met and flowed into each other. They drew from her and she gave readily – she could not have not given. Would it weaken her? Would she be stronger if she put them away and stood by herself, alone? No, that was not her way any more than it was the way of nature. She fed them with her own nutrients, she reared them in her own shade, she was the support on which they leaned as they grew.

Soon they grew tall, soon they grew strong. They wrapped themselves around her, smothering her in leaves and flowers. She laughed at the profusion, the beauty of this little grove that was the whole forest to her, the whole world. If they choked her, if they sucked her dry of substance, she would give in without any sacrifice of will – it seemed in keeping with nature to do so. In the end they would swarm over her, reach up above her, tower into the sky, and she would be just the old log, the dried mass of roots on which they grew. She was the tree, she was the soil, she was the earth.

Touching them, watching them, she saw them as the leaves and flowers and fruit of the earth. So beautiful, she murmured, touching, watching – so beautiful and strong and living.

The first summer that Aunt Mira was with them, Bim and Raja caught typhoid. They were fortunate to have her in the house since she nursed them alone. They were so ill they were often unconscious, drifting about without any moorings in the luminous world of fever and then returning to the edge of consciousness in a kind of daze, not really aware who it was that lifted their heads and spooned barley water into their mouths or held cold sponges to their foreheads so that the water trickled into their eyes and ran down their cheeks onto their pillows. The doctor would come but he had no medicine for them: nursing was all, he said, and nursing was what Aunt Mira did best.

Tara hovered at the door, not allowed in, or played quietly on the veranda, now and then lifting the bamboo screen at their door to peep in, and Aunt Mira would make a great effort and rouse herself from her anxiety and exhaustion and go out and play a game of cat's cradle with her, or give her a poem to memorize, or thread a string of leaves to tie round her waist for a dance or, if she could not leave Bim's and Raja's bedsides when they were delirious, wave gaily to Tara at the door and point out a squirrel on a tree to her. This became the basis of their special relationship – an affectionate, demonstrative one, always assuring each other of their love, while the one that grew up between Aunt Mira and the two older children was silent and instinctive, seldom demonstrated, often quite sarcastic, but organic, a part of their sinews and their blood.

The difference showed when they played their favourite game of questioning each other: 'What will you be when you grow up?'

Raja said promptly and proudly: 'A hero.'

Tara said you could not be a hero, you could only be a heroic soldier, a heroic explorer, a heroic something, but he insisted he would be, simply and purely, a hero.

Then Bim declared, with glistening eyes, that she would be a heroine, although she would secretly have preferred to be a gipsy or a trapeze artist in a circus.

Tara looked from one to the other in incomprehension. '*I* am going to be a mother and knit for my babies,' she said complacently, but the older two laughed at her so uproariously, so scornfully, that she burst into tears and ran to bury her head in her aunt's lap and complain that they made fun of her.

Aunt Mira smiled faintly when she heard of Bim's and Raja's ambitions and was really in complete sympathy with them, but she stroked Tara's head and consoled her. 'There, there, you'll see you grow up to be exactly what you want to be, and I very much doubt if Bim and Raja will be what *they* say they will be.' This consoled Tara entirely and turned out to be true as well.

They had other games to play on summer afternoons, lying on

bamboo matting on the floor under the slowly revolving electric fan, watching the geckoes crawl across the ceiling after the flies, wiping the perspiration from their faces and feeling swollen and flushed by the heat.

'What is the hottest thing you can think of?'

'Melting lead over the kitchen fire and going out in the sun to pour it into a groove in the clay,' said Bim because that was what they had done that morning and she felt sure she had got heat-stroke.

'Holding a magnifying glass over a sheet of paper in the sun and burning a hole into it,' said Raja.

'White chicken feathers lying in the ash heap by the kitchen door,' said Tara unexpectedly, and then instantly mumbled 'No, no, not really,' because she had just remembered what it had felt like to roll off Aunt Mira's bed and crawl under it to visit the cat's newest litter, all lined up against her panting flesh like leeches. The dust under her bed, the cats' fur, matted and grey and marmalade, immobilized by the heat except for their panting breath and little pointed pink tongues hanging out of their open mouths – that was the warmest thing she knew.

'And the coolest thing you can find in summer?' the game continued.

'A long drink of water from the earthen jar on the veranda.'

'Watering the rush matting at the door with a hose-pipe, seeing it trickle down and smelling the wet *khus*.'

'A water-melon cut open and sliced, all red and juicy.'

In search of such balm, they would steal out of the house although forbidden to do so under pain of sun-stroke. They could hear the grass frizzling in the sun, the dust seething in the air, nothing else – even the pigeons were dumb, and the coppersmiths. They made a dash across the scorching earth to the water tap at the end of the rose walk, quietly trickling into the green mud around it. They squirted each other with the water but it was tepid and lifeless. The gardener's family lay on a string cot under the mulberry trees, and their smallest baby cried and cried, its skin angry and sore with prickly heat.

They wandered down to the long row of servants' quarters behind the guava trees. There Tara's old ayah sat like a bag of rags, chewing her betel nut and stirring up a fire of smouldering sticks to boil some tea. The acrid smoke billowed out into their eyes and made them cry. This made her laugh: 'If the smoke follows you like this, it means you will have faithful husbands.' They snorted at her scornfully and went into her room, odorous of cowdung fires and mustard oil, to look through her bags and baskets filled with old rubbish gleaned from their house over the years – bent forks, scraps of lace, curling yellow photographs and empty tins. The sooty walls were papered with bright pictures from the illustrated papers but it was too dark and smoky to make them out, and they soon grew bored and drifted out, stopped to whistle at the bedraggled parrot she kept in a cage, feed it a chilli or two that it only stared at beadily and refused to touch, then went back to the house to collapse onto the bamboo matting spread on the floor for them, pinioned to it like leaves drying and fading into mere brown tissue held together by bleached skeletons.

'What is the most frightening thing you can think of?'

'Finding a centipede inside your slipper just as you are putting it on.'

'The well the cow drowned in.'

'A cholera injection,' said Tara, but immediately followed that by a small gasp for it had led her to think of something far more frightening and disquieting, something she feared to speak of at all. It gave her face a baffled, secretive look as she grappled with a memory that heaved out of her mind like a shape emerging from the surface of dark water, at first grey and indistinguishable, then gradually coming closer and growing larger as she backed away in fright.

She had followed her father into her mother's bedroom on a day when her mother had not emerged at all, very quietly so as not to disturb her and therefore not noticed by her father. Then what she saw made her back into the dusty crimson curtain that hung at the door and hide in its folds, watching something she did not wish to see: her father, with his mouth folded up very primly, his eyes pinpointed with concentration behind the lens of his spectacles, bending over the bed, pressing a syringe into the thick, flabby arm that lay there. As the needle went in, the mother's head tilted back and sank deeper and deeper into the pillow, the trembling chin rose into the air and a little sigh issued through her dry lips as if the needle had punctured an air-bag and it was the very life of her that was being released, withdrawn from her. Then Tara knew she had witnessed a murder – her father had killed her mother. She stumbled out of the room and was sick on the drawing room carpet.

'What is the matter, Tara?'

Tara had crawled into Aunt Mira's bed in the garden that night and lay in a ball, pressing against her aunt's feet as she sat cross-legged, telling them a story that began 'Once upon a time there was a king and he had three sons . . .'

'When will they come home?' Tara whispered. To her baffled

wonder, that evening the car had driven up to the veranda steps and her mother had come out of the house and stepped into the car with the father and driven off to the club as usual, dressed in green silk and several pearls, palpably alive. They had not returned yet and the square of light that was the dining-room door kept Tara awake as a tyrant does its prisoner.

'Soon,' her aunt comforted her.

'Poor Abu, still waiting up with the dinner,' Bim grumbled. 'It's so late, why don't they come home to dinner?'

'When people play cards, they don't notice the time.'

'*Why* do they play cards?'

There seemed to be only one answer, too obvious to make, but that night Aunt Mira gently hinted at another as if she knew what kept Tara so miserably awake and tortured. 'It helps your mother to forget her pain,' she suggested.

Tara stiffened immediately. Bim and Raja were startled. What pains had she? they clamoured to know. Then Tara heard the word: diabetes. Now they understood why the doctor came so often to the house. Injections, said Aunt Mira, it was the daily injections that kept her alive.

'Alive?' wondered Tara, the morning scene unreeling through her mind like a film cut loose in the projector and wildly flying backwards.

Bim and Raja argued 'If she is ill, she should stay in bed. Then she would get better. She should not go to the club,' they said censoriously.

'She is trying to lead a normal life, for your father's sake,' Aunt Mira explained, but such adult clichés could satisfy no child. Unappeased, they continued to question Aunt Mira. Insulin, they wanted to know more about insulin. Their aunt could tell them nothing beyond the need for the daily injection of insulin that their father gave her.

'Oh,' sighed Tara, 'is *that* why she has those little blue marks in her arm?' and she laid her head against her aunt's shoulder, weak with relief and gratitude at having been given an explanation that would cover up the livid, throbbing scene in her mind as a scab covers a cut.

Raja of course outgrew the efficacy of his aunt's answers to his questions and her stories spun shining through their nights like a spider's silver webs. He would make scornful remarks, point out the illogic of her fairy tales. Impatient, he would leave his sisters to his aunt and go off to the servants' quarters or hail the soda-man, a jaunty young Sikh who came to the house driving a cart in which blocks of ice and crates of soda bottles slithered on the wet sacking and smelt pleasantly of damp straw. While the cook exchanged empty bottles for full ones and had a block of ice put in his ice-box, Raja drank a bottle of ginger beer, tingling to its spiciness, and then leapt up onto the cart and, waving the whip over the yellow nag's ears, set off at a rumble down the drive, making the soda-man rush out and abuse him and the girls jump up and down with delight and cheer him. He would drive it at a furious rattle up to the gate and then stop and jump off, surrendering the whip to the angry driver, and smile smugly at the admiring girls. Or he would go and call Hamid, the driver's son who worked in a cinema house in Kashmere Gate and was already a wage-earner although not much older than Raja. Hamid used to take him for rides on his bicycle when he was small, then taught him how to cycle. He also taught him wrestling. The two of them dug a shallow pit behind the garage, beat and crumbled the earth till it was smooth and even and then they would wrestle, grunting and groaning and pushing at each other in mock combat that always ended in being serious. Raja was always beaten and emerged bleary-eyed and dusty but panting with pride at having partaken of this manly sport. For a while he went in for a daily oil massage and for eating blanched almonds with his morning milk, absolutely serious in his pursuit of excellence, but after a while Hamid's own dilettantism infected him. Cutting short a half-hearted wrestling bout, they would get onto their bicycles and set off for the cinema in Kashmere Gate and Hamid would smuggle Raja in without a ticket to see the latest Charlie Chaplin or Douglas Fairbanks or any Bombay film for which Sehgal had sung the songs. Raja had no ear for music but the Urdu lyrics that were sung appealed to him powerfully and he would recite them emotionally and dramatically as they cycled slowly home at night, passing from lamplight to shadow along the pipal-tree lined street, quite sure that the parents would not be back from the club and that the girls would be asleep.

But Bim, a light sleeper, would lift her head when she heard him steal up across the inky lawn and murmur a muffled reprimand at which he would stick out his tongue.

As he grew long-legged and lanky, he became more difficult to catch. Tara, who had always felt at a disadvantage when competing for Raja's attention since she was the smaller and weaker one, born to trail behind the others, while Bim and Raja were not only closer in age but a match for each other in many other ways, began to realize that she and Bim were actually comrades-in-arms for they pursued Raja together now and Raja eluded them both.

In games of hide-and-seek in the garden, on summer evenings when the long, flattened-out afternoon could at last be ripped away so that their refreshed evening selves could spring up and come into being, it was always Raja who was the leader, who did the counting-out, who ran and hid, and it was always the two girls who were left to run about in frenzied pursuit, tearing their dresses and bruising their knees, quite unmindful of stains and scratches and beads of blood while their eyes gleamed and their faces flushed with lust to find and capture him and call him captive.

There was one glorious moment when they cornered him, up against the impenetrable carvanda hedge, and leapt upon him, from east and west, all nails and teeth and banshee screams. But, ducking beneath their arms, he turned and dashed his head madly into that thick, solid hedge behind him and broke his way through it with one desperate, inspired thrust of his body. And they, too, were sucked into the tunnel he had so surprisingly made in that wall of thorns and twigs and leaves, fell into it and blew through it, then streamed after him, made limitless by surprise, into the forbidden area of the back garden. This was the still, uninhabited no-man's land into which the gardener hurled branches of thorn and broken flower pots. Here he built his steaming, fetid compost heaps. Here was the well in which the cow had drowned, the deep stone well that held green scum and black deeds.

Here the girls stopped, halted in their mad stampede by the sad realization that Raja had escaped them again, fled past these barriers and probably found shelter in the servants' quarters where Hamid would help to hide him from them. Out of breath, heated, glaring, they looked down at the thorns they stood in that had scratched long strings of blood-beads out of their brown legs, and at the convolvulus and the castor oil plants that grew thickly about the well.

For a while they panted noisily, unnecessarily noisily, trying to recapture the glory of that moment when they had caught Raja, nearly caught him, up against the hedge. Then they bent to wipe the blood from their legs and straightened to slap at the mosquitoes that rose humming from out of the moist compost heap and hovered about their heads in dark nets.

Then Tara breathed 'Bim, we're right next to the well,' and instinctively they moved closer to each other in order to face together what was such a source of horror to them all and definitely out of bounds as well. But Bim, left flat and emptied out by disappointment at Raja's escape, gave Tara a sudden little push, saying 'Let's look.' When Tara hung back, she took her firmly by the elbow and made her kneel beside her, then bent forward to peer through the weeds into the depths of the well.

The water at the bottom was black, with an oily, green sheen. It was very still except when a small frog plopped in from a crack between the stones, making the girls start slightly. They narrowed their eyes and searched but no white and milky bone lifted out of it. The cow had never been hauled out. Although men had come with ropes and pulleys to help the gardener, it had proved impossible. She had been left to rot: that was what made the horror of it so dense and intolerable. The girls stared, scarcely breathing, till their eyes started out of their heads, but no ghostly ship of bones rode the still water. It must have sunk to the bottom and rooted itself in the mud, like a tree. There was nothing to see – neither hoof nor horn nor one staring, glittering eye. The water had stagnated and blackened, closing over the bones like a new skin. But even the new skin was black now and although it stank, it gave away nothing.

Nothing in their hands, the girls backed away on their knees till it was safe to stand, then turned and hurried away, through the grey thorns and over the midden heap, and finally butted their way through the hedge back into the garden, the familiar and permitted and legitimate part of the garden where they found Raja coolly sitting on a cane stool beside Aunt Mira, eating the slices of guava that she cut and peeled for him.

Rushing forward with renewed fury, they screamed and jeered and raged at him. He stuck out his tongue at them for he had no idea that they were not screaming with rage at his escape from their clutching fingers and pinching nails but at the horror behind the hedge, the well that waited for them at the bottom of the garden, bottomless and black and stinking.

When Bim realized, although incredulously, that Raja was withdrawing, that his maleness and his years were forcing him to withdraw from the cocoon-cosiness spun by his aunt and his sisters out of their femaleness and lack – or surfeit – of years, she grew resentful. She still sat listening to Aunt Mira's fairy tales but with a brooding air, resenting being left there, bored and inactive, by Raja. Her resentment led her at times to be cruel to Tara.

She knew how Tara longed for curls. Tara's hair was as lank and black as Bim's, hanging limp to her shoulders, so that she yearned for a little wave to it, some soft curls. To ask for the golden locks of fairy-tale heroines was too much, Tara knew, but at least she might ask for a slight wave, a bit of a curl. Bim overheard her confiding in her aunt: '*Masi*, I wish God would give me curls. If I pray to him, will he give me curls, *masi*?' Bim went immediately to the sewing box and fetched a pair of scissors. Flashing them at Tara, she whispered 'Come, I'll cut your hair for you. Then it will curl by itself. Long hair never curls – it has to be cut very, very short.' Tara was enticed by this promise and at once slipped out of Aunt Mira's bed and followed her sister.

But when she saw Bim leading her out of the house and up the outer staircase to the rooftop, she grew apprehensive and hung back, putting her hands round her long bunches of hair, protectively. 'Come on, come on,' Bim hurried her roughly, snipping the air with the big heavy sewing scissors and, making Tara crouch down behind the cast-iron water-tank on the roof, she cut through her hair at the ears with great sure crunches of the steel blades. Thick inky swathes lay about their feet, peppered Tara's neck and back with snippets and drifted with the evening breeze to the edge of the terrace, then lifted up and floated over the balustrade and into the garden.

Tara began to whimper as she felt the unaccustomed touch of cool air on her neck, bared and naked, then raised her hands to feel the bristles about her ears, as sharp and rough as stubble, and let out a loud wail of distress. When Bim marched off with the scissors, looking undeniably smug, Tara stayed back and refused to go down.

After a while the strands of hair floating down from the terrace were noticed by those in the garden and in the veranda. They came out to stand in the driveway and gaze with shaded eyes to see where it was coming from. The white sky stared blankly back. A circling kite whistled thinly – and Tara sobbed and whined. They could hear her now.

Bim was asked to go up and fetch her but would not – she was doing her homework, she importantly said. Then Raja and Hamid went and shouted with laughter at the sight that met their eyes – they said Tara looked like a baby pigeon fallen out of its nest, blue-skinned and bristly, crouching behind the water-tank and crying for her lost hair. As the boys roared with laughter, her crying grew wilder. Finally Bim stomped up and grabbed her by the arm. 'Stop howling, you booby,' she said roughly. 'You wanted curls, now you've got curls. You *said* I could cut your hair and I *did*. How was I to know you didn't mean it?' and she pulled the wailing sister down the stairs and scornfully turned her over to Aunt Mira's tender ministrations.

Tara was sure she would never forgive Bim her cruelty. Bim's big-sisterliness would always be linked with that ruthless and cynical chopping of her long hair, Tara felt. It grew again, as Aunt Mira assured her it would, but as straight and lank as it had been before.

These were the dramas that seemed not so much to make cracks in the dull metal bands that held them all down into a world, an age, of unbearable, total inactivity, eventlessness and apathy, as to emphasize them by hitting them with a hammer so that they clanged and the clangs resounded and echoed. As they grew into adolescence it seemed to Raja, Bim and Tara that they were suffocating in some great grey mass through which they tried to thrust as Raja had thrust through the thorny hedge, and emerge into a different atmosphere. How was it to be different? Oh, they thought, it should have colour and event and company, be rich and vibrant with possibilities. Only they could not – the greyness was so massed as to baffle them and defeat their attempts to fight through. Only Raja sometimes did. On his bicycle, cycling off to the cinema in Kashmere Gate, or in the wrestling pit with Hamid, or rattling down the drive in the soda-man's cart, hallooing and waving a whip over the startled nag's head, or flying kites on the terrace in the evenings, he seemed to come alive and glow, even if briefly, to be followed by a long trough of brooding sullenness and irritability.

Raja also had the faculty of coming alive to ideas, to images picked up in the books he read. The usual boyhood adventure stories, *Robin Hood* and *Beau Geste*, set him on fire till he almost blazed with enthusiasm as he showed Hamid how to fashion swords out of bamboo poles and battle with him, or pictured himself in the desert, in the Foreign Legion, playing some outsize, heroic role in a splendid battle. He cycled to Connaught Place and bought cheap paperbacks printed specially for the American Army and sold on the pavements, and took them home to share with his sisters. 'Book worms, book worms,' Aunt Mira called them, rather proudly and indulgently, as they lay stretched on their beds under the stickily revolving fans, reading with almost audible concentration.

The sisters, however, read themselves not into a blaze but a stupor, sinking lower and lower under the dreadful weight of *Gone With The Wind* and *Lorna Doone*, their eyes growing glazed so that they seemed to read through an opaque film and the stories and characters never quite emerged into the bright light of day and only made vague, blurred impressions on their drowsy, drugged minds, rather than vivid and clear-cut ones. They hadn't the vitality that Raja had, to participate in what they read – they were passive receivers, bulging with all they read, sinking with its weight like water-logged rafts.

While Tara would be dragged helplessly into the underworld of semi-consciousness by the romances she read, Bim was often irritated and would toss them aside in dissatisfaction. She began to realize they were not what she wanted. What did she want? Oh, she jerked her shoulders in irritation, something different – facts, history, chronology, preferably. She was bored by the books Raja brought her and tried not to disappoint him by showing her boredom but of course Raja saw and was hurt. Bim began to read, laboriously, sitting up at a table with her elbows placed on either side of the book, Gibbon's *Decline and Fall* that she had found on the drawing-room bookshelf. Raja secretly admired her for it as he could not have tackled a study of such length himself, but would not show it and said only that she did not know what she was missing, that she had no imagination: to him, the saddest sin. That hurt and puzzled Bim: what need of imagination when one could have knowledge instead? That created a gap between them, a trough or a channel that the books they shared did not bridge.

Yet when they came together it was with a pure and elemental joy that shot up and stood straight and bright above the surrounding dreariness. There were still those shining summer evenings on the banks of the Jumna when they went together, Bim and Raja, barefoot over the sand to wade across the river, at that time of the year no more than a sluggish trickle, to the melon fields on the other bank to pick a ripe, round one and cut it open with Raja's pen-knife and bite into the juice-suffused slices while the sun sank into the saffron west and the cannon boomed in the city to announce the end of the day's fast in the month of Ramzaan and the start of prayers in the great mosque. At this hour the dome of the sky would soften from white-hot metal to a soft mauve tapestry streaked with pink. The washermen would fold the dried washing spread out on the sand and load it onto their donkeys and ride away. Smoke would rise from small fires in the hovels at the bend of the river and from under the thatch of the melon-growers' huts, turning the evening air furry and soft. A lapwing would start out of the dark with a cry and a star wink into life simultaneously, it seemed.

Tara was sent to fetch them home. She came, holding Baba by the hand. Now and then she bent to pick up a small, insignificant river shell and press it confidingly into his hand. Seeing Raja and Bim wading slowly back through the river, muddy and tired, she waved. They shouted. The two pairs of children trudged slowly towards each other over the dry silver of the sand. When they met, they became a blur in the dark, wavering homewards.

As they turned to make their way back to the house, a kind of low drumbeat started up in the pits of their stomachs, reverberated through them, making them stop and clutch each other by the hand.

'*Hato! Hato!*' shouted a man in a khaki uniform and a scarlet turban, and pounded past them on urgent heels, making way for a white horse that loomed up out of the dunes and floated by with a dimmed roar of hoofbeats on the sand, followed by a slim golden dog with a happy plume of a tail waving in the purple air. The pampas grass bent and parted for this procession and then rustled silkily upright into place again.

When the three figures had vanished into a dip in the dunes and then reappeared in the white dust of the road ahead, at a distance, Raja breathed out in awe 'It is Hyder Ali Sahib on his horse. He looks like a general! Like a king!'

'Perhaps he likes to imagine he is one,' said Bim tartly, drawing Baba forward by the hand. Some of the sand had been flung into their eyes. They were all rubbing at the grains.

Tara jumped up and down on her toes, watching them still. 'And his dog,' she cried. 'See the lovely dog running after the horse.'

'I wish he were a friend of Papa's,' Raja said wistfully as they shuffled up the road, sand filling the spaces between their toes. 'Then he might let me ride his horse sometimes.'

'You don't know how to,' Bim said.

Ahead of them, the magical procession turned in at the Hyder Alis' tall wrought-iron gate and a light came on in the porch and, a moment later, another one in their own house behind the trees.

After that the sense of dullness and hoplessness that reigned over their house took on the intense aspect of waiting. They were always waiting now – superficially, for their parents to come home from the club, or Aunt Mira to put Baba to bed and come and tell them a story. Yet when the parents were back and Aunt Mira free, they were still unfulfilled, still waiting. Perhaps for the white horse to appear again on the dunes, followed by the golden dog. Or for some greater event, some more drastic change, a complete reversal of their present lives and the beginning of a new, wondrous phase. They would wander about the garden, peering intently into the phosphorescent green tunnel of a furled banana leaf, or opening a canna lily pod and gazing at its inner compartments and the embedded pearly seeds, or following the path of a silent snail, searching for a track that might lead somewhere, they had no idea where.

Bim felt she knew the answer for at least some of the daylight hours on six days of the week – the hours she spent in school. At school Bim became a different person – active, involved, purposeful. A born organiser, she was patrol leader of the Bluebirds when still a small pig-tailed junior, later of the Girl Guides, then captain of the netball team, class prefect, even – gloriously, in her final year at school – Head Girl. A bright, slapdash student, she spent little time at her studies but did almost as well as those dim, bespectacled daughters of frustrated failures who drove their children frantically, bitterly, to beat everyone else in the exams and to spend all their waking hours poring myopically over their schoolbooks. Bim had an easy, teasing manner with the teachers who liked her for it even if they sometimes scolded her. They were always admonishing Tara in reproachful tones: 'Look at your sister Bimla. You should try to be more like your sister Bimla. *She* plays games, *she* takes part in all activities, *she* is a monitor, the head girl. And you . . .'

Tara hung her head lower and lower, dragging her foot as she walked, irritating them still further. Physically smaller and weaker than Bim, she lacked her vigour, her stamina. The noise, the dense populace, the hustle and jostle of school made her shrink into a still smaller, paler creature who could not rouse herself out of a dismal apathy that made the lessons as irrelevant and meaningless as the buzzing of a fly against the windowpane, and friendship with the loud, vulgar, vigorous young girls in the class, so full of unpleasant secrets and revelations and so quick to betray and mock, an impossibility, vaguely wished for but quite beyond her capacity to undertake.

Whereas school brought out Bim's natural energy and vivacity that was kept damped down at home because of the peculiar atmosphere of their house, school to Tara was a terror, a blight, a gathering of large, loud, malicious forces that threatened and mocked her fragility. When confined within its high stone boundary walls, she thought of home with tearful yearning, almost unable to bear the separation from Aunt Mira, from Baba, from the comfortable, old, accustomed ayah, the rose walk, the somnolent mutter of the pigeons in the sunny veranda eaves, all of which took on an aura of paradise for her when she was separated from it.

To Bim, school and its teachers and lessons were a challenge to her natural intelligence and mental curiosity that she was glad to meet. Tara, on the other hand, wilted when confronted by a challenge, shrank back into a knot of horrified stupor and tended to gaze dully at the teachers when asked a question, making them wonder if she were not somewhat retarded (in the staff room, over tea, they said 'There is a brother, I've heard, who is . . .' and tapped their heads significantly). Tara was capable of spending a whole lesson seemingly hypnotised by a fly exploring a windowpane beside her desk or sticking the broken nib of her pen into a scrap of blotting paper and watching the ink ooze and spread. She did this quite without any curiosity in the scene that might have made her preoccupation excusable. Her teachers did not know that she had only to enter a classroom for the mucous membrane in her nostrils to swell and block her breathing apparatus. She was too polite to sniff but it gave her face a set, congested look that they took to be stubbornness, even insolence. She made them all bridle, teachers and students alike. She made no friends. When the others clustered together, sharing a delicious secret like a lollipop passed from one to the other for an unhygienic lick, Tara was left out. If they were choosing teams for a game, Tara was always left to the last, standing forgotten and wretched, and then one of the leaders would reluctantly agree to include her. She was no good at any game while Bim had a natural affinity with the bat and ball, and had the most splendid coordination, trained in sports as she was by Raja and Hamid who had often made use of her as a fielder when they got up a cricket game between them.

If only Tara had made up by showing some talent in the field of arts, as it was called by the staff, it might have given them cause to excuse her lassitude, her 'insolence'. But her fingers were so stiff, she could neither draw nor paint or even knit or weave paper baskets in the crafts class. She tended to reduce things to the smallest possible circumference as if in the hope they might then vanish altogether – a large brass jug and great pestle and mortar set up on a table in the arts class would appear on her sheet of drawing paper as a series of knobs and buttons, rubbed and rubbed at with her eraser till smudged to a shaky blur; a scrap of weaving or knitting in her hands became a tight knot that had to be cut away from the loom or knitting needles when it could be worked no tighter.

The missionary ladies who ran the grey, austere mission school, found this lack of ability, this lack of will too deplorable. They were all elderly spinsters – had, in fact, taken the vow of celibacy although not the nun's habit – awesomely brisk, cheerful and resourceful. Having left the meadows and hedgerows, the parsonages and village greens of their homes behind in their confident and quixotic youth, they had gone through experiences of a kind others might have buckled under but that they had borne and survived and overcome like boats riding the waves – wars and blitzes, riots and mutinies, famines and droughts, floods, fires and native customs – and they had then retired, not to the parsonages and village greens, but to the running of a sober, disciplined mission school with all their confidence, their cheerfulness and their faith impeccably intact. Tara could not suppress a baleful look as she observed them bustling about the classrooms, cracking open the registers or working out algebraic problems across the blackboards, blowing whistles and rushing across the netball fields, organising sports days and annual school concerts, leading the girls in singing hymns and, every so often, dropping suddenly to their knees, burying their faces in worn and naked hands, and praying with most distinguished intensity. Tara wondered uneasily if hers were one of the lost souls they prayed for.

Yet she preferred them to the Christian converts who made up the rest of the staff. She deplored their taste in clothes and definitely preferred the missionary ladies' grey tunics to the fancifully patterned and embroidered saris of pink and purple georgette that the converts favoured. She was offended by their names which were usually Rose and Lily or even, in one case, Pansy. Many of them were spinsters but even in those who were married and were met at the gate after school by husbands on bicycles or even had some of their children in the school, unnaturally clean and with charity clearly stamped on their subdued faces and shabby clothes, Tara sensed a bank of frustration – surely that was what made them so frighteningly spiteful, bitter and ill-tempered. They had such very sarcastic tongues and always seemed to single out Tara, as if sensing her distaste and disapproval, for their sharpest tongue-lashings. The other girls, instead of siding with her against the enemy, tittered and smirked to see her scolded and have her homework flung at her in rage. The truth was that they all considered Tara unbearably snobbish and conceited. The very fact that she wandered about the playground by herself during the lunch-break, morose and aloof, watching the kites that circled in the white sky waiting to swoop down on an unprotected lunch-box in a flash of claws and beaks, or picking up the neem pods under the scattering, yellowed trees, simply out of an embarrassed need to have something to do with herself, led them to conclude she was too conceited to join them in their songs and their gossip and chatter.

Bim, observing her out of the corner of her eye while she played a wild impromptu game of basketball with the bigger girls, carefully avoided having anything to do with her anti-social misery: it was contagious.

The dreariness of school intensified and reached its intolerable acme, for Tara, on Thursdays when the girls were sent, two by two, with a teacher at the head, to the mission hospital on the other side of the thick stone wall, to distribute fruit and blankets to the non-paying patients. These blankets were made up of squares of red wool that the girls knitted during craft class on thick, blunt wooden needles. White chalk dust became thickly embedded in the coarse wool. Tara suffered genuine physical agonies working the rough wool with her perspiring fingers, getting it knotted tighter and tighter on the thick needles till they couldn't move any more and she had to appeal for help and be soundly castigated by the very cross crafts teacher, a Miss Jacob who had a wart on the side of her nose and whom Tara saw as a medieval witch. When enough squares had accumulated, they were sewn together and these thick, scratchy, hot blankets were borne in triumph to the hospital wards along with baskets of blackened, oozing bananas and green, sour oranges. The girls would form a crocodile and be marched through the hospital wards, stopping at the iron bedsteads to unload their bounty upon women who had just given birth and were obliged to wrap their fragile new babies in these coarse, itching blankets, others who had open, running sores or wore green eye patches or lay groaning and calling upon God to deliver them – nightmare figures emanating an odour as thick as chloroform, compounded of poverty and charity, disease and cure. Sometimes they would meet the hospital kitchen squad dishing out the patients' meals and once when Tara saw the rice and *dal* being ladled out of pails onto aluminium platters in slopping piles, she was obliged to run out behind a hedge to be sick. After that, charity always had, for her, the sour reek of vomit. The next Thursday she pretended to be ill. Other weeks, she made the most preposterous excuses, trying anything to be let off going to school on charity Thursdays. But Bim realized what was going on and told Aunt Mira. Aunt Mira was puzzled and concerned, Bim outraged.

'You could do just that little bit without complaining,' she said severely. 'It's not too much to ask of anyone – just to save up their breakfast fruit and give it to someone who needs it.'

'I don't mind giving them my breakfast fruit,' cried Tara passionately, tearful and red-faced now that she had been found out. 'They can have *all* my fruit, every bit. Only *I* don't want to go and give it to them!'

'Why not?' said Bim. 'Too fine a lady to step into the hospital ward? The smells upset you, do they? The sights keep you awake at night, do they? Oh, you poor little thing, you'd better get a bit tougher, hadn't you – auntie's baby? Otherwise what good will you ever be? If you can't even do this little bit for the poor, what will you ever be able to do when you grow up?'

Bim of course worshipped Florence Nightingale along with Joan of Arc in her private pantheon of saints and goddesses, and Tara did not tell her that she hoped never to have to do anything in the world, that she wanted only to hide under Aunt Mira's quilt or behind the shrubs in the garden and never be asked to come out and do anything, prove herself to be anything. When challenged to name her own particular heroine, she looked vague, tried to shift away, saying she would think about it. Seeing Bim's eyes flash so righteously, her mouth fixed so censoriously, Tara lacked the boldness to make an answer even if she could think of one.

Forced to go back to school, she accepted with a weak abandonment of hope that these grey, wretched days would stretch on forever, blighting her life with their creeping mildew. When she came home in the afternoon, she would embrace her aunt with such fervid passion, with such excellent intentions of helping her more, being patient and sisterly to her little brother, that her family wondered at her intensity, saying 'You're only a day girl, Tara, you haven't been sent to boarding school, after all,' quite failing to gauge the depth of her despondency. She would sit on a stool on the veranda, winding woollen balls for her aunt, or read nursery rhymes to Baba, trying to make him say 'Ba-ba, Black Sheep' after her, till the wool was all in tight knotted balls and Baba failed to make any response beyond the faintest smile, not in her direction but the cat's, and then she would walk off to trail amongst the rose bushes or climb up to the terrace and watch Bim and Raja fly paper kites.

Two episodes cut through the grey chalk dust of school life with stripes of shocking colour.

In the first case, it was the colour of blood itself, perhaps not seen but sensed in all its scandalous outrage. It happened when Tara was still in the primary section. Their class was at the end of the building, and just outside, across a dusty strip of playing field, stood a row of tin-roofed, tin-walled latrines. There was something sinister about them that kept Tara away from them even when desperate to go. She would come home quite frantic with the need to urinate or even with her knickers stained damp and yellow rather than go into them in schooltime.

One day, glancing up from her slate, she saw some unusual activity outside the tin doors: the principal was there, gesticulating excitedly in a way novel to that calm lady, along with a man in a strange costume of khaki shorts, khaki shirt, a large khaki *topee* balanced on his prominent ears, and a rifle over his shoulder, just like a figure in a cartoon from Kipling's days. Tara gave a gasp of alarm that made the other children look too and they all began to scream – Tara had for once not been alone in finding a sight sinister. The teacher was torn between her duty to silence them and her curiosity to see what was going on.

What had happened was that a mad dog had found its way into the school compound and crawled into one of the tin latrines. No one knew who had alerted the municipal dog shooter – nevertheless he was there, with his gun, obviously for the purpose of shooting the dog.

Hearing the alarm spread through the primary school, the principal left him to his abominable duty and came hurrying to herd them indoors, shut the doors and windows and command them not to see. They did not see but could hardly help hearing the shot followed by the squealing of the dog that seemed to spurt and squelch out of its body like blood till it was silenced by a second shot. Some of the children, made wild by the sounds, ran to see the dog dragged by its legs across the playing field by the comic hunter in khaki, and squeaked 'Ooh, look, blood – bl-ood all over'. Tara did not see, kept her fingers pressed into her eyes till blue and red stars burst out of them, but she was aware that blood had been spilt and washed over her feet, warm and thick and living.

Unlike Bim and Raja, she never pestered her parents for a dog. She knew what her father meant when he spoke darkly of the danger of rabies.

The other episode of colour was the more glamorous one of an adolescent crush of a pupil on her teacher. In this case, an unusually young and somehow appealing woman with strange grey cat's eyes set in her narrow face, who was soon seen to be a neurotic by everyone, even Tara, but who nevertheless exercised a fascination over the young girls who longed for an element of colour in a life so singularly monochrome. By being different, by being quite obviously unsuitable, the new teacher made people talk. Very soon after she arrived, while Tara was still making tentative introductory gestures of bringing her a bunch of sweetpeas and offering to carry her load of books, there was a murmur, a susurration of scandal. The teacher had been called out of the classroom. She had been summoned by the principal. The principal had accused her of a misdemeanour. No one knew exactly what, but the girls gossiped. A foreigner, a blonde young man with an ascetic face and the saffron robes of a monk, had been seen loitering at the school gates. Miss Singh had been seen rushing out after school. She would come to class in the mornings, her pale eyes glittering, too bright, and laughingly confess she had not had the time to correct their books or prepare the new lesson: should they read some poetry instead? Tara was charmed. The girls said she had a 'boyfriend.' What had the principal caught her at? Had she tried to elope? With the blonde Buddhist monk? The gossip grew wilder. Miss Singh came out of the principal's office in tears. In class, she broke down completely in front of the appalled girls who did not know whether to rush up with their sympathy and handkerchiefs or drop their heads and pretend decorously not to notice. Miss Singh took a few days off. The principal took her classes. She found the girls in an unruly mood, defiant and excited and strangely rebellious. Five hundred lines were given them to write.

Miss Singh had not been sent away. They found out by standing in the flower bed under her window, trampling the flowers as they lifted each other up to peep in. They saw her lying fully-dressed on her bed, a wet cloth covering her eyes. Her thin wrist dangling helplessly out of the bed aroused their pity. They had read *Lorna Doone*, they had read *Camille*. They tiptoed away, awe-struck. They shot accusing looks at the principal whenever she strode past their classroom, swinging the spectacles that hung on a black ribbon round her neck.

Tara collected a bunch of velvet brown and purple pansies in the garden to take to school next day. But next day Miss Singh was gone. She had left, with her bags, without a word, without a goodbye to a single girl, not even to Tara who stood at the open door of her room, holding the bunch of pansies with their wide-eyed step-child faces. Tara was hurt, offended. She had thought up a plan to help Miss Singh: she was going to offer to carry messages for her, deliver notes to the blonde Buddhist monk or whoever it was who had caused Miss Singh this trouble. Now she could not. One of the big girls swooped down on her, snatched the pansies out of her hand and went laughing away. At home, Bim teased her for moping over Miss Singh so that she burst into tears and ran to Aunt Mira to complain. Bim was scolded for her tactlessness but only stuck out her tongue, unrepentant.

A great cloud of accusation settled over the principal's head: the girls refused to excuse her role in this painful affair. Often the resentment verged on near-rebellion. Some of the more lawless played practical tricks on the old lady. There was even a plan to secretly open the bird-cages that lined the length and breadth of her small private veranda and set all her pet budgerigars free. But Bim appeared on the scene of the conspiracy like a wrathful thunderbolt, her eyes angrily flashing, and stopped them (Tara was one of the guilty band). 'Do you know,' she hissed at them, 'do you know that Miss Stephen is *dying* – dying of *cancer*?' The guilty ones shrank back into the hedge, horrified, disbelieving. 'What do you mean, Bim?' the boldest stuttered. 'You're making up stories. How could you know?' 'I know,' Bim hissed, 'I know because she goes to see Dr Cherian at the hospital and Dr Cherian told my aunt when they met at a tea party. Miss Stephen is *ill*. She has cancer. And she will die. And it's very, very painful. But she's brave enough to carry on working and running the school,' she said through her teeth, glaring at each one so ferociously that they turned and fled.

Miss Stephen faced a strangely subdued assembly the next day.

There were no stink bombs, no water balloons, no rude sounds. Instead, the girls bent their heads dutifully over their hymn books and sang Nearer My God To Thee most soulfully. Some had tears in their eyes. Some blew their noses.

Tara was not one of them. She stood silently, stonily, mourning not the slow death that was settling about Miss Stephen but the abrupt death of romance brought about so effectively by her sister Bim. Back in the classroom, stooped over her needlework, she continued to brood over the figure of Miss Singh lying on the bed, the thin wrist dangling, the blonde Buddhist lingering near the gate – the figures of her first real-life romance – and continued to nurse a grudge against Miss Stephen and Bim till, with time, they faded from her memory, the same dull grey mildew settling upon them as on everything else within the stone walls of the mission school.

As schooldays with their somehow supernatural elasticity stretched and stretched over the years, the girls became infected with something of Raja's restlessness. It made Bim more ambitious at school, working consciously and deliberately at coming first in the examinations and winning honours. She was not quite sure where this would lead but she seemed to realize it was a way out. A way out of what? They still could not say, could not define the unsatisfactory atmosphere of their home. They did not realize now that this unsatisfactoriness was not based only on their parents' continual absence, their seemingly total disinterest in their children, their absorption in each other. The secret, hopeless suffering of their mother was somehow at the root of this subdued greyness, this silent desperation that pervaded the house. Also the disappointment that Baba's very life and existence were to them, his hopeless future, their anxiety over him. The children could only sense all this, they did not share it, except unwillingly. To them Baba was the perpetual baby who would never grow up – that was his charm, they felt, and never thought of his actual age.

When Bim became head girl of her school the principal came to congratulate the parents on her honour. They were not at home, and she had tea with Aunt Mira instead, an Aunt Mira so awkward with joy and pride that she poured the milk into the sugar pot and offered the tea strainer instead of the biscuits, much to her own anguish and the girls'. Then Raja won a poetry prize offered by his school magazine. His poem about the Battle of Panipat was a fine, ringing one with plenty of rhyme and rhythm and nothing to be ashamed of at all – it was recited by his friends and chanted at football games and on bicycle rides. When a teacher referred to 'the young Lord Byron in our midst', Raja's fate seemed sealed, the future was clear. A little crack seemed to open in the stony shell that enclosed them at home, letting in a little tantalising light. The future . . .

Lying on the bamboo matting on yet another summer afternoon, the game they played seemed quite without savour.

'What would you most like to eat?'

'A watermelon.'

'A piece of ice.'

'What would you most like to drink?'

'Ginger beer.'

'Vimto. No. Aa – agh.'

They rolled over onto their stomachs in revolt against the flatness, the insipidity of it all. Then, rolling off the matting, they stole barefoot into Raja's room – he was not back from school. Everyone else in the house was asleep. They could do anything they liked. What should they do that was daring enough, wild and unlawful enough for such a splendid opportunity? They searched. They sniffed and hunted.

There was Raja's copy of Iqbal – stained, much-thumbed, marked and annotated – his scattered papers covered with the beautiful script they could not read and which therefore had an added cachet in their admiring eyes. But today they would have preferred to see an unexpected photograph, a stranger's handkerchief . . . What made the two sisters expect such shocking revelations? Somehow they felt that today such secrets should be revealed, would be in keeping. Squatting, they searched along his bookshelves where Urdu verse lay cheek by jowl with American paperbacks – those long thick flapping American army editions that he picked up second-hand on Connaught Circus pavements: Louis Bromfield's *Night in Bombay*, Saroyan's *The Human Comedy*, *Huckleberry Finn*, *Moby Dick*, *The Postman Always Rings Twice*; also the enormous green volumes containing Keats and Shelley, Blake and Donne; the verses of Zauq and Ghalib, Dagh and Hali in cheap tattered yellow copies – that odd ragbag of reading that went to make up their romantic and inaccessible and wonderful brother.

But they had sat there, cross-legged, beside the long low bookshelf on countless afternoons, reading while Raja lay on his bed, asleep or half-awake and humming the songs that seemed to be always vibrating inside him like a taut, shining, invisible wire. Today they wanted something more from Raja, of Raja. Finally they opened the cupboard into which he threw his clothes. Here they rummaged, shaking out his shirts and rolling them up again, shoving his socks and handkerchiefs into corners as they searched.

'Look, Tara, I'm nearly as tall as he is now,' said Bim, holding up a pair of his trousers at her waist.

'No, you're not,' Tara giggled. 'They're much, much too long.'

'They are not,' protested Bim and suddenly stepped into them. She pulled them up high above her waist, up to her chest, tucked the bunches of her frock into them, then drew them close about her waist. Reaching into the cupboard again, she found a belt with which to fasten it around her. Tara was doubled over with laughter, stuffing her hands into her mouth, and crying tears of laughter to see the preposterous figure of her sister in the bunched up old khaki trousers over her flowered frock, with her black hair tumbling about her hot, excited face. Then Bim found another pair of trousers, the white ones Raja wore for tennis, and handed them to Tara. Tara had even more trouble than Bim in putting them on over her frock and tightening them about her smaller, slighter figure, yet she managed it more neatly and emerged looking like one of those slight, elegant young boys who play girls' roles on stage, pressing her hair close to her head to make her face more boyish. They pranced about the room in their trousers, feeling grotesquely changed by them, not only in appearance but in their movements, their abilities. Great possibilities unexpectedly opened up now they had their legs covered so sensibly and practically and no longer needed to worry about what lay bare beneath ballooning frocks and what was so imperfectly concealed by them. Why did girls have to wear frocks? Suddenly they saw why they were so different from their brother, so inferior and negligible in comparison: it was because they did not wear trousers. Now they thrust their hands into their pockets and felt even more superior – what a sense of possession, of confidence it gave one to have pockets, to shove ones fists into them, as if in simply owning pockets one owned riches, owned independence.

Carried away by the splendour of their trousered selves, Bim suddenly dashed across to the desk and pulled out the small top drawer in which Raja kept cigarettes. She found an opened packet with a few cheap, foul smelling, loosely packed cigarettes spilling out of it. She pushed it into her pocket, along with a box of matches. She strutted about the room, feeling the cigarettes and matches in her pocket, realizing now why Raja walked with that fine, careless swagger. If she had pockets, if she had cigarettes, then it was only natural to swagger, to feel rich and superior and powerful. Crowing with delight, she flashed a look at Tara to see if she shared her exhilaration and whispered 'Let's go out for a walk, Tara.'

'Oh Bim, *no*!' squeaked Tara, squeezing into a corner by the desk in alarm at the very suggestion. 'No, no, Bim!'

'Come on, Tara, no one will see – everyone's asleep.'

'The gardener might be outside,' warned Tara as Bim cautiously opened the door to the veranda and peeped out.

'He's half-blind. He'll think we're Raja's friends,' said Bim, tossing her mane of hair to show how confident she felt, and slipped out onto the veranda, slightly unnerved by the brilliant glare of the afternoon light. 'Come *on*,' she hissed sharply at Tara who then came scurrying and squealing after her. They tumbled down the stairs into the garden together, then the blank white glare and the brazen heat made them blink and falter. 'Come *on*,' hissed Bim again, and dived into a great bush of magenta bougainvillea that bloomed beside the stairs.

Here they crept in, rustling, sat down on the upraised roots and mounds of dry leaves, giggling at their own nervousness. To make up for this lapse of confidence – Bim had thought momentarily of going up to the garage, taking out their bicycles and going for a ride, in their trousers – Bim drew out the cigarettes and matches from her pocket. 'Let's try,' she whispered, bending very low because a thorny branch was scraping at the back of her head, plucking at her hair.

'Oh, Bim, no – o!' cried Tara in fright. Her sister was driving her, forcing her through fear again, as usual. She tried to resist, hopelessly. This was why she distrusted Bim so: Bim never knew when to stop. Discontented with mere fantasy, she insisted on turning their games into reality, usually disastrously. There was always the one sickening moment when she overstepped and began to hurtle downwards into disaster, trying always to drag her sister along with her. 'Oh no,' protested Tara, weakly.

'But why *not*?' demanded Bim, impatiently. 'Raja smokes. Father *knows* he smokes. Mother knows too. We must at least do it once,' and sticking the cigarette between her lips, she struck a match and lit it in a cloud of stinging yellow smoke, puffing hard so that her eyes stood out and watered. Then she passed it to Tara and lit herself another. But Tara threw hers away wildly after one puff, spluttering with disgust.

'Tara!' screamed Bim, seeing the cigarette fall on a heap of dry leaves and grass, and scrambled up to stamp it out before it turned into a blaze. Her hair caught in the bougainvillea, her legs felt suddenly hampered by the trousers that did not fit. She heard Tara struggling to get out of the bush and then someone's voice raised and the garage door swinging open. So there was nothing for it but to fling the cigarette out into the open driveway and race after Tara, up the steps and into Raja's room. Someone was coming up the veranda. It was – was it? – it *was* Raja. Back so early from school – why? Screaming at each other to hurry, they ran into Raja's bathroom to tear off their trouses. By then Raja was already in his room. They heard the crash of an armful of books as they landed on his desk and scattered. He had heard – or seen? – them! He was at the bathroom door, shouting 'Who's in there? Open!' But they had bolted it. Trousers off and flung into a corner, their legs feeling naked and exposed, they opened the outer door and fled, leaving him to rattle at the inner door and shout 'I know it's you – you rascals! Come out at once, you horrors!'

It was not spite or retaliation that made Tara abandon Bim – it was the spider fear that lurked at the centre of the web-world for Tara. Yet she did abandon Bim, it was true that she did.

The Misra family had taken the girls with them to the Lodi Gardens one day in early spring when the *bignonia venustra* was in bloom, enfolding the dark walls of the Lodi tombs in long cloaks of flamboyant orange. The picnickers lay on the grass in the honey-gold sun, eating peanuts out of paper cones and peeling oranges and urging each other to sing songs. Two young men had been invited as well, possible suitors for Jaya and Sarla, and the picnic had been arranged to give their first meeting an air of informality. Yet everyone's eyes were on each other so sharply, sharpening on each other like blades, snip-snip-snip, that they made Bim and Tara feel anything but informal. On the contrary, they were deeply uneasy. The Misra girls had become strangely artificial in their speech and manners – Bim and Tara could scarcely recognise them. The two chosen young men were sullen and mostly silent, their dark heads sunk between their shoulders as they gloomily picked at grass and avoided looking at each other. Only the Misra brothers remained themselves, as jocular and loud and coarse as usual, making foul jokes and managing to suggest vulgarities even when they did not state them. Bim and Tara, infected both by the Misra girls' self-conscious artificiality of manner and the young swains' deep gloom, did not know how to deal with them or with the Misra brothers – how to defend themselves against their jokes or deflect them by repartee as Jaya and Sarla could do, being more practised. So when the others were fussing over the unpacking of the picnic baskets, they wandered away together, saying they would look at the tombs.

They walked in silence up a knoll to one of the smaller tombs and stood uncertainly gazing at its blackened walls and thought of sitting down on the grass outside by themselves, but a boy in striped pyjamas and a cricket cap hung about the small porch, leaning against a pillar, watching them while he tossed a pebble from one hand to the other. After a moment's hesitation, they chose the uninviting dark inside and the dizzying stench of bats that it contained.

The boy must have flung the pebble after them. They heard a small dull thwack as it hit something soft but it was followed by a sinister crepitation that began to stir in the corners of that octagon of pitch darkness, began to swirl invisibly about them, the humming growing louder and more menacing, at the same time descending towards them till they realized what it meant and, with yelps, pushing into each other in their hurry, ran out together.

Tara catapulted out and went hurtling down the grassy slope, her head bent and her hands pressed over her ears, screaming like a whistle as she went. At the foot of the knoll she turned to look for Bim and saw that she was still at the top – she had not got away, the swarm had got her. They had settled about her head and shoulders till they had wrapped her about in a helmet of chainmail that glittered, gun-metal blue, and shivered and crept over her skin, close-fitting, adhesive. Bim, too, had her head bent and her arms crossed over her face but she was not screaming – she seemed locked into the hive, as if she were the chosen queen, made prisoner. The whole hillside, the brilliant cobalt sky, the honey air, the grassy slope and flowering creepers were covered with the pall of bees, shrouded by them as by a thundercloud. It was a bees' festival, a celebration, Bim their appointed victim, the sacrificial victim on whom they had draped the ceremonial shawl, drawing it close about her neck as she stood drooping, shivering under the weight of their gauzy wings, their blue-black humming.

What was Tara to do? Helplessly, she ran back up the hill a little, but instantly the bees rose, hummed a warning, swayed towards her, and she screamed to see them approach so that Bim, spying her out of her swollen eyes, cried in a thick, congested voice 'Get away, go – run, run!' and Tara ran, ran down the knoll back to the Misras, screaming for help.

They heard her at last – or, rather, at last connected the frenzied screams they had heard with Tara's running, maddened figure – and leapt to their feet, left the paper cones and radios and songs behind, and came at a gallop to see what it was all about. Tara was conscious, as she half-stood, half-crouched, shivering, of Jaya and Sarla flying up the knoll and flinging Jaya's pink veil over Bim's head, the men tearing off branches and beating them in the air, someone lighting a rolled newspaper and sending its smoke coiling through the air like a whip, and the young boy who had thrown the stone being dragged across the grass to be thrashed.

Then they were all bustling out of the park and into the waiting cars, and Sarla was dabbing at the bee stings with some lemonade out of a bottle and Bim was sitting with her head in her lap, growling 'Don't *touch* me, don't *touch* me!' She was swollen to a great size, and tinted a strange shade of plum-blue, quite unrecognisable. Tara, squeezed into a corner of the overcrowded car, very small and meek, whimpered to herself. She had one bite to nurse, on her knuckles, but although the sting was still embedded in it like a needle in a pocket, she dared not ask for any attention or sympathy – she knew Bim deserved it all.

That whole episode was an accident that ought to have been followed by a thorough investigation, a cure, each sting withdrawn, put away. But in the uproar that followed, it was all somehow bundled out of sight, hurriedly. Tara had not the opportunity, nor found the courage, to go to Bim and say 'Bim, I'm sorry I ran away – I wasn't brave – I didn't come to help you. I am ashamed – I shall never forgive myself. Forgive me.' Nor did Bim ever care to explain what she meant when she growled at her sister 'You couldn't help it – if you'd stayed, you'd have been stung, like me – you had to run.' Only Raja raged openly 'You nitwit. Why didn't you stay and help Bim to beat them off?' Aunt Mira said instantly 'Tara's just a baby – what could she have done?' and there was the powerful ammoniac stench of vinegar to bring tears to their eyes as she poured out a bottleful onto a napkin and doused Bim with it. The old ayah shook her head over such inefficacious treatment and fetched her betel-nut box and dipped her finger into the jar of lime paste and smeared it on Bim's stings till she looked as if she had dabs of cotton wool stuck to her, or a strange, erratic growth of feathers. Whenever Tara smelt vinegar or tasted lime paste in a betel leaf, her flesh crept, she shivered, she recalled the zig-zag advance of threatening bees emerging from that dark, stinking tomb to capture Bim and leave her bloated and blue like a plum. Aunt Mira and the ayah between them treated Bim and drew out all her stings, but Tara kept hers hidden.

Tara began to avoid both Bim and Raja. Aunt Mira did not provide sufficient defence – so thin, so scrawny, she could no more hide Tara from them than a thin reed. She began to shut herself away in her room, or slip out by herself, quite often to the Misras' house next door.

The Misras had been their neighbours for as long as they could remember (theirs was not a neighbourhood from which people moved – they were born and married and even died in the same houses, no one ever gave one up) and yet the friendship between the two families was only a token one, formal and never close. Bim and Raja, especially, were so scornful of the Misra children that Tara dared not admit openly that she herself did not judge them or find them lacking. Now she found neither Bim nor Raja holding her back – studying hard for their examinations, they hardly noticed Tara any more and had no intention of pursuing her or bullying her – Tara found herself free to edge closer to the warmth she felt emanating from them, from their large, full, bustling household. The two Misra girls who had been to the same school as Bim and Tara, although they were a few years older, responded to her touchingly hesitant advances in a kindly, patronising way that almost developed into a friendship, the closest certainly to friendship in Tara's forlorn experience.

What attracted Tara was the contrast their home provided to hers. Even externally there were such obvious differences – at the Misras' no attempt was made, as at Tara's house, to 'keep up appearances'. They were so sure of their solid, middle-class bourgeois position that it never occurred to them to prove it or substantiate it by curtains at the windows, carpets on the floors, solid pieces of furniture placed at regular intervals, plates that matched each other on the table, white uniforms for the house servants and other such appurtenances considered indispensable by Tara's parents. At the Misras' string beds might be carried into the drawing room for visiting relations, or else mats spread on the veranda floor when an influx of visitors grew so large that it overflowed. Meals were ordered in a haphazard way and when the family smelt something good cooking, they dipped impatiently into the cooking pots as soon as it was ready instead of waiting for the clock hands to move to the appointed hour. The chauffeur might be set to minding a fractious baby, driving it up to the gate and back for its amusement or dandling it on his lap and letting it spin the steering wheel, while the cook might be called out of the kitchen and set to massaging the grandmother's legs. Elaborate arrangements might be made for a prayer meeting on the lawns to please an elderly relative and then suddenly set aside so that the whole clan could go and see the latest film at the Regal. Theirs was a large family of many generations spread through the city, and there was constant coming and going, friends and relations perpetually under one's feet. The Misra girls complained to Tara how difficult it was to study and prepare for exams in such circumstances, and sometimes brought their books across to work in Tara's room, but never for very long since their interest in academic work was weak and wavering at best, and often they would abandon it and set out shopping for clothes and bangles or to attend a family festivity like a wedding or naming ceremony, leaving school-work undone and Tara abandoned and envious.

But now they noticed Tara standing on the edge, watching, with kindly eyes, and often swept her along. Although she was consumed with shyness and embarrassment at finding herself in a society to which she realized she did not belong, she enjoyed the break in routine, the change of scene, and came back flushed and excited, too excited to sleep even if the outing had been no more than a visit to a tailor or a jeweller in the city.

Once she wandered across on a bleak winter day with an old woollen coat drawn over her school uniform that she had not changed out of through laziness, to find the whole family on the lawn, posing for a photographer who kept darting out from behind his black cloth and cyclopean instrument to marshal them into straight rows, some on chairs and some on their feet, little ones in front, big ones at the back. Tara backed away, hoping to disappear through the hedge, but the Misra girls spied her, broke rank and darted at her, dragged her along to stand beside them and be photographed. That was their kindliness, their easy, careless hospitality, and the result was the incongruous appearance of Tara, bundled into her grey woollen coat and looking like a mouse with a bad cold, standing along with the ranks of Misras in their silk and brocade finery, posing for a family photograph. Whenever she saw it, silver-framed, up on the cabinet in their hall, she looked away in embarrassment. Had she been a little younger, she might have attempted stealing it and cutting it out, but she was too big for such adventures now, she was quite big enough for adventures of another kind.

The Misra girls realized that, in their prosaic, accepting way, and often invited her to come to cinema shows with them, or to the Roshonara club where she sat on the lawn, sipping lemonade, listening to the band, stiff as a puppet in her consciousness of being looked at by young men returning from the tennis courts or the cricket field or standing around the bar. It was a novel experience for Tara whose own parents sat playing bridge in the green-lit, soundless aquarium of the card-room, unaware of their daughter's presence outside, and to whom it had never occurred that the child was now a young girl and might like to be taken out with them. The Misra girls themselves found the Roshonara club too boring – they did not play tennis, they did not dance, they knew all the Old Delhi families spread over the verandas and lawns in clusters of cane chairs, had known them all their lives and knew they could not offer them any novelty, any excitement.

Besides, they were already engaged to be married – the picnic at Lodi Gardens, so disastrous for Bim and Tara, had reaped a different harvest for Jaya and Sarla – and life did not hold out the shadowy promises and expectations that it still did to Tara. They enjoyed seeing Tara perch, trembling, on the edge of her chair, casting her eyes quickly around the prospect, then dropping them, half-frightened by what she saw. They gave her Vimto to drink, lent her bits of jewellery to wear, introduced her to the families they had known all their lives but who had been screened away from Tara by the particular circumstances of her home and family. They were touched to see Tara blinking as she looked about her – it made them feel matronly and condescending, experienced and wise.

It was to their engagement party that Tara wore her first silk sari – a pale shell-pink edged with silver that Aunt Mira had thought suitable for her youngest niece. There were two parties thrown on the same day – an afternoon affair for all the women of the family and the two sisters' girl friends, to be followed by a formal evening affair. Bim and Tara were invited to the first, their parents to the second. Bim was forced to accompany Tara and sat glumly on the carpet at the far end of the room, bored and irritated by it all – the musicians who had been invited to play and sat grouped decoratively on a white sheet spread over the carpet with their instruments before them, the songs sung by the ladies and the young girls, invariably mournful ones of heart-break and romantic yearning – till she could stand no more and, beckoning sternly to Tara, got up and slipped out into the garden where gardeners and electricians were at work on strings of lights and pyramids of potted plants in preparation for the evening party. A group of workmen, staggering under the weight of a long table, shouted to them to keep out of the way and as they turned they bumped into a servant hurrying up with white tablecloths and silver vases stuffed with papery zinnias and gomphrenias.

'Let's go up on the roof, it'll be quieter there,' said Bim, and Tara was forced to follow her up the stairs to the terrace. Tara felt they might as well have stayed at home if this was all they were going to do at the party, and Bim leant on the balustrade and looked across the hedge at their own silent, already darkening house as if that were exactly what she wished she had done.

They watched the workmen scurrying about the lawn, dropping a ladder, setting up a branched tree of electric lights over the porch and draping tangled strips of fairy lights on the domed trees along the drive with the maximum possible amount of argument and contradiction and muddle. The Misra boys were standing about on straddled legs, shouting orders and abuse in their lordly, uncivilised way that made Bim direct dark looks at them.

'I don't know how those two girls are going to study and pass their finals with all this going on,' she said.

'I don't think it matters to them,' said Tara, picking at flakes of blackened lichen on the balustrade sulkily. 'They're getting married afterwards anyway.'

The Misra boy standing below shouted 'Donkey! Fool! Look, you've smashed another bulb. D'you think they belong to your father that you can go smashing them up as you like?'

Bim gave a snort of disgust. 'I don't know why they're in such a hurry to get married,' she said. 'Why don't they go to college instead?'

'Their mother wanted them to be married soon. She said she married when she was twelve and Jaya and Sarla are already sixteen and seventeen years old.'

'But they're not *educated* yet,' Bim said sharply. 'They haven't any degrees. They should go to college,' she insisted.

'Why?' said Tara, suddenly rebellious, impatient to go back down the stairs, get away from Bim and join the women who were now streaming out of the house, laughing, calling to each other, flocking to the long tables on which platters of sweetmeats, pink and yellow and topped with silver, had been placed between the silver vases with the zinnias and gomphrenias, while a waiter in a white coat with something embroidered in red across the pocket, frenziedly uncapped bottles of lemonade and stuck straws into them and handed them out with automatic efficiency. The hired band arrived just then in an open lorry and began jumping out of it with huge instruments of shining brass clutched in their arms. The Misra brothers rushed up and began to bawl at them for being late. They hurried off into a brightly striped pavilion that had been set up at the far end of the garden. The Hyder Alis' dog was barking as though in pain at all this noise and confusion.

'Why?' repeated Bim indignantly. 'Why, because they might find marriage isn't enough to last them the whole of their lives,' she said darkly, mysteriously.

'What else could there be?' countered Tara. 'I mean,' she fumbled, 'for them.'

'What *else*?' asked Bim. 'Can't you think? I can think of hundreds of things to do instead. *I* won't marry,' she added, very firmly.

Tara glanced at her sideways with a slightly sceptical smile.

'I won't,' repeated Bim, adding 'I shall never leave Baba and Raja and Mira-*masi*,' making Tara look away before her face could betray her admission that she, closely attached as she was to home and family, would leave them instantly if the opportunity arose. Bim did not notice her. She was looking down, across the lighted, bustling garden to her own house, dark and smouldering with a few dim lights behind the trees, and raised her hands to her hair, lifting it up and letting it fall with a luxuriant, abundant motion. 'I shall work – I shall *do* things,' she went on, 'I shall earn my own living – and look after Mira-*masi* and Baba and – and be independent.

There'll be so many things to do – when we are grown up – when all this is over –' and she swept an arm out over the garden party, dismissing it. 'When we are grown up at last – then – then –' but she couldn't finish for emotion, and her eyes shone in the dusk.

In the garden below, the little blue buds of lights in the trees bloomed suddenly to the sound of excited twittering from the guests.

# IV

Bim was correcting papers at the dining table, her own desk being insufficient for their size and number. All the doors were shut against the dust storm raging outside so that they could only hear the sand and gravel scraping past the walls and window-panes but not see it. It seeped in through every crack and opening, however, so that every surface of wood or stone or paper in the room was coated with it, yellow and gritty. It coloured the light too, made the daylight so pallid that they had to have the electric light on and that was turned to a lurid shade of orange which, far from being festive, was actually sinister.

Tara, trying to pen a letter to her daughters, one last hurried one before they arrived in India, felt she was being roasted like a chicken under the burning orange bulb. She wished she could switch it off and she and Bim could put their papers aside and sit in a companionable dusk, but Bim's concentration on her work was so intense, it crackled a warning through the air. So she huddled inside her kimono and tore at her hair, trying to get on with the letter. It would not go. She laid down the pen. Suddenly coming to a decision that pinched her nostrils and made her look almost severe, she said 'Bim, you *must* come. With Baba. It will be so good for you.'

'What do you mean?' Bim asked, pushing her spectacles up onto the bridge of her nose. They reflected the orange light that was swaying in the breeze that had somehow got into the closed room, a ghostly reflection of the storm outside. The lenses reflected the darting light, swinging from left to right crazily, dangerously.

'I mean,' said Tara, looking away,' I mean – you need a change.'

'What makes you think that?' asked Bim in wonder, and her sister's expression which was rather as if a tooth were being extracted from her mouth very slowly, made her take off her spectacles and hold them in her hand so that they could face each other directly.

'I mean – I've been watching you, Bim. Do – d'you know you talk to yourself? I've heard you – muttering – as you walk along – when you think you're alone –'

'I didn't know I was being watched,' Bim broke in, flushing with anger.

'I – I couldn't help overhearing. And then – your hands. You keep gesturing with them, you know. I don't think you know, Bim.'

'I don't – and I didn't know I was supposed to keep my hands still when I talked. The girls in college did a skit once – one of them acted me, waving her hands while she talked. It was quite funny.'

'No, Bim, you do it even when you're not talking. I mean, you must be talking to yourself.'

'Don't we all?' Bim enquired, her voice and her eyebrows rising simultaneously.

It was a look that would have made Tara quail as a child. But now she insisted 'Not *aloud*, Bim.'

'I must be getting old then,' Bim said, with a careless sniff. 'I *am* getting old, of course.'

'You're not. You're worrying.'

'Worrying? I have no more worries,' cried Bim, laying down her spectacles and slapping the tabletop with one hand. 'No worries at all.' She lifted her hand and touched the white lock of hair over her ear.

'About Raja,' insisted Tara, grimly determined to have it all out and be done.

'Oh, you want to talk about Raja *again*,' Bim groaned disgustedly. She picked up her spectacles and made to put them on, bending over the stack of papers on the table with an exaggerated air of interest. But she gave it up in an instant, laying the spectacles down on top of the papers. 'I'm *bored* with Raja. Utterly bored,' she said evenly. 'He is too rich to be interesting any more, too fat and too successful. Rich, fat and successful people are *boring*. I'm not interested, Tara.'

Tara threw herself forward on her arms, her hair in its long curls – yes, at last she had achieved the curls she had prayed for as a little girl; now they were as luxuriant as vines, thanks to the best hairdressers of the international capitals – sweeping over her ears and across her cheeks, casting purple shadows. Between them, her eyes and her mouth agonised. '*Why* do you imagine such things about Raja? You haven't even seen him – in how many years, Bim? You live in the same country and never visit each other. I come, from abroad, every three years, to see you, to see Baba and Raja. I know more about Raja's home and family than you do, Bim. You don't know anything about his life, about his family or his work.'

'Yes, I *do* know,' Bim replied loudly. 'He is invited to weddings, engagement parties, anniversaries – they spread out carpets and cushions for him to recline on, like a pasha – and he recites his poems.' She made a clownish face, ridiculing such pomp, such show, such empty vanity. 'I can imagine the scene – all those perfumed verses about wine, the empty goblet, the flame, and ash . . .' she laughed derisively.

'You haven't read any of it in years – how do you know?'

'I know Raja. I know his poems.'

'Why can't it have changed? Grown better?'

'How can it – when he lives in that style? Living in his father-in-law's house, making money on his father-in-law's property, fathering one baby after another –'

'Five. And they're quite grown up now – the girls are anyway.'

'And the little boy is so spoilt, he's impossible.'

'You've never even seen him, Bim!'

'I couldn't bear to – I can imagine it all – after four daughters, much lamented, at last the little boy, the little prince arrives. What a dumpling he must be, what a rice-ball – with all the feeding that goes on in that house, Benazir cooking and tasting and eating all day, and in between meals little snacks arriving to help them on their way. Imagine what he must look like, and Raja! Imagine eating so much!'

'Why do you imagine they eat all day?' cried Tara in distress.

'I *know*. They *did* visit me once. Have you forgotten? After their marriage, after their first baby was born, they did come to visit us. And Benazir was already so plump, and Raja – Raja looked like a pasha, he was so fat. They were visiting too, as if they were pashas, with presents to dazzle us with. He brought me a string of pearls – imagine, pearls! – and told me how Hyderabad was known for them. And I just told him "But Raja, you know I don't wear jewellery!" Then he brought a hi-fi set for Baba – "the latest model", he told us,' she went on, laughing. 'And Baba just smiled and never touched it. He only loves his old HMV gramophone, he loves to wind it up and sit by it, watching the record turn. All through their visit he was so afraid Benazir might ask for it back – it was hers, you know. Then Raja sulked and sulked. "Tara would have worn the pearls," he said, "and Bakul would have known what a fine hi-fi set that is – you two know nothing."' Bim laughed again and repeated, mockingly, 'No, we know nothing, we two – nothing.'

They sat in silence together, listening to the storm blow itself out, so that the roar of the trees bending and the creepers dashing against the walls and the gravel flying gradually lessened, seemed to recede, leaving them in a kind of grey cave that still echoed with the tides.

'And now that baby is to be married,' Bim mused, drumming her fingers on the table. 'Moyna. I wonder if she's as plump as Benazir used to be? Benazir must be huge. She never liked to get up or move if she could get someone to fetch and carry for her. And she fed that baby all day long. Little silver dishes of milk puddings would arrive – she'd brought along a woman to cook for them, she didn't trust Janaki or me – and she would spoon it into her mouth, fattening her up. And Raja – how he'd grown to *enjoy* Benazir's food –'

'It's very good,' Tara said earnestly. 'It really is.'

'Yes, I know, but it's disgusting to enjoy it so much, and eat so much of it. Such rich foods. They must be bad for him, I kept telling him that, but of course he wouldn't listen.' She shook her head, a bit saddened now. Then she sat up straight. 'It's unhappy people who eat like that,' she said suddenly, authoritatively. 'I read that somewhere. They compensate themselves with the food they eat for the things they missed.'

'*What* things has Raja missed, Bim? He has a wife, children, his own house, his business, his hobby –'

'But that's just it,' Bim exploded. 'All – all that nonsense. That's not what Raja had wanted from life. He doesn't need a hobby, he needs a vocation. He knows he has given his up, just given up what used to be his vocation, turned it into a silly, laughable little hobby . . . That is why he needs to console himself with food and more food. Don't you *see*?'

Tara's mouth was open, she was full of protest. She felt it was wrong to allow Bim to follow the path of such misunderstanding. But she only wrung her hands in a distressed way, wondering how to persuade someone so headstrong, so habitually headstrong, as her sister. Finally she said 'You should go and visit them, Bim, and see for yourself how it is. There's the wedding. They want you there. Here's a letter. Let me read it to you . . .'

'No, it's for you,' said Bim, waving it away as Tara started to draw it out of its envelope.

But Tara pretended not to notice. She opened out the sheets of blue paper and began to read. '"It's time you met your young nephew. We have just bought him a pony, a plump young white one that the girls say looks like a pearl so they call her Moti. Benazir has made him a velvet suit and when he sits on her back he looks like a prince in a Persian miniature . . ."'

Bim slapped the tabletop with her hand, loudly. 'You see,' she said, in triumph, 'what did I tell you? He may be a grown man, respectable citizen, father of a family and all that – but what is he still trying to do, to be? Remember Hyder Ali Sahib's white horse and how we would see him riding by while we played in the sand by the Jumna?'

'Of course,' Tara nodded, with a sentimental list to her head.

'That's what Raja was thinking of when he bought the white pony. Raja always admired Hyder Ali Sahib – probably envied him cutting such a fine figure on the white horse, a servant running ahead of him to clear the way of rabble like us and a dog to bring up the rear. Impressive, I suppose – and wasn't Raja impressed! See, this late in life, he's still trying to be Hyder Ali Sahib,' she laughed. 'Hyder Ali Sahib was his ideal in life and it's the ideal he's still pursuing, poor Raja. To gratify his own boyhood desire, he now forces his poor little boy to ride. Terrible, isn't it, how parents drive their children to fulfil their own ungratified desires?' Her face shone with vindication as if it were oily.

Tara drew back, affronted. 'I don't think little Riyaz is at all aware of his father's ungratified desires,' she said, primly.

'No, but he will be. When that pony throws him and he howls and no longer wants to ride and his father insists he get back on, *then* he will know what it's all for.'

'Why do you foresee such terrible things?' Tara protested, wincing, her maternal instinct touched as if with a knife-point. 'The pony won't throw little Riyaz. What a terrible thing to imagine, Bim.'

Bim was holding her head in both her hands, shaking it slowly from side to side. 'That's my trouble,' she mumbled. 'I do foresee all these terrible things. I see them all,' she said, closing her eyes, as if tired, or in pain.

Tara, afraid of that expression, said gently 'Well, when one grows old, one is said to have all kinds of fears, become very apprehensive,' and then looked down at the letter in her hands and read on, details of the arrangements for Moyna's wedding that were going on in Raja's household, elaborate and expensive arrangements, for she was the first of his daughters to marry and it was to be a grand affair. There were to be lighted torches along the driveway, a *shehnai* player from Benares to play at the wedding, ice carved into swans on the tables . . .

But Bim did not make any response. Although she opened her eyes and stared at all the books and papers and letters scattered over the dusty table, she did not seem to be seeing anything. If she was listening to anything, it was to the sounds of returning normality outside, the usual summer morning sounds of mynahs quarrelling and shrieking on the lawn, the pigeons beginning to mutter comfortably to each other in the veranda, dry leaves and scraps of paper swirling down the drive and blowing into hedges and corners. Leaving Tara to read on, she stood up and picked up a plate of orange peels that had been lying on the table since breakfast.

Roughly interrupting Tara's low, monotonous recital, she said sharply 'Why do you peel oranges and then leave them uneaten, Tara? It's such a waste.' Tara, startled, put down the letter but did not say it was Bakul who had left the orange on the plate.

'It's half-rotten, Bim,' she said. 'I only left the rotten bits.'

'It's not rotten,' Bim retorted. 'It's perfectly all right. I do hate waste,' she added and went out of the room with an oddly uncertain step. Tara was disconcerted by it but would have been far more upset if she had seen how Bim's lip was trembling and how her hand shook so that the orange peels slipped off the plate and littered the way to the kitchen. Something about Raja's letter, Tara's comments, the world of luxury and extravagance created by them and approved by both of them, excluding her, her standards, too rough and too austere for them, made anger flower in her like some wild red tropical bloom, and a kind of resentment mixed with fear made her stutter, half-aloud, 'I mean – I mean she's only five years younger than I am and she thinks I'm *old*. And she spies on me – she's been spying. She is cruel, Tara, and cold. And Raja selfish, too selfish to care. And what about the letter he wrote *me*? Oh yes, he writes beautiful letters to Tara – all wedding, all gold – but what about the letter he wrote *me*? *My* letter? Has Tara forgotten it – in my desk? And I –'

She pottered about the kitchen for a while – Janaki must have gone out to roll herself a betel leaf and chew it quietly out by the servants' quarters – washing the plate, putting it away, seeing if there were any more oranges left in spite of her sister's and brother-in-law's wasteful ways, and then went out on the veranda to find that the dust-storm had left the whole garden shrouded in grey. Each leaf, each bush drooped with the weight of dust. Even the sun appeared to be swathed in grey cobwebs. Everything seemed ancient and bent. Everything seemed to have gone into eclipse. The house would need a thorough cleaning. She stood on the steps and shouted 'Janaki! Janaki!' both angrily and desperately.

Tara began to keep an eye on Bim as she moved about the house, watchful and wary. She wondered why she had not noticed before how very queerly Bim ran the house – or was this queerness something new, something that had happened just now under pressure? She could not help noticing Bim's excessive meanness – the way she would scrape all left-overs onto saucers and keep them for the next meal so that some of the meals that arrived on the table were just a long procession of little saucers with little portions smudged onto them, like meals for a family of kittens. Tara felt ashamed of them, knowing how Bakul's fastidious nostrils would crinkle at the sight. She noticed that he tried to have luncheon and dinner engagements in the city as often as possible, telephoning old colleagues and cronies, finding something he had to discuss with them over a meal, at the club, almost every day. She was glad. She was more relaxed sitting at the meagre table with just Bim and Baba. At the same time she worried that they didn't eat properly. Then she noticed a pound of the best, the most expensive tea turning to dust on the kitchen shelf. Bim had bought it long ago, in a moment of largesse, then obviously suffered pangs of remorse and not been able to bring herself to use it. And yet packets of books kept arriving – expensive volumes of history and art. They must cost a great deal. When she hinted at the expense, Bim said of course, but she needed them for her work. Were they not available at the library? ventured Tara, and Bim gave her a withering look.

Then, while perambulating the garden early in the morning when it was still fresh although the day's heat was beginning to rise at the fringes and form shimmering banks like cumulus clouds, she found a great mound of manure lying behind the garage. When she asked the gardener who was squatting by the garage door, mending some broken tool, she learnt Bim had ordered a cartload of manure one day and then claimed to have no money left for seeds. The gardener began to wheeze self-pityingly to Tara, 'What am I to do? Times are bad. I have to grow vegetables, I have to grow food – but how? When there is no fertilizer, no seed, and whenever I turn on the tap, Bim – missahib comes and tells me not to waste water?' Tara, embarrassed, gathered her kimono about her and walked on, confused.

She had always thought Bim so competent, so capable. Everyone had thought that – Aunt Mira, the teachers at school, even Raja. But Bim seemed to stampede through the house like a dishevelled storm, creating more havoc than order. Tara would be ashamed to run a house like this. Bakul would have been horrified if she did. Then how had Bim acquired her fine reputation? Or had her old capability, her old competence begun to crumble now and go to seed? Tara saw how little she had really observed – either as a child or as a grown woman. She had seen Bim through the lenses of her own self, as she had wanted to see her. And now, when she tried to be objective, when she was old enough, grown enough and removed enough to study her objectively, she found she could not – her vision was strewn, obscured and screened by too much of the past.

'What did we really *see*?' she wondered aloud in the evening when the dark laid a comfortingly protective blanket on her and no one could make out too much in the dark or the dust as they sat idly flapping palm-leaf fans against the turgid heat and the swarming mosquitoes that rose from the lawn or dropped from the trees, making walls about them: a form of torture that was well-known to them; it was simply summer. 'I think it's simply amazing – how very little one sees or understands even about one's own home or family,' she felt obliged to explain when the silence grew too strained.

'What have you seen now that you had not known before?' Bakul asked in a slow, amused tone. He was smoking a cigar. It made his voice riper than ever. Juice might run, through the cracks, purple.

'Only that I had noticed nothing before,' Tara said, thrown into confusion by his measured tone. She would have preferred simply to ramble.

'What else do children ever do?' Bakul asked. He had been out all day, he had eaten and drunk well, he was in a mood to be indulgent this evening. 'Do you think our own daughters notice anything about us? Of course not – they are too occupied with themselves. Children may see – but they don't comprehend.'

'No one,' said Bim, slowly and precisely, 'comprehends better than children do. No one feels the atmosphere more keenly – or catches all the nuances, all the insinuations in the air – or notes those details that escape elders because their senses have atrophied, or calcified.'

Bakul gave an uncomfortable laugh. 'Only if they stop to think, surely, and children don't. They are too busy playing, or chattering, or –'

'Or dreaming,' mused Tara, dreamily.

'No.' Bim rejected that. '*We* were not busy – *we* hardly ever chattered. Most of the time we simply sat there on the veranda steps, staring at the gate. Didn't we, Tara?'

Tara nodded silently. She felt Bim's hold on her again – that rough, strong, sure grasp – dragging her down, down into a well of oppression, of lethargy, of ennui. She felt the waters of her childhood closing over her head again – black and scummy as in the well at the back.

'Or we lay on our backs at night, and stared up at the stars,' Bim went on, more easily now. 'Thinking. Wondering. Oh, we thought and we felt all right. Yes, Bakul, in our family at least we had the time. We felt everything in the air – Mira-*masi*'s insignificance and her need to apologise for it, mother's illness and father's preoccupation – only we did nothing about it. Nothing.'

Tara gave a sudden small moan and dipped her face into her hands so that her long curls fell about her head. 'Oh Bim,' she moaned through her fingers. 'I didn't come and help – help chase those bees away –'

'What can you be talking about?' Bakul asked in amazement.

'Bim knows,' moaned Tara. 'Bim knows what I'm talking about.'

Bim flapped her palm-leaf fan with a brisk clatter as if to call Tara to attention, remind her of the need to be sensible. Bakul said, when a little light dawned, 'You've always had this thing about bees, Tara.'

'So would you,' she cried, 'if you'd seen that swarm that attacked Bim – that *huge* black swarm.'

'Oh,' said Bim, seeing at last what Tara saw. She laughed and flapped her fan airily. 'You mean in the Lodi Gardens. That awful picnic when the Misra girls were being looked over by those boys. And we felt so awkward, we walked away to that tomb. And a boy threw a stone, I think, and that was how the bees were disturbed and attacked us.'

'And I ran away,' moaned Tara, rocking back and forth. 'I just turned and *fled*.'

'What else could you do?' asked Bim, genuinely surprised that Tara should find in it any matter for debate.

'They would have attacked you too if you had stayed,' Bakul agreed.

'You ran for help,' said Bim in the voice of a sensible nurse applying medicine to a wound. 'I *sent* you to fetch help.'

Tara raised her face and gave her a quick look to see if she were aware she was telling a lie, if she were deliberately doing to it salve Tara's conscience. It was too dark that moonless night to make out an expression on any face, and Tara had to calm her agitation by accepting that Bim had genuinely forgotten the details, not blurred or distorted them for Tara's sake. She felt a certain relief that time had blurred the events of that bizarre day, even if only in others' minds and not hers.

'You still remember that?' Bim asked. 'I had quite forgotten.'

Tara opened her mouth to say something more – now that she had brought it out in the open, even if only under cover of darkness, she wanted to pursue it to its end. She wanted to ask for forgiveness and understanding, not simply forgetfulness and incomprehension. But neither Bim nor Bakul was interested. They were talking about the Misra family.

'It is very strange,' said Bakul, 'meeting them at intervals of several years.' He drew on his cigar. 'One imagines they too have spent the time in travelling, working, having all kinds of experiences – and then one comes back and finds them exactly as they were, exactly where they were.'

'Only more so,' said Bim, laughing.

'Yes, that is true – more so,' he said and gave her an approving look. He had always admired Bim, even if she infuriated him often, and Tara sensed this admiration in the murky air. She sensed it with a small prick of jealousy – a minute prick that simply reminded her how very close she was to Bakul, how entirely dependent on him for her own calm and happiness. She felt very vulnerable that evening.

Perhaps it was the prickly heat spreading over her skin like a red map.

'The boys never were any good,' he was saying, 'and now they are grown men they are even more silly and idle and obese. Where are their wives, by the way? The last time we came to Delhi, I think we saw a wife or two.'

'The wives come sometimes but soon go back to their families in disgust. Women like change, you know,' said Bim. ''The wives wanted the new life, they wanted to be modern women. I think they wanted to move into their own separate homes, in New Delhi, and cut their hair short and give card parties, or open boutiques or learn modelling. They can't stand our sort of Old Delhi life – the way the Misras vegetate here in the bosom of the family. So they spend as much time as they can away.'

'And Jaya and Sarla,' Tara said sympathetically, almost tearfully, feeling for them as well as for herself, feeling for all women, helpless and abandoned. 'Poor things.'

'Yes, abandoned by their husbands. Isn't it odd how they were married together and abandoned together?'

'Abandoned? Are they actually divorced?'

'I think they are – but it's not a word that's used in their family, you know. In their case, it was the husbands who were too modern, too smart. They played golf and they danced and gave cocktail parties. Imagine, poor Jaya and Sarla who only ever wanted to knit them sweaters and make them pickles. They soon came home to Papa and Mama – were *sent* home, actually. For years they used to talk of going back to their husbands and make up reasons for not joining them where they were – they were in the army and the navy, I think, which was convenient. Now I notice they no longer do. Now all they talk about is their school.'

'At least they have that.'

'Least is the right word – the very least,' said Bim with asperity. 'I think they hate it really – they hate children, they hate teaching.'

'Do they?' said Tara, shocked. Hate was a word that always shocked her. The image of a dead dog immediately rose before her, bleeding. 'Then they shouldn't teach.'

'Oh they don't say they do – perhaps they don't even know they do – but you can see it by the way they look, so haggard and eaten up.' Having said that, she fell silent quite abruptly and would say nothing more. Tara wondered if she were drawing a parallel between her own life and those of the Misra girls. There had been that doctor once, she recalled. The memory came whining out of the dark like a mosquito, dangling its long legs and hovering just out of reach. Tara could not remember his name. How stupid, when he had been in and out of their house all that year that Raja had been ill. And Aunt Mira. Tara recalled his narrow, underprivileged face, his cautious way of holding his bag close to him as he came up the drive as if afraid that Bim would bark at him or even bite.

Amused in spite of herself, she uncharacteristically interrupted some tediously long-drawn platitude of Bakul's to say 'Oh, and Bim, do you ever see Dr – Dr – what was his name?'

Bim sat very still, very rigid, a shape in grey wedged into a canvas chair. She turned her face slightly towards Tara like an elderly bird inclining its beak. 'Who do you mean?' she asked, and her voice was like a bird's, a little hoarse, cracked.

'Oh, the doctor who used to look after Raja,' said Tara, striking her forehead with her hand. But she sensed Bim's disapproval – or was it distress? – and wished now to withdraw. 'I've forgotten. It doesn't matter.'

'Dr Biswas,' Bim told her flatly. 'No, I haven't seen him since Mira-*masi* died,' she added.

Then they were all three silent. All three were annoyed – Bakul at not being listened to, Tara at her own obtuseness, and Bim at having to listen to her and Bakul and not be left alone. She gathered her feet under the hem of her sari and looked straight ahead of her, into the screen of shrubs, absolutely remote from them.

And Tara, who had thought of redeeming herself tonight from years of sticky guilt, felt she had thoughtlessly plunged into greater depths – murkier, blacker depths – and was coated with the scum of an even greater guilt. She looked despairingly towards Bakul to help her out. But Bakul was glaring. Bakul was wagging his foot in disapproval and distaste at this unsatisfactory audience.

They all sat together as if at the bottom of a well, caught by its stone walls, trapped in its gelatinous waters. Till Bim gave her arm one loud thwack with her palm-leaf fan and exclaimed 'Mosquitoes! They are *impossible*.'

Badshah started up out of his sleep at the whack which had resounded like a shot in the night. Ready to charge, he looked wildly about him. It made Bim laugh. 'Lie down, lie down,' she placated him, pushing at him with her bare foot and he lay down again with a sigh, edging a little closer to her.

The mosquitoes that night were like the thoughts of the day embodied in monster form, invisible in the dark but present everywhere, most of all in and around the ears, piercingly audible. Bim could hear Tara's voice repeating all the cruel things she had so gently said – 'Do you ever see Dr – Dr – what was his name?' and 'When one is old, one has all kinds of fears, apprehensions' – and

Tara reading aloud a letter from Raja, a letter Raja had written to her, not to Bim. Her own name was not mentioned in that letter. Raja had not written to her or referred to her. Had there not been a quiet, primly folded-up pride in Tara's tone as she read that letter addressed to her? At last the adored, the admired elder brother was paying attention to her, whom he had always ignored, for now he had turned his back on Bim.

Bim saw all their backs, turned on her, a row of backs, turned. She folded her arms across her face – she did not want to see the ugly sight. She wanted them to go away and leave her.

They had come like mosquitoes – Tara and Bakul, and behind them the Misras, and somewhere in the distance Raja and Benazir – only to torment her and, mosquito-like, sip her blood. All of them fed on her blood, at some time or the other had fed – it must have been good blood, sweet and nourishing. Now, when they were full, they rose in swarms, humming away, turning their backs on her.

All these years she had felt herself to be the centre – she had watched them all circling in the air, then returning, landing like birds, folding up their wings and letting down their legs till they touched solid ground. Solid ground. That was what the house had been – the lawn, the rose walk, the guava trees, the veranda: Bim's domain. The sound of Baba's gramophone and the pigeons. Summer days and nights. In winter, flower-beds and nuts and cotton quilts. Aunt Mira and the dog, roses and the cat – and Bim. Bim, who had stayed, and become part of the pattern, inseparable. They had needed her as much as they had needed the sound of the pigeons in the veranda and the ritual of the family gathering on the lawn in the evening.

But the pattern was now very old. Tara called it old. It had all faded. The childhood colours, blood-red and pigeon-blue, were all faded and sunk into the muddy greys and browns of the Jumna river itself. Bim, too, grey-haired, mud-faced, was only a brown fleck in the faded pattern. If you struck her, dust would fly. If you sniffed, she'd make you sneeze. An heirloom, that was all – not valuable, not beautiful, but precious on account of age. Precious – to whom?

Turning on her side, her cheek glued with sweat to the thick fold of her elbow, she stared at Baba lying stretched out so peacefully, so passively on the cot next to hers on the dark veranda. Was she precious to him? But he was unaware of her, as unaware in waking as in sleep. He never raised his eyes from the gramophone turntable, never noticed if she were gay or sad, grey or young. If she were to vanish, if a loop of the Jumna river were to catch her round the waist and swirl her away like an earthen pot, or urn of ashes, then Baba would not know. He would not see. He would beautifully continue to sleep.

And that was for the best, that was how it should be, she told herself. But a mosquito came circling round her head, inserted its drill into her ear and began to whine. She flapped at it in fury.

When a letter arrived from their father's office in the familiar long brown envelope, she marched straight into Baba's room with it and said, abruptly, 'Baba, here's another letter from Sharma. He wants one of us to come to the office to attend a meeting. He doesn't say what it's about but he says it is important for one of us to come. Will you go?'

Baba, who had given a start when she bounded in, her hair streaming, with such decision and determination, shrank against the pillow on his bed, shrivelled up as at some too great blaze of heat, while the gramophone wailed on. He compressed his white lips, inclined his head towards the record with the most acute attention, as though it might supply him with an answer.

Bim paced up and down quickly, making abrupt turns. 'Or would you like me to go? Hmm, yes, I suppose I should. But Sharma hates that – I embarrass him. He hates having to talk to me, so he doesn't. Shall I send Bakul? Ask Bakul?' She looked at Baba so fiercely that his head began to wag as if she had tapped it. 'Yes? You think so? I could ask him – but I won't,' she immediately added, grimly. 'He'll go, and he'll be so patronising, and he'll come back full of advice. I have to make up my own mind. And yours,' she said, with a small, vicious stab. Then seeing him helplessly wagging his head, she clutched her head and burst out 'Oh, if only Raja would take care of these things.'

Baba's head wagged in agreement and, when she had stalked out of the room, continued to wag as if he could not stop. Then the record ran down and he put out his hand to wind it up again. As he wound, he became intent on the winding, and it calmed him. His head steadied itself. He forgot Bim. Music unfurled itself. On and on like a long scroll that he held in his hands.

'You see,' she pounced on Tara next when she saw Bakul leaving the house, freshly redolent of shaving cream, lotions and colognes, in his uncle's chauffeur-driven car, and found Tara folding clothes and packing them into suitcases opened out on her bed, with a happy air of preoccupation and of imagining the busy days ahead with her daughters, at the wedding, in Raja's house. Bim's sudden interruption made her drop a bag of shoes onto her toes and start.

'*This* is what I mean,' Bim was almost shouting, waving a letter in her face. 'It's all very well for Raja to write sentimental letters and say how he cares, and how he will never, and how he will ever – but who is to deal with Sharma? He writes letter upon letter to say we must attend an important meeting, he wants to discuss – then who is to go down to Chandni Chowk and do it? Where is Raja then? Then Raja isn't there – ever, never.'

'But he hasn't been here for years, Bim,' Tara said in amazement. 'He's been in Hyderabad all his adult life. Sharma knows that. He must be used to dealing with you.'

'He may be – but I am not. I don't understand the insurance business. Father never bothered to teach me. For all father cared, I could have grown up illiterate and – and *cooked* for my living, or *swept.* So I had to teach myself history, and teach myself to teach. But father never realized – and Raja doesn't realize – that that doesn't prepare you for running an insurance business. Sometimes I think we should just sell our shares in it – sell out to Sharma. What do you think?'

Tara sat down on the edge of the bed and frowned to show she was considering the matter although she was too alarmed by Bim's wild appearance and wild speech to think. 'Why not speak to Bakul first?' she said at last, with great relief at this piece of inspiration. 'Let me discuss it with Bakul – he may be able to advise you.'

But although this had been Bim's own initial idea, now she pulled a sour face at it and went on with her tirade as if Tara's suggestion were not worth considering. 'Because one's parents never considered the future, never made provisions for it, one is left to feel a fool – to make a fool of oneself,' she stormed on. 'Why must I appeal to Bakul, to Raja, for help? Yet that is what I am doing, going down on my knees to them –'

'Oh Bim, just asking for a bit of advice,' Tara clucked, a little afraid of her tone.

'How my students would laugh at me. I'm always trying to teach them, *train* them to be different from what we were at their age – to be a new kind of woman from you or me – and if they knew how badly handicapped I still am, how I myself haven't been able to manage on my own – they'd laugh, wouldn't they? They'd *despise* me.'

'I don't see why, Bim,' Tara said as consolingly as she could. She was so frightened by this revelation of Bim's fears and anxieties that she was too unnerved to be tactful. 'Don't see it as a man's business or a woman's business – that is silly nowadays. Just see it as a – a family business. Yes, a family business,' she repeated, happy to have come upon such a felicitous expression. 'The whole family should be consulted – Raja and Bakul and everyone – before you do anything. Yes, we should have a family consultation,' she said excitedly, seeing a way at last to bring about the family gathering she pined for.

'And will Raja come?' said Bim bitterly, in a quieter tone, as she settled down on the windowsill and leaned against the netting that covered it. It sagged beneath her weight, holding her back like a hammock.

'If you asked him to – I think he'd be *thrilled*,' Tara assured her at once.

'Oh yes, *thrilled*,' Bim made a sour face. 'Who would be thrilled to return to this – this dead old house?' She thwacked the wire screen with her fist so that the dust flew out of it. 'Anyone would be horrified to return to it. Weren't you horrified?' she demanded. 'To see it so dead and stale – just as it's always been?'

'But it's not,' Tara assured her earnestly. 'I mean – only superficially, Bim. Yes, when we arrived, I did notice the house hadn't been painted and the garden is neglected – that sort of thing. But I think the *atmosphere* has changed – ever since you took over, Bim. The kind of atmosphere that used to fill it when father and mother were alive, always ill or playing cards or at the club, always *away*, always leaving us out, leaving us behind – and then Mira-*masi* becoming so – so strange, and Raja so ill – till it seemed that the house was ill, illness passing from one generation to the other so that anyone who lived in it was bound to become ill and the only thing to do was to get away from it, *escape* . . .' she stuttered to a halt, quite pale with the passion she had allowed into her words, and aghast at it.

Bim's eyes narrowed as she sat listening to her sister's outburst. 'Did you feel that way?' she asked, coolly curious. 'I didn't know. I think I was so occupied with Raja and Mira-*masi* that I didn't notice what effect it had on you. Why didn't I?' she mused, swinging her leg casually. 'And that is why you married Bakul instead of going to college?'

'Oh Bim, I couldn't have stood college – not Indraprastha College, just down the road, no further. And the high walls, and the gate, and the hedges – it would have been like school all over again. I couldn't have borne that – I *had* to escape.'

'But was that why you married Bakul?' Bim pursued, hardly able to credit her little sister with such cool calculation.

Yet Tara did not deny it altogether. 'I didn't think of it that way then,' she said seriously. 'At that time I was just – just swept off my feet,' she giggled a bit. 'Bakul was so much older, and so impressive, wasn't he? And then, he picked *me*, paid *me* attention – it seemed too wonderful, and I was overwhelmed.'

They sat together in the dusty, darkened room, running their fingers through their hair with a twin gesture of distracted contemplation, and listened to Baba's record 'The Donkey Serenade' trotting in endless circles and the parrots quarrelling over the ripe guavas in the garden.

'Of course now I do see,' Tara went on at last, 'that I must have used him as an instrument of escape. The completest escape I could have made – right out of the country.' She laughed a small artificial laugh.

Bim gave her a curious look. She thought of Tara as a child – moody, touchy, passionately affectionate, with the high-pitched voice of a much smaller child, an irritating habit of clinging to Aunt Mira long after she ought to have outgrown cuddling and caresses, a love of lying in bed, clutching a pillow and sucking her thumb – and she shook her head in disbelief. She could not believe that these feelings that the adult Tara laid claim to had actually sprung up in her as a child. 'Did you think that all out? Did you think like that?'

'No,' Tara readily admitted. 'I only felt it. The thoughts – the words – came later. Have only come now!' she exclaimed in surprise.

Bim nodded, accepting that. 'You used to be happiest at home – never even wanted to go to school,' she reminded her.

'And *you* were the rebel – *you* used to want the world outside,' Tara agreed. 'Can you remember how we used to ask each other "What will you be when you grow up?" and I only said "A mother" and you and Raja said "Hero and heroine"' She began to laugh. After all these years, she found she could laugh at that.

But Bim did not. Her head sank low, her chin settled into her neck. There was a dark shadow across her face from which her eyes glinted with a kind of anger.

'Oh Bim,' said Tara, in fear.

Bim raised her chin, looked up at her with a little crooked smile – a horrible smile, thought Tara. 'And how have we ended?' she asked, mockingly. 'The hero and heroine – where are they? Down at the bottom of the well – gone, disappeared.'

'What well?' asked Tara with dry lips, afraid.

'The well at the back – the well the cow drowned in,' Bim waved at the darkness outside the window. 'I always did feel that – that I shall end up in that well myself one day.'

'Oh, Bim, don't.'

Bim laughed. She got to her feet and made for the door leaving Tara to wonder, in a panic, if she were serious or if she were only acting a melodramatic scene to impress Tara. Either was possible.

'I feel afraid for her,' Tara said, in a low voice, holding her kimono close about her neck as she sat at the foot of her bed that had been made for the night at the end of the moonlit veranda. 'I don't know what has happened to her. When we first came, she seemed so normal and everyday and – contented, I felt, as if Bim had found everything she wanted in life. It seemed so incredible that she hadn't had to go anywhere to find it, that she had stayed on here in the old house, taught in the old college, and yet it had given her everything she wanted. Isn't that strange, Bakul?'

Bakul, in his white pyjamas, was pacing up and down the veranda, smoking a last cigar before lying down to sleep. He was going over all the arrangements he had made for his tour of India after the week-long family reunion in Hyderabad was over. He was mentally checking all the bookings he had made, the tickets he had bought. He felt vaguely uneasy – somehow he no longer trusted the Indian railway system or the Indian travel agencies. He was wondering if it would not have been better to spend the entire vacation in his uncle's house in New Delhi. And Tara's rambling, disconnected chatter interrupted his line of thought like the chirping of a single sparrow that would not quieten down at night. Tara was repeating her question.

'She did not find it – she made it,' he replied sagely, knocking off half an inch of cigar ash into a flowerpot that contained a spider lily. Its heavy, luxuriant scent, feminine and glamorous, combined with the smell of the cigar in a heady, stifling way, stopping just short of the fetid. 'She *made* what she wanted.'

'Yes,' Tara agreed, quite thrilled. 'And she seemed contented, too, didn't she?'

'Contented?' he asked. 'Contented enough,' he answered. 'No more and no less than most of us.'

Now Tara was not satisfied. She wanted the question, the problem of Bim solved and resolved tonight. The light of the full moon was so clear, surely it could illuminate everything tonight. Like snow, or whitewash, it fell upon the house and the veranda and the garden, covering everything with its white drifts except where the shadows lay or the trees reared up, black as carbon. Like snow, its touch was cold, marmoreal, and made Tara shiver. 'And now she's simply lost all control,' she complained to Bakul. 'So angry and unhappy and upset.'

'I hadn't noticed,' he confessed. Perhaps another travel agency – not the small new one just started by his nephew on the wrong side of Connaught Circus. He would have felt more confident about Thomas Cook. Or he could have taken his wife and children to Kashmir and they could have had a houseboat holiday together. But then Tara would have insisted on Bim and Baba coming with her. She could not free herself of them, of this shabby old house that looked like a tomb in the moonlight, a whitewashed tomb rising in the midst of the inky shadows of trees and hedges, so silent – everyone asleep, or stunned by moonlight.

'Haven't you?' cried Tara in that voice of the anguished sparrow, chirping. 'Haven't you noticed how angry she seems all the time – how she snaps even at Baba and walks about the house all day, doing nothing?'

'What is the matter with her?' asked Bakul, realizing Tara had to talk. He had his own suspicions about Bim but thought better of telling them to Tara. 'Is it that business with Sharma you told me about? Surely it can't be – she's been dealing with him for years.'

'It can't be that then,' Tara agreed. 'It seems to be Raja again, as far as I can see.'

'What, haven't they made up that quarrel yet?' Bakul asked in a bored voice. Really, the house had an atmosphere – a chilling one, like a cemetery. 'I can't even remember what it was about – it was so long ago.'

'It wasn't really a quarrel – it was a letter – it's just that Bim can't forget old grudges. They make her so miserable – I wish I could end them for her.'

Bakul paid her some attention now. He could always find a solution to any problem, he liked to think. He rather relished problems. He relished solving them for anyone as easily impressed as Tara. He thought how nice it would be to have Tara stop looking so preoccupied and concerned and be impressed by him instead. Really, it was a night of Persian glamour and beauty. They should be sitting together in the moonlight, looking together at the moon that hung over the garden like some great priceless pearl, flawed and blemished with grey shadowy ridges as only a very great beauty can risk being. Why were they worrying instead about Bim, and Raja? He came and stood close to Tara, his large solid thighs in their white pyjamas just before her eyes like two solid pillars, and his cigar glowing between two fingers. 'You must arrange for them to meet and speak,' he said in a thick, rich voice.

But Tara made no response to his presence. She seemed to fly apart in rejection and agitation, the bird that would not be stilled. 'But that's what I've been trying to do all the time that we've been here!' she cried. She did not sound satisfied or grateful at all.

'Oh, have you?' he muttered, moving away towards his own bed. 'I didn't know, I've had so much on my own mind. Must check the girls' flight arrival time tomorrow. Remind me, Tara.' He yawned, flung the cigar stub out into the drive and sank, creaking, onto his bed. 'Another night on this damn uncomfortable bed,' he grumbled. 'All the strings loose. Need tightening.' He creaked and groaned and sighed till he found a comfortable position and then lay there like a bolster.

Tara remained stiffly upright on the foot of her bed, staring miserably into the brilliant, pierrot-shaded garden. The moon had struck everything in it speechless, even the crickets were silenced by its white incandescence. They sat in the shadows, intimidated. Only Badshah was not intimidated. Excited by the great flat mask hanging over the trees, looking down and mocking him as he sat, shivering slightly, on the whitewashed steps, he bounded up and raced down the drive to sit by the gate and bellow at it as if it were an intruder he had to guard his property against, warning the sleeping household of its unearthly presence. His barks rang out in the night like notes on a bugle.

On his way to the airlines office next morning, Bakul stopped at Bim's door and, seeing her sitting at her desk with her papers, said 'Tara spoke to me about Sharma's letter to you. Would you like me to stop at the office and find out what it's about?'

She answered immediately, brusquely, 'No, it doesn't matter. I have decided to sell out.'

'Decided?' Bakul exclaimed. His face was already wet with the sheen of perspiration. The light was brassy and remorseless as the heat. 'Now Bim, slow down. Why don't we sit down, all of us, around a table, and discuss it thoroughly before deciding what to do?'

'Discuss it with whom? Baba?' Bim laughed in that coarse way that always offended him. 'He and I are the only ones concerned any more. I have to decide for him.'

'Hmm,' said Bakul, perplexed, and wiped his face carefully with the clean linen handkerchief Tara had handed him that morning. Remembering all Tara had said to him, he went on 'But why not consult Raja first? He has had a great deal of experience in business, in property – he will know how to get the best deal from Sharma. His advice will be worth listening to, Bim.'

Bim shook her head positively. 'No, not Raja,' she said. 'He wouldn't care.' She gave her hand a small wave, dismissing him.

Tara was ready to appeal to anyone now. When Jaya's little visit one morning was over, she insisted on accompanying her down to the gate although the sun was already white-hot and they had to cover their heads with the ends of their saris and keep their eyes on the ground. It had burnt everything into a landscape of black and white, of coal and ash. Tara felt giddy under its blaze.

'What strange ideas Bim does have,' Jaya said.

'Yes,' Tara agreed, happy to have this opportunity to ask for Jaya's advice. But Jaya was only referring to their conversation over glasses of fresh lemonade under the cantankerously complaining and squeaking fan of the drawing room. Jaya had herself come for advice. 'The school is shut for the summer now so Sarla and I thought we'd renovate everything, paint the furniture. What colour do you think we should paint the children's tables and chairs?' While Tara pretended to consider the question seriously, Bim answered at once: 'Red.' 'Oh no.' Jaya was appalled. 'Not *red*. Pink or blue – it must be pink or blue.' 'Why?' demanded Bim argumentatively. Jaya had not been able to say, but 'It must be pink or blue,' she had insisted.

Now she appealed to Tara. 'It can't be red,' she complained. 'Red would be *awful*. It must be something soft, like pink or blue.'

'What?' said Tara, not having realized this was what had brought Jaya to visit them.

'The furniture,' said Jaya, hurt at her lack of interest. 'The school tables and chairs.'

'Oh,' said Tara. 'Bim is – is in a strange mood these days,' she explained, trying to bring in her own anxieties for Jaya's attention. 'I'm worried about her, Jaya.'

'About Bim?' Jaya was scornful. Indignation still burnt in her. How burnt and blackened her skin was, Tara noted, staring at their feet in slippers, making their way through the heavy white dust of the driveway. Jaya's feet were like the claws of an old rook, twisted and charred. Her voice, too, sounded like a burnt twig breaking, brittle and dry. 'No need to worry about Bim – she's always looked after herself. She can take care of herself.'

'For how long?' worried Tara, holding her white cotton sari like a veil across her face against the blinding light. 'Bim's not young. And Baba's not young either. And here they are, just the two of them, while we are all away.'

'There are two of them – they have each other,' Jaya's voice angrily smouldered. 'Bim has Baba to look after – she has always liked to rule others – and he needs her. Bim's all right.'

There seemed no way of conveying her anxiety to Jaya. Tara paused by the gate. Here a mulberry tree cast its shade over them and they stood adjusting their eyes to the shade that seemed pitch-black in comparison with the white heat shimmering outside its dusky circle. Ripe mulberries lay in the dust, blackening. Some had been squashed underfoot, their juice soaked into the earth like blood. Their resemblance to worms made Tara squirm. She tried to keep her feet off them but they were everywhere.

'We'll be going away to the wedding, Jaya, as soon as the girls arrive,' Tara said.

'Is Bim going with you?'

'No,' Tara shook her head mournfully. 'That's the trouble – she won't come. She refuses to come.'

Jaya gave a horsey snort. 'Bim has her own mind,' she said. 'Bim always did. You were always so different, you two sisters.' She gave Tara an almost maternal look, both approving and preening.

But Tara would not accept that. 'We're not really,' she said. 'We may seem to be – but we have everything in common. That makes us one. No one else knows all we share, Bim and I.'

'Of course,' said Jaya carelessly. 'That is only natural. But Bim is so stubborn. Not like you. *You* were never stubborn. I hope you enjoy the wedding, Tara. Give our love to Raja, to Benazir. Thank them for the invitation – we got such a grand one,' and she went off into the sun's blaze again and Tara stood amongst the fallen, mutilated mulberries and their smeared juice in the shade of the tree, watching her till her eyes smarted and her head reeled. She would have to go back to the house if she were not to faint from the heat.

Tara's concern quivering in the air, like the moist nose of a dog that is restless and won't lie down, made Bim want to stamp on it and stamp it out, rudely and roughly, just as she would have done when they were children. 'Must you wear those jingle-bells at your waist, Tara?' she asked irritably as Tara came in, veiled, from outdoors. 'All those gold bangles on your wrists – and then all those silver bells at your waist, too. I never thought you'd be the kind of woman that carries a bunch of keys at the waist.'

'Our suitcases,' Tara explained apologetically, startled into feeling guilty. 'Our trunks. Bakul gives me the keys to keep.'

'Yes, but how can you bear them jingling so?' Bim asked querulously, pressing her hand to her head. The electric fan creaked and complained over their heads for want of an oiling. A gecko on the wall let loose a series of clucked warnings. Its tail flicked at the tip, spitefully. Tara edged past it and past Bim at the table, keeping a safe distance from both, her hand pressed against the key chain to silence it.

But Bim was not appeased. Her anger was as raw as a rash of prickly heat that she compulsively scratched and made worse. At lunch there was a hot curry that Tara could not bear to eat and tried to pass down the table unobtrusively. Bim pounced on her. 'What's the matter? Don't you like Janaki's curry? It isn't very good – Janaki can't cook – but one mustn't *fuss*. Take some, Tara.' When Tara shook her head, she insisted till Tara nearly cried and finally took a spoonful, splashing the red gravy onto the plate and onto the tablecloth which made Bim go pale with anger.

When she swung down the veranda for a baleful afternoon rest, she nearly stepped on a smashed pigeon's egg and the unsightly corpse of a baby bird that had plunged to its death at birth from its disastrously inadequate nest. The scattered bits of shell, the shapeless smudge of yellow-tipped feathers and bluish-red flesh and outsize beak made Bim draw back for a moment, then plunge on with a gasp of anger, as if the pigeon had made its nest so crudely, so insecurely, simply to lose its egg and anger her and give her the trouble of clearing it. It was a piece of filth – Bim nearly sobbed – not sad, not pathetic, just filthy.

All afternoon her anger swelled and spread, acquiring demonic proportions. It was like the summer itself, rising to its peak, or like the mercury in the barometer that hung on the veranda wall, swelling and bulging and glinting.

Then Baba, shaded and sequestered in his own room, played 'Don't Fence Me In' once too often. It was what Bim needed to break her in two, decapitate her with anger. Clutching at her throat, she strode into his room and jerked the needle-head off the record and twisted back the arm. In the silence that gaped like a wound left by a tooth that has been pulled, she said in a loud, loose voice, 'I want to have a talk with you, Baba. You'll have to leave that off and listen to me,' and sitting down in a canvas chair by his bed, she rattled down a straight line aimed at Baba, shocked and confused before her, like a train racing down a line, driven by a mad driver. She would not look at Baba's widening eyes, more white than black, as she rattled on, straight at him, for he was the target she had chosen to hit – and hit and hit. She was telling him of her idea of selling their shares of the firm to Sharma, using that as a line on which to run. 'If I sell, it'll mean the end of that part of our income. It was too small to count anyway, but it did cover some of the expenses. With my salary, I'll be able to pay the rent, keep on the house, I'll manage – but I might have to send you to live with Raja. I came to ask you – what would you think of that?' She was hitting the target now – hitting and hitting it. 'Are you willing to go and live with Raja in Hyderabad?'

She had not known she was going to say that till she had said it. She had only walked in to talk to Baba – cut down his defence and demand some kind of a response from him, some kind of justification from him for herself, her own life, her ways and attitudes, like a blessing from Baba. She had not known she would be led into making such a threat, or blackmailing Baba. She was still hardly aware of what she had said, only something seemed to slam inside her head, painfully, when she looked at Baba.

He did not say anything. He only sat on the edge of his bed as he always did, his long hands dangling loosely over his knees, but he seemed to draw back from her, as far as he could, and his mouth was drawn awry as if he had been slapped, hard.

'I mean,' she cried, leaning out of her chair towards him, 'I mean – it's just an idea – I've been wondering – I wanted to ask you, Baba – what you thought.'

But Baba never told what he thought. No one knew if he thought.

'I didn't mean,' she said hoarsely, 'Baba, I didn't mean –'

Then Bim's rage was spent at last. It had reached its peak, its acme, like a great glittering wave that had hovered over everyone and that now collapsed, fell on the sand and seeped away, leaving nothing but a soggy shadow in the shape of Baba's silence.

No afternoon in all that summer had been so quiet, so empty as the one Bim spent that day, lying as still as a bone left on the sand by the river.

Silence roared around the house and thundered through it, making her press her hands against her ears. She would have relished the sound of the gramophone if it could have drowned out the sound of silence.

Now she pressed her hands across her eyes but the resulting flashes and pin-pricks of light darting and dashing across her eyelids did not amount to an answer. Only the questions thundered and thundered, one dark wave succeeding another. Why had she chosen Baba to vent her hurt and pain and frustration on? Why had she not written a letter to Raja, pouring out all she had to say to him over the years? Or attacked Tara instead since she could never be driven quite away, but always came back crawling to cling out of the habit of affection and her own insecurity? Or Bakul, smashing his complacence into satisfying smithereens with one judicious blow for he would only pretend nothing had happened, remain certain no one could do this to him?

She knew why of course: she could so easily have drawn an answer out of them – she already knew the answers they would have yielded up. Their answers were all so open, so strident, so blatant, she knew every line and nuance of them.

It was Baba's silence and reserve and otherworldliness that she had wanted to break open and ransack and rob, like the hunter who, moved by the white bird's grace as it hovers in the air above him, raises his crossbow and shoots to claim it for his own – his treasure, his loot – and brings it hurtling down to his feet – no white spirit or symbol of grace but only a dead albatross, a cold package of death.

Like the smashed egg and the bird with a broken neck outside. Filth to be cleaned up.

Her eyes opened at this sight against her will and she looked around the room almost in fear. But it was dark and shadowy, shaded by the bamboo screen at the door, the damp rush mats at the windows, the old heavy curtains and the spotted, peeling walls, and in their shade she saw how she loved him, loved Raja and Tara and all of them who had lived in this house with her. There could be no love more deep and full and wide than this one, she knew. No other love had started so far back in time and had had so much time in which to grow and spread. They were really all parts of her, inseparable, so many aspects of her as she was of them, so that the anger or the disappointment she felt in them was only the anger and disappointment she felt at herself. Whatever hurt they felt, she felt. Whatever diminished them, diminished her. What attacked them, attacked her. Nor was there anyone else on earth whom she was willing to forgive more readily or completely, or defend more instinctively and instantly. She could hardly believe, at that moment, that she would live on after they did or they would continue after she had ended. If such an unimaginable phenomenon could take place, then surely they would remain flawed, damaged for life. The wholeness of the pattern, its perfection, would be gone.

She lay absolutely still, almost ceasing to breathe, afraid to diminish by even a breath the wholeness of that love.

Although it was shadowy and dark, Bim could see as well as by the clear light of day that she felt only love and yearning for them all, and if there were hurts, these gashes and wounds in her side that bled, then it was only because her love was imperfect and did not encompass them thoroughly enough, and because it had flaws and inadequacies and did not extend to all equally. She did not feel enough for her dead parents, her understanding of them was incomplete and she would have to work and labour to acquire it. Her love for Raja had had too much of a battering, she had felt herself so humiliated by his going away and leaving her, by his reversal of role from brother to landlord, that it had never recovered and become the tall, shining thing it had been once. Her love for Baba was too inarticulate, too unthinking: she had not given him enough thought, her concern had not been keen, acute enough. All these would have to be mended, these rents and tears, she would have to mend and make her net whole so that it would suffice her in her passage through the ocean.

Somehow she would have to forgive Raja that unforgivable letter. Somehow she would have to wrest forgiveness from Baba for herself. These were great rents torn in the net that the knife of love had made. Stains of blood that the arrow of love had left. Stains that darkened the light that afternoon. She laid her hands across her eyes again.

When she took Baba's tea in to him later that afternoon, she found him asleep. That was why the gramophone had been silent in the afternoon – not because he was sulking, or wished to punish her, but simply because he was asleep. She ought to have known – Baba knew neither grudge nor punishment. She touched him on the cheek with one finger – its whiteness seemed to be like a saint's that suffers itself to be kissed. He woke at once and, seeing her, smiled.

'Your tea, Baba,' she murmured. 'I brought you your tea.' She felt an immense, almost irresistible yearning to lie down beside him on the bed, stretch out limb to limb, silent and immobile together. She felt that they must be the same length, that his slightness would fit in beside her size, that his concavities would mould together with her convexities. Together they would form a whole that would be perfect and pure. She needed only to lie down and stretch out beside him to become whole and perfect.

Instead, she went out. In the garden, a koel lifted itself out of the heavy torpor of the afternoon and called tentatively, as if enquiring into the existence of the evening.

In the evening, the sisters paced the terrace, waiting for a bit of breeze to come and lighten the air. Tara tried to talk – there were not many evenings left to them – but Bim was silent and seemed tired. After a while they stopped and leaned on the balustrade together, looking out over the stretch of sand to the still-standing river and above it the gauzy screen of dust into which the sun was sinking – a serene glass bubble filled with a pale liquid that did not quiver or ripple but was absolutely calm, weighting it down and forcing it to fall. The scene beneath reflected its lack of colour and its stillness. The river did not seem to run, the ferry boat was static and the egrets stood stock-still in the shallows.

'I'm going to bed early tonight,' said Tara and Bim nodded, her eyelids drooping with tiredness. She, too, wanted to sleep. She was exhausted – by Tara, by Baba, by all of them. Loving them and not loving them. Accepting them and not accepting them. Understanding them and not understanding them. The conflicts that rose inside her with every word they spoke and every gesture they made had been an enormous strain, she now felt, leaving her worn out. In spite of her exhaustion, she feared the night and the long hours and the dark when she would have to face herself. How would she swim through that ocean and come out again? she wondered.

In the event, she decided not to go to bed. She ignored the bed laid out for her at the end of the veranda, next to Baba's. She dreaded seeing his sleeping shape, unresponsive as a god, guilt-arousing as a saint. She dreaded the unreal light of the moon and Badshah's crazed barking. She dreaded hearing Tara's and Bakul's voices murmuring at their end of the veranda, forcing her to imagine their conversations and tones. No, she would stay in her stifling, dust-choked room, propped up by cushions on her hard wooden divan, the lamp with the brown paper shade lit and her books beside her to help her through the night. While she listened to the others switch off their lights and settle into bed, she rustled through page after page, the leaves of her mind falling one on top of the other as thick as cards, the cards her mother's, her father's hands had so expertly shuffled. They still shuffled and the cards, the leaves, fell upon each other with a dry, dusty crepitation, as meaningless and endless as their games.

To try and halt this crazy paper-dance, she reached out towards her bookshelf for a book that would draw the tattered shreds of her mind together and plait them into a composed and concentrated whole after a day of fraying and unravelling. It was the *Life of Aurangzeb* that lay at the top of the stack and came away from it between her fingers. Bim gave a little sigh and sank down on her cushions with relief at finding some history, a table of dates and facts with which to steady her mind. But, as if by instinct, she opened it to an account of the emperor's death:

> *Alone he had lived and alone he made ready to die . . . he wrote to Prince A'zam: . . . 'Many were around me when I was born. but now I am going alone. I know not why I am or wherefore I came into the world . . . Life is transient and the lost moment never comes back . . . When I have lost hope in myself, how can I hope in others? Come what will, I have launched my bark upon the waters . . .'*
>
> *To his favourite Kam-Baksh he wrote: 'Soul of my soul . . . Now I am going alone. I grieve for your helplessness, but what is the use? Every torment I have inflicted, every sin I have committed, every wrong I have done, I carry the consequences with me. Strange that I came with nothing into the world, and now go away with this stupendous caravan of sin!'*
>
> *. . . In accordance with his command 'Carry this creature of dust to the nearest burial-place, and lay him in the earth with no useless coffin,' he was buried simply near Daulatabad beside the*

*tombs of Muslim saints.*

Then Bim's mind seemed stilled at last. A silence settled upon it as a shroud that is drawn up over the dead. Laying her open book across her chest, she lay with her eyes closed, repeating the emperor's last words to herself like a prayer. She felt tears seep from under her eyelids involuntarily: they were warm as they ran down the sides of her face into the wells of her ears. They left a map of river-beds in the dust, trickling a little and then drying.

When she moved, it was to go to her desk and carefully draw out the entire lower drawer and carry it, heavily loaded with papers, to the divan where she could kneel beside it as she took out the papers in bundles and read them intently by the dim brown-papered light for the first time in many years.

They were not her papers, they were the translations she had made once of Raja's poems. They would be difficult to read, she feared, and her face was white as if with fear, or pain. Then it proved easy. The years had made them impersonal. Nowhere in them could she find Raja, not the Raja now and not the young Raja, the child Raja. For the poems were really very derivative. On each of them she could clearly see the influence of the poets he loved and copied. There was no image, no metaphor, no turn of phrase that was original. Each was a meticulous imitation of what he had read, memorised and recited. He had made no effort to break the iron rings of clichés, he had seemed content to link them, ring to ring, so that they clinked and jingled down the lengths of his verses. He had not, it seemed, really set out to startle by originality, to burst upon the literary world as a new star, fresh and vivid. One could see in them only a wish to emulate and to step where his heroes had stepped before him.

Touched, Bim laid them carefully in a heap beside her knees, one sheet on the other, like so many cards in a game. She had not realized that Raja's ambitions were so modest and unassertive. Far from playing the hero, he had only worshipped the heroes of his youth. Since he had set about imitating them and deriving from them so meticulously and painstakingly, they were not quite so bad as they might have been if he had trusted only in his own worth. Bim had to admit that he had learnt his craft well. He had acquired a surprising command over the craft of writing Urdu verse. He had learnt his lessons in metre, rhyme and rhythm and acquitted himself well.

But would he like her still to keep them? Would he want to be shown them again? Would they embarrass him, pain him, dismay him? She sat half the night wondering. She had thought of tearing them to bits, emptying her desk of them so that no trace should be left of those 'heroic' days of theirs. Now she was not certain. Her eyelids flickered with tiredness as her fingers shuffled through them again and again, and even her sand-coloured lips moved silently as she debated with herself what to do.

*'Strange that I came with nothing into the world and now go away with this stupendous caravan of sin!'*

Why load the bark with this accumulation made through a thoughtless life? Would it not sink? Would it not be better to jettison everything, to lighten the bark and go free, with ease?

*'Many were around me when I was born but now I am going alone.'*

But they were Raja's papers, not hers. It was not for her to decide whether he would take them with him or disown them and discard them, the litter and rubble left by the human picnic.

In the end, the only paper she tore that night was the letter he had written her and she had never answered. It was too late to answer it now. The only course left was to pretend it had never been written.

Having torn it, she felt she had begun the clearing of her own decks, the lightening of her own bark. After that, she spent the rest of the night in tearing and throwing away great piles of her own papers – old, dry, impersonal things, examination papers she had set her students, notes she had made in her own student days, tutorial papers she had forgotten to hand back, trivial letters that did not bear re-reading, pamphlets and catalogues sent by bookshops and academic journals, empty cheque books and full pass books, files dating back to her father's lifetime . . . Why had she kept them all these years? Now she flung them in a heap in the centre of the floor, and her shelves and desk were bare except for dust.

While she worked, she felt a sharp, fiery pining for college to re-open and her ordinary working life to be resumed. Then she would be able to end all this storm of emotion in which she had been dragged back and forth all summer as in a vast, warm ocean, and return to what she did best, most efficiently, with least expense of spirit – the keeping to a schedule, the following of a time-table, the application of the mind to facts, figures, rules and analyses. Once again, she felt with a certain bitterness, what a strain Tara's visit had been, what it had cost her by constantly dragging her apart into love and hostility, resentment and acceptance, forgiveness and hate. Worn out by it, she threw away the last paper, lifted the empty drawer off the divan and then lay down and slept. Even Badshah had fallen silent by then.

When Bim woke in the morning, she found her nieces sitting on the edge of the divan, looking into her confused face and laughing. They leaned forward to kiss her, and Tara came in, laughing too, to kiss them. Tara and Bakul had been, early that morning, in the dark, to fetch them. 'Here they are,' she was saying with such pride, such triumph, that they might have been fruit she had raised, or prizes she had secured. 'Look, Bim, here are your nieces again,' she laughed and Bim, struggling to free herself from the night and reach them, reached out to touch their faces and draw them to hers to be kissed.

She had not held anyone so close for years. Their young faces loomed, their brightness and pinkness filled her vision, and the scent of their fresh skin and fine hair and the soap and water with which they had just washed wafted down to her, making her draw back into her cushions, overwhelmed.

'Are you tired, Bim-*masi*?' they laughed at her. 'Aren't you awake yet? What have you been doing all night? Your room looks like a storm's been through it.'

'Tired? Not awake?' She sat up then, as straight as she could, feeling a dreadful pain in her back from the hard wooden divan on which she had spent the night. 'You just wait – you just see – I'll be up and have your tea ready and we'll be out on the veranda, all of us, in five minutes, and then Tara will have her family gathering at last,' and she plunged past them and stood over them, tall and refreshed.

'What *are* you wearing, *masi*?' they teased. 'The very latest fashion – a caftan! Ma, you never told us how fashionable Bim-*masi* has grown.' No one mentioned that her face seemed made of clay – old dried clay that had cracked. Only Bim felt it, with the tips of trembling fingers.

'You're making fun of me now,' said Bim, finding her way back to her aunt-self, her aunt-persona. 'Come along, come out to the veranda – I want some light – I want my tea. Have you seen Badshah? Have you seen my jet black cat?'

It was with Baba that the nieces chiefly spent their time. They would slip into his room and sit cross-legged on his bed, listening to the old records that they had listened to on all their previous visits to the house, playing with his gramophone as if it were the most novel toy of the year. They squabbled so much for turns at winding it up that Bim and Tara would have to go in and see that they were fair about taking turns. Baba, sitting in the canvas chair by the bed with his knees looming up under his chin, watched them, chuckling.

Then they found the old bagatelle board and insisted he play with them, noisy games that led them all to shriek and roar with laughter and howl with rage as they watched the metal balls roll inexorably into the traps and channels set for them. Once Bim and Tara even heard Baba calling out excitedly on winning five hundred points and turned to each other in disbelief.

When Bakul enquired 'When will you take them shopping? You said they needed saris for the wedding. Shall I send for the car?' Tara shook her head fiercely, refusing to break up Baba's party.

They were to leave early in the morning. There was just time for Bim to give them tea out on the veranda. Still sleepy, they were all subdued. The girls sat side by side on the divan, petting the cat that lay stretched out like a black string between them and drawing it out longer and longer with their caressing fingers till Bim begged them to stop.

The pigeons strutted up and down on their spidery pink claws, dipping their beaks into their breasts and drawing out from them those chiding, gossiping sounds as if they were long thick worms.

Out on the lawn Badshah was following a suspicious scent laid invisibly in the night. His paws made saucers of colour on the pale dew drawn across the grass like a gauzy sheen.

Teacups clinked on the saucers, tinnily.

The sunlight spread like warm oil, slowly oozing and staining the tiles.

Of course it was Bakul who spoke then, as Bim knew he would. Placing his empty cup in the centre of an empty saucer, he said, blowing his words through his lips like bubbles through a pipe, 'Our last day in Delhi. The last day of this family gathering. Tomorrow, another one in Hyderabad.' The bubbles sailed over their heads, bloated and slow, then sank to earth with their weight.

'Oh it will be more than just a family gathering,' said Tara, worriedly tightening the belt around her kimono. 'A wedding always means such crowds – Benazir has relations coming all the way from Pakistan – there'll be such confusion – we won't have time to sit about our tea like this.'

One of the girls let out a little shriek as the cat suddenly swatted at her with its quick paw. Laughing, they both began to tickle her belly, making her kick.

'But, Bim, we'll soon be back,' said Tara, lifting her voice above their giggles. 'You'll have me and the girls back after the wedding. That's what I'm really looking forward to – a few quiet weeks while Bakul does all the travelling. The girls will love it.'

The cat sprang up in protest and fled. The girls rocked with laughter.

'Do they love quiet times?' Bim asked, whacking one of them on her knee.

'They *will*,' Tara was certain. 'But perhaps not all that quiet – they do have fun with Baba, don't they? Did you hear them playing bagatelle? The way they squabble over his gramophone! Did you hear Baba laughing?'

Bim nodded. She kept her hand on Mala's knee. It seemed to her its round shape was the size and consistency of a ripe apple.

'They must do something besides sit and listen to Baba's records,' Bakul said fussily, getting up and pacing up and down the veranda. 'D'you hear, you two? You are to visit all the relatives. They want to meet you. They want to introduce you to young people in New Delhi . . .'

'And marry you off as soon as they can arrange it,' Bim interrupted, giving the little knee a shake.

The girls went pink and looked and winked at each other, but Tara protested, 'No, no. What makes you think so? They're still studying, Bim.'

'That won't stand in your way,' said Bim. 'If you can find two eligible young men – *you* wouldn't insist on their going back to college.'

'No,' Tara agreed, 'but *they* might,' and the girls gazed into her face, a bit warily. 'Mightn't you?' Tara asked them gently. They seemed not quite out of their cocoons yet, they were somehow still fuzzy and moist, their eyes half-open, like kittens'.

'Now *that*' said Bim, standing up to collect the tea-tray, 'is good news. You must give me a little time with my nieces and give me a licence to influence them – an aunt has that prerogative, surely.'

'You can have all the time you want with them,' Tara said graciously, helping to hand over the empty cups, 'and influence them as much as you like. In our family, aunts have that prerogative. Like Mira-*masi* had.'

Bim gave a little start, scattering sugar, and her hand jerked to one side. The others looked at her. She was staring at the ranks of flowerpots on the steps and the dusty shrubbery outside as if she saw something there. Then 'Hmm,' she said, settling her chin into her neck, and lifted the tray and went off down the veranda and heard Tara say 'Mala! Maya! Why don't you get up? Why don't you help your aunt? You *should*, girls.'

'They must go and dress,' Bakul boomed. 'Why is everyone sitting around here? Hurry!'

When they had all disappeared into their rooms, Bim came out of the kitchen slowly and went down the steps into the garden. She was tired, had not slept well, there was a mist before her eyes that bothered her. The bright light of day cut into her temples, leaving a wake of pain. She wanted shade, quiet. She went down to the rose walk to be by herself for a bit.

As summer advanced, any pretence the garden made during milder seasons shrivelled up and disappeared. The stretches of arid yellow dust extended and the strips of green shrank. Now there was really nothing left but these two long beds of roses, the grey-green domes of the mulberry and eucalyptus trees at the far end, and the water tap that trickled into a puddle of green mud. A party of parched mynahs stood around it, drinking and bathing. As they saw Bim and Badshah shuffling up the path, they rose and twittered with loud indignation from the tree tops. Drops of water flew, bright and sharp as nails, from their agitated wings.

Bim trailed up the path, looking at her toes, not at the hedges where white things might slip ghost-like in the blaze of day, or even at the crimson roses, all edged with black now in this scorching heat. She thought how Aunt Mira would have trembled if told to influence her nieces, how her hands would have shaken when she lifted the tumbler that concealed her brandy, how it would have rattled against her nervous teeth as she drank, and then the long hands would have shaken even more . . .

'Bim!' called Tara, quickly crossing the frizzling lawn to the shade of the rose walk, her hand shielding her eyes from the sun.

Bim watched her come with tired resignation. She would have liked to wave Tara away, to be alone to mutter to herself, make gestures, groan aloud and behave like the solitary old woman she was, not as a sister or an aunt. 'Haven't you to pack?' she asked, a bit coldly. Perhaps that was what Aunt Mira had needed, she felt, and missed – they had never allowed her to be alone, never stopped pursuing her and surrounding her for a minute. They had not realized and she had not told. Nor could she tell Tara.

'All done,' Tara called back. 'Bakul and the girls are getting ready.'

'And you?'

Tara came up to her and for a fleeting moment Bim thought she was going to take her by the arm. They had never held hands, not even as children. How would she do it? She stood with her arms hanging stiffly by her sides. But Tara only brushed against her faintly and then, side by side, they strolled up the path, the dog leading the way, his tail rising into the air like a plume as he pranced to annoy the mynahs, giving them just a glint of his eye as a warning.

Then when Bim thought the danger over and relaxed, Tara's hand did suddenly creep up and her fingers closed on Bim's arm with sudden urgency. She pulled at Bim's elbow, urging her to stop, to listen. They stumbled on the hems of their long dresses and came to a stop, clumsily. Hurriedly, Tara said in a rush that made Bim realize that she had kept these words bottled up till they burst: 'Bim, I always wanted to say – I can't go away without saying – *I'm sorry* – I can never forgive myself – or forget –'

'Oh Tara,' Bim groaned. 'Not those bloody bees again!'

'No, no, Bim, much worse, Bim,' Tara hurried on, clutching her kimono at the knees, 'much worse. When I married – and left – and didn't even come back and help you nurse Mira-*masi*, Bim – whenever I think of that – how *could* I?'

'What! You'd only just married and gone. You couldn't have come back here immediately after you'd gone. It wasn't as if you were in New Delhi – you had gone all the way to Ceylon.'

'I could have come – I *should* have come,' Tara cried, and bit her lip. She tried to tell Bim what was even worse, still worse – that, taken up with her husband, her new home and her new life, she had not even thought of Aunt Mira, had not once worried about her. Not till after her death. And of that she heard only after the funeral. 'I didn't even come to the funeral,' she wailed.

Bim's feet kicked impatiently into the hem of her nightdress. She must stop this. She must bring all this to a stop. To Tara's visit, to this summer, all those summers before. Looking desperately about her, she shaded her eyes against the sun, and said 'There's Bakul – on the veranda – calling you.'

'Tara! Tara!' Bakul called, and Bim felt well-disposed to him for the first time that summer. 'Go, Tara,' she said.

But Tara clung to her arm, her face puffy and angry. She wanted something of Bim – a punishment or at least a reprimand with which she could finally plaster the episode, medicate it. 'I never even came to the funeral,' she repeated, as if Bim might not have heard.

'I didn't ask you to it,' Bim said roughly. 'You didn't need to. Don't be so *silly*, Tara – it was all so long ago.'

'Yes, but' cried Tara desperately, turning towards the house now, and Bakul, as if against her will 'but it's never over. Nothing's *over*, ever.'

'No,' Bim agreed, growing gentler. She saw in Tara's desperation a reflection of her own despairs. They were not so unalike. They were more alike than any other two people could be. They had to be, their hands were so deep in the same water, their faces reflected it together. 'Nothing's over,' she agreed. 'Ever,' she accepted.

Tara seemed comforted to have Bim's corroboration. When Bim repeated 'Go, Tara,' she went. At least they had agreed to a continuation.

Bim's agitation rose humming out of her depths as the family got ready to depart. Bakul's uncle's car had arrived to take them to the station. It was standing in the drive. The gardener had come to help the driver load it with their smart American suitcases. The girls, in their travelling jeans and T-shirts, hopped about, crying with alarm every time a suitcase tilted or bulged or threatened to fall. Bakul was handing out tips to the servants who had gathered on the veranda steps as if posing for an old-fashioned photograph of family retainers: they even smirked uncharacteristically ingratiating smirks as they stretched out their palms and salaamed. Bakul looked in his element, his lower lip moistly pouting with fulfilment. Tara darted back into the house, remembering something. Baba's gramophone was churning out 'The Donkey Serenade' like a jolly concrete-mixer. The gardener and driver were lashing a rope around the bags, strapping them to the carrier. Bakul shouted orders to them. Then he turned to Bim and shouted, having forgotten to lower his voice in turning from one to the other, 'Where's that sister of yours gone now?'

'Tara, Tara,' Bim shouted, as tense and impatient as Bakul. She stood staring at the shuttered door in fear that Tara might bring Baba out with her, or that Baba might follow Tara and get into the car with her to go to Hyderabad. Had she not ordered him to go, asked him to go? At any moment, at any second, Baba might come out and leave with them. 'You'll be late,' she fretted aloud, shifting from one foot to the other as if it were she who was to travel.

'I know,' he fumed. 'Tara!'

Then Tara darted out. Alone. Bim felt herself go limp, her tension recede. 'Hurry, hurry,' she said, brushing aside Tara's last affectionate squeeze and trying to propel her towards the open door of the car. But Tara put out her hand to block the door and would not go in. She stood stiffly, stubbornly, beside the car, refusing to let everyone's impatience budge her. She was frowning with the distress of unfulfilment.

'Baba won't come out,' she murmured to Bim who still tried to bundle her physically into the car.

'Let him be,' Bim said, relief blowing her words into large light bubbles that rolled off her tongue and floated effervescently into the orange air. 'He feels frightened by all this – this coming and going. You know he's not used to it.'

Tara nodded sadly. But this was not all that was on her mind. There was another block, halting her. She tried to force her voice past that block. 'Shall I tell Raja – ?'

'Yes,' Bim urged, her voice flying, buoyant. 'Tell him how we're not used to it – Baba and I. Tell him we never travel any more. Tell him we couldn't come – but *he* should come. Bring him back with you, Tara – or tell him to come in the winter. All of them. And he can see Sharma about the firm – and settle things. And see to Hyder Ali's old house – and repair it. Tell him I'm – I'm waiting for him – I want him to come – I want to see him.'

As if frightened by this breakdown in Bim's innermost self, this crumbling of a great block of stone and concrete, a dam, to release a flood of roaring water, Tara unexpectedly let go Bim's hand and fell forwards into the car. At once, the driver, who had been waiting with his foot on the accelerator, released the brake so that the car gave a sudden jolt, then stalled, throwing them all backwards. The girls laughed, Tara squealed. The driver started the engine again. Bakul sank back with a groan of relief. The suitcases on the carrier wobbled. Tara and the girls began to wave their hands at Bim and the servants lined on the steps, as the car glided forwards, at first slowly in first gear, then accelerating with a spurt, making the gravel fly from under the wheels and Tara sink back so that her face was wiped out from the window with a brisk suddenness. It reappeared at the rear window now, and again her hand rose, to wave. Bim waved back, laughing, doubled over as if she were gasping for breath, heaving with laughter helplessly. Badshah sprang after the car, barking. It turned out of the gate. The bougainvillea closed upon it.

It had grown too long, it needed trimming.

'Chandu,' Bim said, straightening up and turning soberly towards the servants who were watching with her, 'that bougainvillea needs to be trimmed.'

But now they had all lost their ingratiating smiles. They looked sullen again. The tips had been moderate ones, nothing lavish. Chandu nodded noncommittally and sidled off. When they had all gone, Bim went up the steps and sank down into one of the cane chairs with the slow movements of an old woman who feels she is no longer watched and need no longer make a pretence. Her black cat came to her and climbed into her lap.

Then the terribly familiar rattling and churning of Baba's record slowed down and came to a stop. The bamboo screen lifted and Baba came out. For a moment he stood blinking as if he could not quite believe that the veranda was so empty, so quiet.

'They've left,' Bim assured him.

He came and sat down beside her. It was very still. Lifting her black cat's chin on one finger, Bim said, staring directly into her green glass eyes, 'Would you have liked to go with them, Baba – to the wedding, I mean?' With the cat's chin still balanced on her finger, she looked at his face from under heavy, tired lids.

Baba, gazing at the cat, too, shook his head quietly. Then the cat grew irritated and jumped off Bim's lap and twitched the tip of her tail angrily.

They sat in silence then, the three of them, for now there seemed no need to say another word. Everything had been said at last, cleared out of the way finally. There was nothing left in the way of a barrier or a shadow, only the clear light pouring down from the sun. They might be floating in the light – it was as vast as the ocean, but clear, without colour or substance or form. It was the lightest and most pervasive of all elements and they floated in it. They found the courage, after all, to float in it and bathe in it and allow it to pour onto them, illuminating them wholly, without allowing them a single shadow to shelter in.

They were sitting – wordlessly and expressionlessly – inside this great bubble of light when a black smudge beetle-like entered it at its circumference and came crawling up the drive, in the shade of a white cotton sari, for it was only Jaya. They waited, almost without breathing, for her to come within screeching distance.

'What, just sitting about?' she screeched. 'Oh, and I'm so busy – so busy – but I had to come myself to tell you. Of course, Tara's left, hasn't she? Is that why you are sitting like that?' She came up the steps, her slippers striking each one emphatically. 'But I have so much to do. You know, Mulk is going to sing. It is Mulk's guru's birthday and Papa has given him permission to celebrate it. He is to come on a visit and sing for us, and Mulk will sing, too.' She sat down on a creaking chair and began to fan herself with the end of her sari. 'So many people are to come – Mulk has invited everybody – and you must come too – it will be a big affair – out in the garden – just like old times again – Sarla and I are to make all the arrangements – I'm so busy – so little time left – will you help, Bim? And you must come, with Baba –'

'It's Moyna's wedding day,' Bim told Jaya and Sarla as they met her in the porch, and at once they clasped her to their plain cotton bosoms, crying excitedly 'Mubarak! Mubarak! And it's Mulk's guru's birthday, too, you know,' and then rushing away because it wasn't the wedding that excited them – they tended now to brush aside weddings as so much fluff, rather unsightly and not at all necessary – it was really the unaccustomed noise and bustle in the old house, the return to old times and the hectic effect of music that made them fly and flap about, screaming at the servants to bring out more trays, more cushions and rugs, and greeting the guests who were pouring in at this late hour, all having dined fully and at leisure and now come out of the steamy city to the cool dark lawn in Old Delhi to listen to a little music under the dusty stars.

Bim and Baba lowered themselves onto a cotton rug spread over the prickly dry grass, close to the edge of the lawn where cannas, hibiscus and oleanders grappled together in a green combat for life. 'Can you see, Baba?' Bim murmured, tucking her feet under her sari, and he inclined his head a little and blinked worriedly. They could just make out, between the shoulders and over the heads in front of them, the wooden divan that had been carried out and placed in front of the dry fountain, spread with a white cloth, a Persian carpet and some coloured bolsters, and on which the musicians were already seated, having first been fed by the sisters, and were tuning their instruments with the absorption of grasshoppers or bees. The sounds, too, were insect-like and buzzed and chirruped and zoomed in the spotty dark of the lamplit garden, and the atmosphere was as busy and complicated as *sitar* strings.

The *tanpura* player had the rapt, wall-eyed stare of a madman or a fanatic. Tall and thin as a charred pole, his face was completely disfigured by pockmarks, huge black pits that seemed to carve up the whole of his face into grossly uneven surfaces, and one eye was quite blinded by smallpox. He did not need his eyes, however, and strummed the *tanpura* strings as if in a mesmerised state, his eyes gazing sightlessly into the dark. The *tabla* player, on the other hand, was as round and fat as a marrow, a little plump man who bounced on his buttocks with excitement, rolled his eyes at the audience as if to say 'Just wait! See what's coming – hold on!' and then threw back his head and chortled in anticipation of their applause.

Mulk, who was one of the two star performers of the evening, sat cross-legged, jovial and at ease in the centre of the fiddling, drumming, waggling musicians, dressed in fresh white pyjamas and a sky-blue embroidered Lucknow shirt, passing round betel leaves on a silver tray to his accompanists and laughing at jokes flung at him from the audience with exaggerated enjoyment.

His brothers were sitting in the front row, relaxing against large, thick bolsters, with somewhat selfconscious looks of scepticism and indulgence on their faces as if they weren't quite sure they could digest the huge and festive dinner they had just had. 'Mulk-*bhai*, begin with a lullaby,' one of them shouted loud enough for Bim and Baba at the back to hear. 'First put us to sleep – then you can do what you like,' and Mulk threw back his head and opened a mouth crimson with betel-juice to make a raucous pretence at laughter and good humour. An instrument loudly whined, then was stilled.

All the instruments were stilled. The drums ceased to tap, the *tanpura* to strum. Fingers steadied, held them still. Mulk, letting his chin sink down into the folds of his neck, appeared to be plunged in deep thought. Then he lifted one hand, the one with the opal ring that gleamed in a shaft of light from the lamp in the porch, raised his heavy triple chin, looked vaguely upwards at the dim stars, and then sang a tentative phrase in his rich, dark voice. He roved from note to note, searching for harmony, experimenting with sequences, till at last he found the right combination, the sequence that pleased him by its harmony. He sang it in a voice that resounded with the pride of discovery, rang out in triumph. Now all the instruments joined in, made confident by his success. The *tabla* rollicked with delight at the rhythm he had found for it, the *tanpura* skipped and hurried to keep up with him. Swaying their heads with approval, the musicians followed Mulk with perfect accord. He had launched their boat, now they were all in motion. Now they rose upon a crest, now they moved forward upon a wave of sound.

Bim, swaying slightly too with the melody that swelled about them, let her eyes rove over the audience that was scattered over the lawn, partly lit by the light that fell through the pillars of the veranda and partly shadowed by the nervous dancing shadows of the foliage so that they were like pierrot figures in a theatre. There were people only just coming up the drive, others milling restlessly about, settling on the cotton rugs only to rise again and move closer to friends, form new groups and then break up and shift again. Some fanned themselves with the palm-leaf fans they had brought along, either languidly or frenziedly as they forgot or recalled the heat. Others opened up their silver *pan* boxes and rolled themselves betel leaves or shared them with their families or friends. The quieter ones merely smoked cigarettes, each no more than a small pinpoint of flame in the darkness. Bim had just lit herself one when she had to draw in her feet and make room for a young couple who came and settled down before her with their small daughter in a crackling violet dress trimmed with silver and little gold rings in her ears. She peeped at Bim over a shoulder with great, kohl-rimmed eyes, then clutched her mother's soft, powdered neck and hissed 'Look, Ma, a woman is smoking!' making Bim remove the cigarette from her mouth and smile. The child stared and stared till a packet of biscuits was opened for her and then she concentrated mouse-like on them till she was patted to sleep on her mother's lap by hands that jingled in time to the music with their load of glass bangles.

All this commotion, confusion and uproar might have drowned out Mulk's song and yet it did not. It simply formed a part of the scene, like the lamps and the dark and the scent of night-flowering plants, a kind of crepitating tapestry through which Mulk's song wound purposefully, never losing the thread but following a kind of clear, infallible instinct with his musicians to accompany him, and the purpose and the harmony and the melody of his song were a part of the tapestry too, the gold thread that traced a picture on the shimmering background, and no one minded if it was haphazard or arbitrary.

Mulk's brothers were no longer lolling against the bolsters. They were sitting cross-legged and bolt upright, beating out the rhythm on their knees and swaying their heads to the melody and crying 'Vah! Vah!' loudly with pleasure and congratulation at every pleasant or unexpected piece of inspiration on Mulk's part, or of intuitive accord and foresight on that of the accompanists. No one would ever have thought that they disapproved of their brother's singing or grudged him what he spent on his musicians, for their delight and sympathy was obvious in every wag of their heads and slap of their hand on their knees. They were also a part of the tapestry, as much as the singer and the musicians forming that composed, absorbed group before them. Mulk's song sung in that pleasant, resonant voice, bound them all together in a pattern, a picture as perfectly composed as a Moghul miniature of a garden scene by night, peopled with lovers, princes and musicians at play.

And there was still another element to this composition. Now the sisters were hurrying down the veranda steps, followed by men with great kettles and small, smoking braziers, and others with trays loaded with cups. As they busily set up a kind of open-air tea shop beside the cannas and the oleanders, Mulk's song rose to a joyful climax, his voice swelling to its fullest strength and the *tanpura* and the *tabla* rising and expanding with it, so that they all arrived together at the peak from which they could do nothing but come rolling down, hilariously, into laughter, congratulation and joviality.

'Tea, tea – come get your tea,' Sarla and Jaya were calling, and the servants were bustling to pass the cups up and down the rows seated on the rugs. Bim chose to rise, stretching her cramped limbs, to go and fetch two cups. 'Wonderful music, Jaya,' she said as she bent to pick up the cups held beneath the spout of a great black kettle by a little grubby servant boy. 'What a voice Mulk still has – it's wonderful,' she said, but Jaya and Sarla, with sweat pouring down their faces and glittering on their foreheads, pumping their arms up and down at the elbows, only smiled worriedly and hardly seemed to hear. The time for them to hear and to think had not come yet. The tea was only a break for refreshment, for the chief part of the programme was still to follow and Mulk's singing was not the star performance as Bim had imagined.

There was a shuffle taking place on the divan. While the accompanists were drinking their tea with loud, appreciative smacks and slurps, an aged little man in a crumpled *dhoti* and faded shirt, wearing a small black cap on his head, was being helped up onto the divan by the Misra brothers and settled onto the centre of it while the others shifted aside and made room for him with an air of both affection and respect.

'Mulk's guru,' Sarla explained quickly as Bim moved away with two cups of tea in her hands. 'Mulk has asked his guru to sing tonight.'

'Ah,' said Bim and all round her people were saying 'Ahh' with the same note of awe and expectation for the guru, once a famous singer, now lived in retirement and hardly ever appeared in public.

'Mulk's guru is going to sing now,' Bim told Baba as she handed down a tea cup to him, slopping, and then carefully settled down beside him to stir and sip the scalding, sweet, milky tea. All round them there was a babble, a hubbub, as the audience prepared for the chief treat of the evening. On the divan too, there was a continuing stir and an atmosphere of both relaxation and mounting anticipation as the musicians exchanged jokes and compliments, sipped tea, chewed betel leaves, flexed their muscles, cleared their throats, tuned their instruments and prepared themselves.

Pleasure and confidence and well-being exuded from all of them, as if music were food and drink to them, a rich nourishment that they had imbibed and gave away generously to all – all except for the elderly guru whose face and little, wizened figure were so dried and aged, so brown and faded and wrinkled, that they could exude nothing at all except a kind of weary acquiescence. Mulk was chaffing him now, teasing him, but the old man, resting the palms of his hands on his knees and leaning forwards, did not smile or in any way respond. He seemed to be having trouble with his teeth which were false and did not fit.

Then he turned one palm upwards on his knee, and immediately Mulk and the accompanists fell silent. Out of that silence his ancient voice crept out and began to circle in the dark, a skeletal bird making its swoops and darts hesitantly, enquiringly. The accompanist followed at a little distance, discreetly, as if not to disturb him. Mulk sank into a listening pose, rapt, swaying his large head very, very gently.

Up on the veranda, on a large white bed, the old father had been lying, listening, quite mute. Now his heavy bulk seemed to stir for a shadow loomed up against the whitewashed wall and swayed like a monument that is crumbling.

Watching that pyramidal shadow that had risen in the night on hearing the old singer's voice, Bim listened to the small, ancient voice, too, rough-edged and raw as if in pain. There was about that voice a tinge of snuff, of crimson betel spittle, of phlegm. Also of conflict, failure and disappointment. The contrast between Mulk's voice and his was great: whereas Mulk's voice had been almost like a child's, so sweet and clear, or a young man's full and ripe and with a touch of sweetness to it, the old man's was sharp, even a little cracked, inclined to break, although not merely with age but with the bitterness of his experiences, the sadness and passion and frustration. All the storms and rages and pains of his life were in that voice, impinging on every song he chose to sing, giving the verses of love and romance a harsh edge that was mocking and disturbing. He sang like a man who had come, at the end of his journey, within sighting distance of death so that he already stood in its looming presence and measured the earth and his life on it by that great shadow. One day perhaps Mulk would also sing like this, if Mulk were to take the same journey his guru had. After all, they belonged to the same school and had the same style of singing and there was this similarity despite the gulf between them.

Listening to him, Bim was suddenly overcome with the memory of reading, in Raja's well-thumbed copy of Eliot's *Four Quartets*, the line:

'*Time the destroyer is time the preserver.*'

Its meaning seemed to fall out of the dark sky and settle upon her like a cloak, or like a great pair of feathered wings. She huddled in its comfort, its solace. She saw before her eyes how one ancient school of music contained both Mulk, still an immature disciple, and his aged, exhausted guru with all the disillusionments and defeats of his long experience. With her inner eye she saw how her own house and its particular history linked and contained her as well as her whole family with all their separate histories and experiences – not binding them within some dead and airless cell but giving them the soil in which to send down their roots, and food to make them grow and spread, reach out to new experiences and new lives, but always drawing from the same soil, the same secret darkness. That soil contained all time, past and future, in it. It was dark with time, rich with time. It was where her deepest self lived, and the deepest selves of her sister and brothers and all those who shared that time with her.

Now the guru sang:

'Your world is the world of fish and fowl. My world is the cry at dawn.'

Bim's hand flew up to brush aside the grey hair at her face, and she leant excitedly towards Baba. 'Iqbal's,' she whispered. 'Raja's favourite.'

Baba gave a single nod. His face was grave, like an image carved in stone, listening.

The old singer's voice rose higher, in an upward spiral of passion and pain:

'In your world I am subjected and constrained, but over my world You have dominion.'

'Vah! Vah!' someone called out in rapture – it might have been the old man listening alone on the veranda – and the singer lifted a shaking hand in acknowledgment.